MW00979448

Claire's Dilemmas

The Life of a Student Nurse

Marlene Ritchie

Produced by:

FriesenPress

Suite 300 – 852 Fort Street
Victoria, BC, Canada V8W 1H8

www.friesenpress.com

Distributed to the trade by The Ingram Book Company

Table of Contents

For Eric and Sarah, my son and daughter, who bring joy into my life. And for my grandmother, Eliza Lutz McClelland, who was innovative and inspired others to be adventurous.

Chapter 1
Claire's First Dilemma

I was planning something terrible. Really awful, and I wasn't that kind of girl. I was the kind that went to church every Sunday with her parents—well until a couple of years ago anyway, when I turned eighteen. Even though it was outrageous, I followed the curfew Dad put on me and had my boyfriends take me home by eleven-thirty. *Eleven-thirty!* No movie or party we went to would be over that early, not really. My brothers borrowed Dad's car without asking. I never did. I was such a goodie goodie, but it wasn't fair. I should be able to do things that I wanted to do. I could take care of myself. Well, then why did I feel so guilty? I used to go to Grandma when I had a problem or a tough decision to make, and she'd make tea for us and listen. With her help, any dilemma could be resolved easily. But she was gone. How I missed her! She died two years ago. No one else understood how I felt. I was on my own. My parents, and brothers too, were going to be so disappointed in me, but if I just went along with what *they* wanted for me, I would be disappointing myself! Could I really go through with it?

I was already dressed in jeans and a t-shirt, with my bed made—except for fluffing up the pillow. Dad would have left for work. Mom would be waiting to pop in the toast for my breakfast. She liked to sit across from me in the breakfast nook and complain about Tommy, my brother, who didn't write home enough. So? Tommy was a teacher with a life of his own. Mom didn't see it that way. "You'll always be my kids," she often said.

I don't care. Well, yes ... I do. But I'm tired of studying. Fifteen years of it: kindergarten, grade school, high school, junior college. How many times did I say I would like to go to some resort, work as a waitress for a year or two ... be on my own for a change? Twenty years old and I'm treated like a baby. I've never lived away from home.

While looking in the mirror, I ran the brush through my straight brown hair and then threw the brush onto my dresser. As I fastened the barrette, a lock of hair flipped forward onto my cheek.

Crummy hair! Wish I were beautiful. Oh well, at least I'm not ugly.

Henry, my high school boyfriend, used to say that I had nice eyes, and Kingsley, my boyfriend at junior college, told me to wear short skirts to show my legs. I checked my posture in the mirror, held out one leg and pointed my toes, while resting one hand on my hip in what I considered a fetching pose.

Damn, damn, this isn't about boys. I just can't stand to go to another class. Not yet. I do want to make my life count. I just don't know how. Grandma, Grandma, I need you.

The conversations I'd had with my mom played over and over in my brain. "You can be anything you want to be." Those were my mother's words. I'd sarcastically repeated them out loud. I'm not a swearing person, but she is sooo wrong! Suppose I wanted to be a star basketball player? I'm only five foot four and absolutely no good at sports. See what I mean? No one can be anything they want to be. By my age, most girls are into a career or getting married. My classmate, Isabel, is going to be a doctor. It's what she always wanted to be, or so she keeps saying. Neat! Bully for her. I can't picture myself as a doctor. Mom wants me to be a nurse. Dad says that's a good job for a girl. He says that Mom is a great mother because she studied nursing. I never remind him that she quit after the first year, got married to him, and had my brother. This is 1960, you know. In this age girls are supposed to have lots of options, but they're the same old choices that my mom had.

And other thoughts repeated, as I sat on the stool in front of my dresser. Marriage was out of the question—for now anyway. Even if Henry came back on the scene, I wouldn't respond. No, he wasn't for me. He'd worked part time in his uncle's general store, for a pittance, during high school, and took a full-time job there after we graduated. He had no ambition. Kingsley was different. He made me laugh, but he was constantly scheming to get rich. He studied management at our junior college and was working as assistant manager at a motel, which he said he'd own before long. He always talked like it was a given that we'd get married, but he never asked what *I* wanted. He boasted that we'd be loaded, have a swimming pool, meet exotic people. Yeah, and work scrubbing my knuckles to the bone. Ambition was good, but not when it was only about getting rich. If he phoned again, I felt inclined to say that I was busy.

Life is hard—too hard! I've just got to get away or the next thing I know Kingsley will have set a wedding date, and then I'll have to disappoint everyone and leave him. That's worse than what I'm actually doing. Yes, a lot worse.

After reading the biography of Albert Schweitzer, years back, I thought I should go to Africa to be a sort of social worker. All those stories about Tarzan made me feel like I could survive there. I'd like to help people, and make their lives easier, but how? What do social workers do in Africa anyway?

Well, one couldn't escape all the bad news. Russia shot down the U-2 with Francis Powers aboard in May. Khrushchev was on the warpath, and had killed the Paris Summit. War was raging in Vietnam, and Dad said American military advisers have gone to help. Cuba revolted and now a man named Fidel Castro was sounding off like a dictator communist. Who was to say if any of us even have a future?

Charlotte concocted our plan. When we were kids we used to tent in our backyards and dream about travelling. We'd discussed visiting Buckingham palace, seeing Jane Austin country, sailing down the Nile, eating curry in India, wearing *geta* and *kimonos* and sitting on the floor in Japan. Wow, that was living—seeing what other people are really like, and what they value. Charlotte had great ideas. I don't think either of us really thought that the dream was possible, but would you believe it? Charlotte's dad gave her money for a ticket around the world, and I'd agreed to use the tuition money Dad had given me to join her when she got to Hawaii. The plan was that I would attend nursing school for one term, and then either flunk out or plead with my parents that I couldn't stand nursing and be allowed to drop out.

Certainly they don't want me to be unhappy! I only applied to nursing to please them after I'd ruled out other suggestions. No, I don't want to be a teacher. No, I'm not going to be a secretary, or a clerk, or a hair stylist.

My grades were good, so of course I got accepted, but I kept asking myself if I was doing the right thing—just pretending to contract for a three-year university course in nursing to appease my parents while my heart was elsewhere.

Charlotte and I met, maybe for the last time, so that she could tell me her schedule. She'd brought a ton of brochures. After giving our order, we slid into a booth at Keys Restaurant.

"Claire, I wish you were going to London with me," Charlotte said, playing with the thick blonde braid that was falling onto her chest. Charlotte usually wore her voluminous hair loose so that cascading waves fell down her back, but when she was getting down-to-business, she didn't bother with style and plaited it instead.

My shoulders drooped. "I know, but I've only saved three hundred dollars, and anyway, I've got to show my folks that I'm not suited for nursing."

The waitress brought our drinks. I looked through the window at the traffic. Cars flashed by, all aimed for a destination, and there I sat with my destination on hold. This was so hard. I forced a smile for Charlotte's benefit and made my voice sound peppy. "So, London is your first stop."

"You brought the money?" Charlotte asked.

"It's for the second tuition instalment. When it's due, I'll buy my ticket."

Charlotte put her hands on her hips. "No way. We're getting our tickets today. You're so weak sometimes—no backbone. Are you trying to back out?"

"No, no, of course not. I just thought—"

"Well, stop thinking. You made the decision. Now we act." She lifted her Coke bottle, and took a sip. "Of course, if you want to stay around here and wind up keeping house, playing bridge, and attending the Ladies' Aid Society, well…"

Half-heartedly, I unwrapped my straw and dunked it in my Coke, bobbing it up and down in the dark liquid.

"You've got to live your own life," she continued. "You've been a dutiful daughter. Your mom and dad's dreams aren't *your* dreams. You're nearly twenty-one years old. You're entitled to live." Charlotte lifted her Coke bottle and plunked it back down onto the table with a thud.

Charlotte had a lot more self assurance than I did.

"Missy, you are so stubborn. No imagination."

Missy was a nickname Charlotte had given me—a secret name that only she and I used. It was a way of bonding. In turn, when we were alone, I called her Charlie. That fit the tomboy image of a girl in control, which she liked to convey. I caught the significance of her referring to me as Missy at that moment. She hoped I'd feel obligated to fulfil our pledge. That girl had a way with everyone: she had persuaded our biology prof to raise her grade; could get any fellow to take her out; and could manipulate her dad to buy her new outfits. And to think that such a self-confident girl had chosen me as her best friend.

Charlotte sighed. "Your mom wants to live vicariously through you." She looked straight into my eyes, checking to see if I agreed. "My mom does too, but I'm lucky. She persuaded Dad to cough up the money for this trip. She thinks I'll meet a prince—be another Princess Grace." Charlotte smoothed her braid, then flipped it over her shoulder and continued. "If I don't meet royalty, I'll still see great art, and learn the lingo of the rich and famous. I mean people more cultured than we are. I'm not going to wind up living such a routine life in a teeny burg."

Pictures of my mom working away in our kitchen, folding clean laundry, and lugging home bags of groceries flashed through my brain.

"Mom seems happy," I said.

Of course she'd appear to like what she is doing, but I wonder if she has regrets. She wouldn't want me to have regrets.

"Sure. She knows she's burned her bridges. Can't walk away now that she's got kids and is married to a man who wants her home cooking."

I laughed. "Charlotte, I wouldn't put it past you to woo some guy and move to his castle. Then I'll lose you forever."

"We'll both marry millionaires."

Neither of us spoke for a few minutes.

"Claire, don't be so inflexible. I hate to say this, but since your mom is a preacher's daughter, she's raised you to be obedient. I worry about you." Looking peeved, Charlotte crossed her arms over her chest.

Charlotte, that hurts. I don't just do what my folks dictate. I do have a mind of my own. True I weigh the pros and cons of every choice many times, but I can change directions. Last summer my folks let me take a job selling ice cream cones at the Rexall drugstore instead of being a camp counsellor, like they would have preferred.

Charlotte had been my best friend and supporter for ages. She was the idea girl and swept me along, but at that moment, she was making me miserable.

Charlotte must have read the dejected look on my face. She reached across the table and took my hand. "Forget what I said, Missy. You've got to live your own life."

I shrugged and squeezed her hand. "I am going to join you. It's just that I have to let my folks down slowly. You know, in six months we'll both be in Hawaii ... if you don't marry a prince before then."

Charlotte scowled. "If I find my prince, I'll drag him along. I won't miss being with my best soul mate, Missy." Charlotte fished into her bag until she found the brochure about Honolulu and passed it over. We looked at glamourous shots of the hotels where I might work. We joked about surfing, hula dancing in grass skirts, eating sizzling meat off a pig rotating over an open pit, and maybe looking down into a volcano.

Across from us, two girls were in a heated discussion. The book on their table attracted my attention: *Psychology for Nurses*. I glanced at the girls to see if they were the kind of friends I wanted to spend three years with. They were arguing about the pros and cons of electric shock therapy, a subject which didn't interest me in the least.

It's an omen. I can't just be a nurse to please my parents no matter how much I owe them. I need to find my own way.

Charlotte dragged me out of the booth, and we stopped at the cashier to pay for our drinks.

I deposited part of Dad's check in the bank, but held onto enough to buy a ticket to Honolulu.

I'll buy it with the date open. I won't even have to tell Mom and Dad for months.

Following our visit to the travel agency, where Charlotte bought her ticket to London and I got mine to Hawaii, we parted, but with big hugs—knowing that we wouldn't be apart for long. Charlotte left two days later, after one more goodbye conversation on the phone, and I began to pack for my move to the nurses' residence. Mom, I could tell, was happy. Teddy, my Border Collie, sensed that something was different. When I went to Hawaii, I wouldn't see him for months, but by that time he'd be used to having me away at nursing school. Nevertheless, it hurt to see his sad eyes as he watched me pack one suitcase with summer clothing, and the Honolulu ticket tucked inside a beach towel. I hugged him and told him that Dad and Mom needed his company, and that during the next little while I would still see him often.

Two Sundays later, Dad and Mom helped me move my belongings to my assigned dorm room. They didn't stay around though, since I needed to change and go to the Dean's welcoming tea. I told them to be good to Teddy and watched them sigh and smile at each other before driving off down the circular driveway in front of the residence. A pang of guilt ruined the elation I'd expected to enjoy.

They won't be happy for long. I hope they'll forgive me. I've never done anything to displease them until now. I feel so deceitful. Grandma, you would say I shouldn't be swayed by others, wouldn't you? Or do you put parents in a different category? I really should take more responsibility for my own actions. But when I do, I feel terrible.

I crossed the threshold into the foyer of the mansion where the tea was being held. Walking arm in arm, their long hair swaying, three giggling girls barged around me.

They have to be around my age, but they act like immature high school kids.

I shrugged. All three went into an adjoining room. They wore name tags, which I assumed the girl seated at the foot of the red-carpeted staircase was dispensing.

"Claire Winchester," I said, and the receptionist ticked my name off her list and handed me a tag to wear. "Tea is in the salon," she said, motioning to the room the girls had entered. "All first year students are expected to attend."

Well, I'm not going to be a student for long.

In my mind, I counted the months until I'd be living in Hawaii, but I could be cool and sophisticated when the situation demanded, and so I said, "Thanks," and sauntered across the hardwood floor, as though mingling with professors and fellow students of a university was old hat.

I entered a large room, the floor of which was covered with red, floral, Oriental rugs.

The sun beamed through windows, which were draped with heavy burgundy velvet. The space smelled of dusty crevices, blistering varnish, and gas from the kitchen range, which had permeated the furnishing. The brown-painted radiators had been turned on in spite of the fact that it was a warm September day. Candles in the candelabra centrepiece sent out delicate flashes of light. *Petit fours*, veggies, and sandwich strips filled silver trays.

I really don't belong here.

My mind drifted. In Hawaii there would be the scent of flowers, salt water, tanned flesh, and moonlight on the waves. I'd worn a short-sleeved, tailored, print dress—one my mother had chosen. The other girls were already into long sleeves or suits. I felt conspicuous, but I was sorrier for the coloured girl—even though she didn't seem to mind being out of place—in pants, a yellow pullover, and a red head scarf. Furthermore, she was the only coloured person in the room.

That girl got in line behind me to fill her plate. "Janette Francis," she said. "Call me Jan. I just got back from my run. What floor are you on? Do you know Norma Wilson?" She pointed to a girl with short, wavy, brown hair and pearl earrings. "She lives down the hall from me. She brought *a skeleton.*"

Jan expected me to be shocked. I lifted my eyebrows feigning surprise. My heart was elsewhere.

"Norma said we could borrow it to learn the bones. She's in 110 and …" Jan went on, naming three other girls. When our plates were full, Jan motioned that I should follow her and led me to Norma, who was sitting on a linen-upholstered sofa. We were introduced.

A lady in a navy suit came toward the head of the table and tapped a glass tumbler with a spoon. She was of average build, wore little makeup, had nails lacquered clear, and wore pumps that matched her suit.

Here comes a dumb speech.

I pictured the box of books in my dorm room, which would certainly be more interesting.

The din of voices continued.

"Girls, girls," the woman in blue called and then, noticing a male student, changed the summons to include him. "Students, students, please …" The room began to hush. She patted the crimped waves of her bobbed hair, which was grey in front. "I guess you all know me: Dean Jacks. And you've met our anatomy professor, Dr. Freeman." She nodded in the direction of the wizened woman seated at the head of the banquet table, who was serving tea into English porcelain cups from a silver-plated urn.

The cup and saucer in the server's hands rattled as Dr. Freeman smiled.

The Dean introduced other professors. She held her hands out to the sides, like paintings one sees of Jesus blessing the flock. "I want to welcome you all to the nursing program. The 60s will bring enormous changes to medicine. You are at a threshold. Though you are still students, you will assume the responsibilities of adults. The lives of your patients are in your hands."

Hmm. My life is going to be in my own hands before long.

The Dean continued, "You enter a noble profession, pioneered by Florence Nightingale. You may laugh at her preoccupation with fresh air, but no one laughs at her dedication to the soldiers in the Crimean War. If America goes to war again, nurses will be called forth, even drafted. You have chosen a noble life of service."

Are you trying to scare us or what? Drafted! Are we that close to another war? If I'm drafted, I'll aim to be sent to the front line. Well, maybe I'll join the Red Cross. I suppose Red Cross nurses look after enemy soldiers at times. Well, they're just boys. Just like my brothers. I'll bet they don't really want to kill people, either.

Dean Jacks was saying, "There is pride in serving one's country. I, myself, was an army nurse and served abroad during World War II."

I could see that woman in the military, even as a General. Thank goodness I was going to escape her tyranny. Charlotte would be amused, but my dad would be applauding and saying that she appeared to be an organized administrator.

She continued, "Today you are not called to wartime service, but you will serve our community with the same dedication. Remember that the physician is the head of our team. You will follow the directions of your superiors. The course ahead of you will not be easy. I urge you to study. It is sad to realize that more than half of you will not be here at graduation." She paused.

Can she possibly read my intentions?

"Study, perfect nursing procedures, learn empathy. I want each and every one of you to receive a diploma from me in three years' time." She cleared her throat. "Since its founding, this school," she raised her voice, "has had the top scores on the board exam every year but one." She wagged her finger. "Don't let your school down a second time." She stepped back and we all applauded.

She didn't persuade me. Nursing sounds like an assembly line to turn out clones following orders. I want a job that needs some ingenuity.

Many of the girls left. The rest of us went to the table for seconds. I hadn't had lunch so I was hungry and loaded my plate with meatballs. One dropped onto the carpet and rolled until it hit the Dean's blue pump. It was funny but embarrassing. I intended to use my napkin to pick up the meatball, but I was too late.

The Dean squashed it with her shoe and the juice sprayed up her leg. Startled, she stiffened. "Oh, my," she said, looking down to see what had happened. Her eyes scanned the room for a culprit. I wanted to shrink into the woodwork, but decided that I should acknowledge my *faux pas* and was about to step up and do so, but Jan stood up, blocking me from the Dean's line of vision.

Was that coloured girl protecting me?

As I tried to maneuver around Jan, I saw that one of the waitresses was wiping the Dean's shoe and another was cleaning the carpet. The Dean brushed her skirt and threw back her shoulders, like whatever had happened was of no consequence. During the ensuing quarter hour, she made the rounds of the room, greeting us by the names she read on our tags. She knew a lot about me. "You've got a fine average. If I'm not mistaken, your father is a banker. We can use his help with our funding drives. Now tell me why you chose nursing."

I wasn't in the mood for this question, and anyway, it was obvious that her interest in me was because my father might use his financial skills to benefit the school.

Hmm. Should I be flippant, say that I came to find a rich doctor to marry? That is probably Mom's wish, so it is not entirely a lie.

Instead, I repeated some of the sugary words about serving the community that she had reiterated in her speech. The Dean nodded in agreement and smiled. Charlotte would get a kick out of that scene.

I am a slick actress when I need to be!

The girls were exchanging personal information when the Dean clapped her hands to gain our attention again. "Now students, stay as long as you like." She gestured toward the food. "I just want to say that you can come to me with any problem—any problem whatsoever. I'm sorry, but I have another appointment and can't stay longer."

Everyone moved aside so that she could exit, and some of the girls thanked her for her encouragement.

There must have been some signal given that I missed. Immediately, about ten young men strode casually through the foyer and joined us.

"Bud," called the girl with dark frizzy hair. She rushed up to him, and on tiptoe, gave him a loud smack on his lips. Speaking loudly, she said, "Meet Bud. He's an intern, and he's brought some of the med school guys. He told me he'd come, but I didn't think he'd have the nerve."

Bud responded by locking his arm around the girl's waist. "Kelly, don't underestimate me." His eyes twinkled, as though he had a lot of mischief in mind.

I was not the only girl sizing up his appearance. He'd be on many want lists for sure. The girl Kelly was too cutesie, but Bud was something else. He must have been a star athlete at one time, with his large shoulders, narrow hips, and long legs. He had dark eyes, wavy, blond hair, and was clean shaven.

The guys helped themselves to the food and punch. There was one coloured guy, Keith, but he made no effort to talk to Jan. He held back, and when Norma was free, he talked with her. After they'd all eaten, Bud suggested that we go somewhere for drinks. One of the guys, who wore horn-rimmed glasses, knew a road house. Some said that they had to finish unpacking.

I had nothing better to do, so I said I'd go.

If I am going to run off to Hawaii, I've got to be more daring. Charlotte is probably meeting some guy in an English pub at this very moment.

They had two cars. We piled in—nine of us in Bud's wagon, and six in a sedan. I had to sit on the lap of a fellow named Kenji.

It took us nearly an hour to reach the clapboard, thirties, saltbox that had been converted into a dance hall. The guys talked about the winter Olympics coming up in Squaw Valley. Bud wanted to sing the praises of Jack Kennedy. "No question he'll defeat Nixon in November," he said. I was thinking of Charlotte.

What time is it in London? I wonder if she went to see the crown jewels. I hope she remembers to write.

When the cars were parked, we filed out, and stretched. A breeze had come up and I shivered. Kenji peeled off his navy jacket and offered it to me, but I declined. "Thanks. I'll be okay inside."

A jukebox recording of Neil Sedaka singing, "Laughter in the Rain" was blaring through the room. Above the wainscot, the walls were decorated with pictures of movie stars. The wide pine boards sufficed as a dance floor. The guy who wore horn-rimmed glasses pulled a couple of the girls over to the machine. They fed it coins and selected "Mrs. Robinson". I was about to slide into a booth, but Bud, the blond athletic guy, tugged on my arm. "Come on. We'll pull four tables together." I followed his direction and sat on one of the arched-back chairs he had arranged around the oak tables. Pitchers of beer arrived. One of the guys bought a package of peanuts and another bought pretzels. They slit the wrappers with pen knives, and we all reached for handfuls.

Several people had coupled up and were doing the Twist. A redheaded guy named Jeff asked me to dance. I'd seen the dance on American Bandstand, and fortified with my first glass of beer, I felt more comfortable with the crowd and had the courage to try.

If Charlotte could see me now!

Kenji had been quietly watching the dancing and listening to the joking around. After the dance with Jeff, and another glass of beer, I felt brazen. "Want to dance?" I asked him.

He shrugged. "You'll have to teach. I never danced."

"Sure. This is an easy one," I said. "Just pretend that you dropped the stub of a cigarette and twist your foot to put it out." I showed him the movement I had heard described on TV.

Laughing to cover up his bashfulness, he imitated the action.

"Now pretend you have a towel and you need to dry your back. You slide the towel from side to side, like so." I demonstrated.

As we faced each other, ready to follow the accompaniment when the record started, Kelly passed by and teasingly ruffled Kenji's black hair. I thought the tousled hair and dimple in his right cheek made him look cute, but I don't suppose he would have liked that description. He was quite stately looking, and appeared to be Asian. He was very well turned out in a white shirt, a striped tie, and black pants. He seemed tall to me, maybe five eight, but since I'm only five four, many people seem tall to me. I could see that his hair might be curly if he let it grow. He had a high forehead and receding hairline.

Don't they say that people with high foreheads are brainy?

He was slim, too—nothing but muscles on those bones. Thick eyebrows and black eyelashes framed his eyes, which were his most notable features. They focused on me and twinkled.

Gee, I feel important.

Appearing embarrassed to try gyrating his hips, he made a funny face, but let his hips sway to the beat. "How do I do?" he asked.

"You're good. Really good."

"What do you call dance?"

"Twist. The Twist. Actually I never did it before tonight either."

"You don't dance?" He was still into the action, and separated by some distance, I tried to match his timing. His smile was infectious.

"I do now," I said. "Where are you from?"

"I come from Japan. I've been here two months."

"Wow, your English is good."

"Wow, your dance is good," he said with a hearty laugh.

"I never drank beer before either," I said, giggling as the music changed and we headed back to our table and took seats side by side. "It's okay. I'm of age." He looked at me blankly, so I explained, "Past eighteen, the legal age to drink."

"Beer is good, wow," he said, reaching to fill a glass tankard for me. "Wow ... wow." He seemed amused by the sound of the word. We grinned as our eyes met. He tapped his fingers against the table in time with the music as though he were enjoying himself.

Kelly and Bud approached our table. Hips rocking, frizzy hair flying over and off her face, Kelly was swinging her arms back and forth when, all at once, her knees collapsed, and she dropped onto the floor. Bud must have thought that she'd tripped, because he was attempting to lift her. I thought that it was the beer until I saw her body jerk into a rigid position on the floor. Then her arms and legs began to contort as she kicked and punched randomly. Her head fell to the left and her eyes rolled.

"Quick, she's having a grand mal," I said.

Bud pushed back the chairs.

I knelt beside her and positioned her onto her left side. Then I loosened the scarf that she wore around her neck. Her teeth were grinding together and foam escaped her lips.

The others had crowded around, looking horrified and uncertain of how to help.

"Aren't we supposed to put something in her mouth so she doesn't bite her tongue?" someone asked.

"She'll be okay on her side. She might vomit, but on her side she won't aspirate," I said, as I accepted a rolled-up jacket someone offered as a pillow to place under her head.

"Is she an epileptic? Does she have a tag?" Bud asked.

Jan pushed up her jacket sleeves to look for a bracelet, while I checked for a neck tag.

"We better call an ambulance," Norma said.

"Can you?" Bud asked, and Norma went to take the phone the waitress had brought.

Kelly's movements had stopped. We watched for several moments and then she opened her eyes and, with a dazed expression, looked up at us.

"Just rest quietly," I said. She closed her eyes. Her breathing became regular so I stood up.

"You did fine," Kenji said to me. "How did you know what to do?"

I shrugged. "Read it in a novel."

"Novel!" he laughed. His smile made me feel tingly all over.

"You are a born nurse," Bud said.

"Yeah," someone else said. "The way you took charge."

Norma patted my arm. "It's a gift. You have the instinct to handle a medical emergency."

I just shrugged.

I guess babysitting taught me something about staying calm in emergencies.

The ambulance arrived. By this time Kelly was sitting up, but the two ambulance attendants took her vital signs. Even though her pulse and respirations seemed good, the men wanted to take her to the hospital.

She protested, "No, no. I'm okay. It's just that … I'm not supposed to have alcohol, but well … everyone else was. I'm such an idiot." She began to cry. "I didn't want any of you to know."

"Kelly, we understand," I said. "Come on, I'll ride in the ambulance with you."

"No," Kelly said. "Just leave me alone. I'm just drowsy. I'll be okay." Her head tipped to the side, and I wondered if another seizure was coming.

The ambulance guys stood back. I could guess that they wanted to leave, but I gestured with my hand for them to wait. They nodded understanding and sat at a vacant table.

"Go on dancing," Kelly said, as she rested her head on her cupped palm.

The crowd paired up again and began to gyrate on the dance floor.

I stayed with Kelly. "So? How do you feel?"

"Must be my sinuses," she said, clamping her head with both hands like a vice.

"You've got a legitimate reason to have a headache. Me, I think I have a hangover. I never drank before."

"You never drank?"

"Wine for communion."

"I don't think that counts." Kelly tried to smile.

"Come on; let's ride back in the ambulance." I took her arm. "We'll all feel better if the doctors check you out."

Reluctantly, Kelly let one of the drivers help us into the emergency vehicle.

Inside the ambulance, Kelly lay on the stretcher. She squeezed my hand. "You're a good nurse, Claire Winchester."

I was about to tell her about my plan, but this wasn't the time to focus on me. Instead, I made a face and tried to sound stern. "Ahem. Miss, you should have a medical alert bracelet."

"Oh, I have," she said, "but I don't wear it, because then people will know."

"Know what? That you could have a medical emergency. I know; Bud knows. The whole lot of us know, and we still like you. So? I'm always doing something silly. You like me, don't you?"

I sound so confident. Surprise, surprise, but really this isn't very different from the times I had to step up and look after some kid who got hurt in the playground when I was babysitting.

She laughed. "I was just remembering the Dean's face when that meatball splattered up her leg. Hey, wait. Was that you?"

"I didn't do it intentionally."

"Oh God, her face," Kelly said. "She must have thought she'd been hit by a grenade." Laughing, Kelly dropped her head back onto the pillow.

In the ambulance I held Kelly's hand. *Wow, wow,* I thought, remembering Kenji's infatuation with the word. *Nice girls. Nice guys.*

Five months in training isn't going to be so bad.

Chapter 2
On the Ward

After a month of lectures and preparation, we students were turned loose to look after patients. My first day working as a nurse was eventful, to say the least. Each student had practised giving bed baths to classmates, and now we were being assigned to bathe our first patients. I was sent to the men's surgical floor, which meant I'd be looking after men who were going to have surgery or were recovering from operations. My instructor, Miss Westlake, met me upon my arrival for duty on the ward. "Bed B, Mr. Clements, is having a laparotomy at three this afternoon. He's in a lot of pain and will require a bed bath," she said. "His roommate, Mr. Bronsky, Bed A, is waiting for a prosthesis. He can take a shower. I'll be around to check." She nodded and left.

Don't I need more directions?

I was stunned—too stunned to ask the meaning of lapara ... laparo ... well, whatever that word was. But then maybe I was supposed to already know. Maybe she'd pull me off the floor and send me to Dean Jacks if I admitted such ignorance. Had I been asleep during a lecture when lapor—that word—was mentioned? Darn. How could I prepare him for a procedure if I didn't know what it was?

I feel like I'm being pushed out of an airplane and told to fly.

Norma, my classmate, was entering her patient's room.

"I don't have any idea," Norma said when I asked her. "Gee, could it be some x-ray? Lapar must come from the Latin. Did you ever take Latin?"

The head nurse was approaching us. "You're not here to socialize," she said.

Norma whispered, "Good luck," and entered the room where her patients awaited.

"What about you, Claire Winchester," the head nurse said to me. "Can't you find your patients?" To no one in particular she said, "Girls are so immature these days."

I walked away in a purposeful manner. Mr. Bronsky was getting a prosthesis. So what?

How am I supposed to prepare him for that? Nursing is complicated.

In class, Miss Westlake had said, "The patients know that you're a student from your blue-checked uniform and white apron. To get their cooperation, you've got to act confident."

I squared my shoulders and continued down the hall. A man with a beard came swinging out of my patients' room on crutches. His striped robe billowed behind him as he passed me, heading toward the lounge.

When I arrived at the door to my patients' room, the shades were still drawn. Bed A was empty and Bed B was occupied by Mr. Clements, whose back was turned toward me.

The man on crutches must be Mr. Bronsky. Should I run after him and introduce myself? No, I'll track him down later and take him to the shower. His prosthesis is undoubtedly a wooden leg. Should I know how he lost his leg? Was it recent? "A shower," she'd said. Did his stump need special care? I should have read his chart. My instructor could have reminded me, but of course she wouldn't. Half of us are supposed to fail. Thank goodness I have my ticket to Hawaii.

Stepping into the darkened room and turning toward the patients' washroom, I called, "Mr. Clements, time for your bath." A nasty smell emanated from somewhere nearby. Even without turning on the overhead light, I could see that the toilet was empty, but I flushed it anyway. Then I filled the ready basin with bath water from the sink and tested the temperature. Glancing in the mirror, I could make out that my brown hair was slicked to the side and fastened with the tortoise-shell clip. My uniform looked neat and the white bib apron cover was clean and starched so stiff that it could have stood on its own.

Very professional. I'm ready.

I stepped toward the doorway from the washroom, holding the stainless steel basin like it was a presentation trophy. Two steps later, my feet slipped from under me. I went down on my bottom. The basin flew across the room. Water drenched the tile floor, the back of my uniform, and the foot of Mr. Clements' bed.

As I pulled myself up off the floor, I realized where the smell had been coming from—a pool of feces.

I'm not sitting in water; I'm sitting in excrement.

"Nurse," Mr. Clements said, rising up onto his elbow. "Are you all right? I had an accident."

He could have told me that when he'd heard me enter his room. No use to scold. I had to hold my temper and contend with the mess. Trying not to breathe in the odour, I pulled myself back up to a standing position.

Mr. Clements continued, "The night nurse gave me an enema. Before she left, we thought I was cleaned out. Sorry. I couldn't make it."

I faked a smile. "I'll get housekeeping," I said, stepping around the foul puddle.

"You all right?" Mr. Clements asked again.

"Fine," I said. I pulled my uniform around to see how much of it was soaked. *Heavens. Is every day going to be like this? Can I stick it out for five months?*

Charlotte is probably having a wonderful time.

I pictured her tripping around Oxford University, crawling through the wee door to the garden that had inspired Lewis Carol to write about Alice in Wonderland. Then I had a thought.

I'll go back to the dorm and change, and while I'm there I can look up the word lapara ... whatever that word was.

Instead, the head nurse offered to loan me one of her wraparounds and got underwear for me that was ordinarily reserved for patient use. I could go without hose for the rest of the day. By the time she had retrieved her spare uniform from the locker and I had changed, Mr. Clements' room had been mopped, the floor was dry, and two nurse's aides had changed Mr. Clements' bed linen. I filled the basin again, put it on his over-the-bed table, pulled the curtain, draped him with a cotton blanket, and proceeded to uncover one arm to bathe it, and then the other, as I assisted him with a sponge bath.

At the end of the bath, we were supposed to hand the patient a wet washcloth and tell them they could finish their bath in private while we were out of the room. It had seemed a clear message when we had practised in class, but when I returned to Mr. Clement's bedside after a suitable interval, I found that he was shampooing his bald head. I gasped, though I did see the humour of the situation. I filled his water pitcher from the washroom and helped him rinse away the soap. Something must have clicked in his brain, and he asked if I could step aside again while he washed his privates.

Bath finished, I was opening the curtains, when one of the other patients put his head inside our room. "You looking after Mr. Bronsky today?"

"Yes, he's my patient."

"Well, he's smoking."

I shrugged. "I wish no one smoked, but what can I do? The doctors condone it. They all smoke," I said.

I should add that most nurses take a cigarette during coffee breaks as well.

"No, I mean his chair is smoking. Come on." He beckoned impatiently.

The two of us raced down the hall to the lounge. The man with the beard had fallen asleep in one of the upholstered armchairs. The stench of smouldering fabric and a cloud of black smoke bellowed up around him.

I shook him. "Mr. Bronsky," I said. "Wake up. Wake up! Your chair is on fire!" I called down the corridor, "Someone please set off the fire alarm."

The head nurse came running with a fire extinguisher.

By the time two towering firemen arrived, dressed in padded jackets, hip boots, and protective gloves, the head nurse had sprayed the chair. It looked like a giant ice-cream sundae. White foam spilled onto the floor. The men lifted the cushion, punched holes in the under padding, said that there was no more danger, and stomped off down the hall while amused patients watched from their doorways.

Mr. Bronsky watched the entire hullabaloo with a grin. I held up a fresh towel to suggest that it was time for his shower. He headed toward the shower stall, walking with crutches, and swinging his stump between them. Afterwards, I handed him fresh pyjamas.

He told me that he'd lost his leg in the war. "Used crutches for years, then after I fell from the ladder—"

"You were climbing a ladder?" I asked.

"Sure. You just hang on to the sides tight and swing your good foot up to the next rung, and up, and up. Nothing I can't do. The surgery put it right. The stump is about healed, you see."

I didn't realize that he'd had surgery on his stump. Missed that by not reading his records.

I should be checking for what? Redness, swelling, signs of an infection? I'm going to have to chart what I've seen at the end of my shift. I guess I'll have to wing it!

"Sit there," I said, pointing to a chair. I washed my hands and did the examination which confirmed that all was well.

Mr. Bronsky grinned. "See, it's doing fine. That fall paid off. They're making a new leg for me so that I can run races pretty soon."

"You're a good model for all of us," I said with a laugh.

When I got back from lunch, Mr. Clements was dozing. Mr. Bronsky's lunch tray was still there, but the food was uneaten, and he was gone.

Heavens, what now? Better find him before he sets fire to his chair again.

I went looking for him, but he wasn't in the lounge. I peeked in every private room, in all the wards, and then went back along the corridor to check every bathroom. He wasn't anywhere.

How can I lose a patient? Is it my fault if he's missing?

The head nurse was bound to ask me when I'd seen him last. That would have been after his shower, an hour and a half ago.

Am I supposed to keep tabs on my patients at all times?

I realized that he might have gone for some test. I did what I should have done earlier; I sat down at the nurses' station and read his chart. No tests were ordered for that day. No fitting for his prosthesis either. My head hurt. I wrung my hands.

I'm just going to have to face that head nurse and tell her that Mr. Bronsky is lost.

Then I heard some woman's voice say, "Mr. Bronsky, you're a real athlete on those crutches." And I heard the plunk, plunk of the crutches against the tile floor.

I wanted to run and put my arms around him, I was so glad to have him in sight. But the nearer I got to him, the more I sensed that something was amiss.

"'Ello nurse," he said, when I caught up with him. He wasn't handling the crutches very well.

"Just a minute," I said.

I want him to stop, so I can ask him why he hasn't eaten. If he'd like something else, I'll check today's menu and order something different.

He halted quite suddenly; one crutch slid out of line so that he was about to fall, but I caught him and looked at him, face to face. His eyes were bloodshot. My stomach turned from the stench of liquor on his breath.

"You've been drinking," I said, fanning his breath away and feeling my stomach contract again.

What now? Am I responsible for his binge? Heavens, what next?

As we came nearer to his room, he leaned on one crutch and put a finger over his lips. "Shush."

"What is it?" I asked, still preoccupied with whom I should tell and what reprimand I'd get.

"Is he gone?" He meant his roommate.

"No, he goes at three o'clock. He's sleeping."

Mr. Bronsky sped up his swing toward their room. There was no one in the corridor, luckily. I don't know how I would have explained his condition. I wanted to hear his story before I went to an authority.

In the room, he climbed onto his bed.

I closed his curtain, helped him take off his shoe, and pulled up the spread. "You've got some explaining to do," I whispered, in a good-humoured tone. "Where have you been? How did you get the alcohol?"

No response. He'd fallen asleep.

I shook him, but he only moaned and moved into a more comfortable position.

Oh dear. He's so plastered that he's passed out.

I called to him, and shook him again and again. He began to snore. There was nothing I could do until he slept off the drunken state, and by then I'd be off duty.

Maybe that's a good thing.

For a moment, I smiled to myself. Then I felt glum again.

The next shift will find him, but I won't be off the hook. I'll be called to my supervisor, and then my instructor, and I'll have to account for where he got the alcohol. This day is a disaster, but don't cry, for heaven's sake. There must be some clever explanation you can concoct.

The aide came to take the lunch tray with the untouched food. She raised her eyebrows. Obviously she smelled the liquor. Should I report his condition to the head nurse before she did? She shrugged, and I took that to mean that the situation wasn't a concern to her.

I felt in his robe pocket and found a flask.

What should I do with this?

I didn't need the head nurse on my back. He was asleep, so for the time being, I put the container in the drawer of his bedside table.

They'll find him drunk, but hopefully I'll be off duty. The evening nurse won't realize that I was around when he got the booze.

I'd been brought up to always be truthful, but maybe omitting some details didn't mean that I was untruthful. I couldn't remember ever being tested about telling the truth before, at least not when my grades were at stake.

As I lumbered back toward the station to put in some time there, the head nurse stopped me. "What's taking you so long? You better hurry and prep Mr. Clements for his surgery. The doctors marked the line of incision. He'll be getting his pre-op meds soon."

"Thanks. I'm just on my way," I said.

So, lapar-whatever is some kind of surgery. Where is the incision being made and why? We haven't been shown how to shave a patient, or did I just miss that somehow?

I'm not one to ever skip a class, but lately I found it easy to daydream and not pay attention. I would picture Charlotte going to see the royal jewels or running into the Queen at Harrods. I wondered if the Queen ever went there to shop. Somewhere I read that you could go to a flea market and find a scarf or a bottle of perfume that the Queen had gifted. Royal memorabilia didn't interest me, but Charlotte would go for that. I pulled my attention back to the task at hand, and in the supply cupboard, I found a wrapped, sterilized tray marked "Pre-op." I opened it gingerly to see what else I'd need.

Soap.

I scanned the shelves but saw nothing indicating that it was for shaving. There were bottles of *pHisoHex*.

It has good germicidal properties. Maybe that's what they use. Can't hurt.

I squirted some into one of the basins.

Water.

It didn't need to be sterile, so I could fill the basin from the taps in Mr. Clements' washroom.

Gloves?

There were autoclaved packages in the cupboard.

I need something to brush up a lather. What is there? Nothing on the tray.

I surveyed the shelves until I saw a jar of paint brushes. They were pretty big, but one of those would do.

Should I autoclave it? Don't think it needs to be sterile. I'll wash it in hot water. I rewrapped the tray and headed to find my patient and pin him down for the prep.

Mr. Clements was a hairy man. I changed the safety razor blade three times before I had finished scraping all the fuzz off his belly, where the doctor had left a mark for the line of incision. I was tense all the while.

What happens if I nick him? Can't let that happen. There would be hell to pay if he went to the operating theatre with bandages. Is he on any blood thinners? The consequences of a nick was unthinkable.

I worked slowly and carefully.

Every hair must be removed.

I knew that from when I'd had an appendectomy. If a stray hair got into the open wound, an infection could result. Mr. Clements protested that it was going to be itchy when the hairs grew back. I didn't tell him that the itching would be minor compared with the pain of pulling off the tape that held his dressings in place. We talked, but he didn't seem to know what was going to happen during surgery. The head nurse peeked inside the curtain a few times, and when I was done, she tapped me on the shoulder as a way of passing on a compliment.

Just as she was leaving, Miss Westlake stepped into the room. "What are you doing?" my instructor asked. She glared at me. Her hands went to her hips.

Oh God. I've displeased my teacher again. It's hopeless.

I flicked the cover over the tray, since I didn't want her to see the paint brush.

"She's just prepped her patient," the head nurse said.

Miss Westlake asked me to step outside the room. "You haven't been taught that procedure. Why did you think you could do it?"

I couldn't find words. I wanted to say that he needed to be prepped, and since he was my patient, I thought that I was responsible and was supposed to figure it out. Fortunately the head nurse joined us. "I asked your student to prep him, and she did a good job. We have to let the students show some initiative, don't you think?"

Miss Westlake wouldn't agree, but obviously didn't want to argue with this head nurse. As soon as the nurse had breezed away, Miss Westlake backed me up against the wall. "In future, if this head nurse or any other person, doctor, or supervisor, or *anyone* asks you to do a procedure, which hasn't been taught, you must call me. I'm responsible for everything you do. Call me and I'll supervise you on the spot, or *I'll do it for you*. Is that clear?"

"Yes, I understand," I said, feeling helplessly wounded.

In a friendlier voice, Miss Westlake said, "How is the rest of your day going?"

Obviously she hadn't heard about the other fiascos, which certainly weren't my fault, but Miss Westlake would undoubtedly attribute them to my bungling. In my mind, I heard her earlier instruction to act confident. I replied, "Fine. Mr. Clements has had his bed bath and Mr. Bronsky took a shower. His stump is healing nicely. No sign of an infection." We hadn't been taught the signs of an infection, but after all, I did bring *some* previous knowledge to this profession—even though it wasn't a vocation that I particularly liked.

"Good. I'm glad that you knew to check the wound. I'll see you before you go off duty." She left me standing in the hallway and feeling quite deflated.

Meantime the medication nurse had gone into the room and given Mr. Clements his medication; the orderlies had transferred him to a gurney and were moving him by me toward the elevator.

I suppose I should say something to encourage him. Decisions, decisions. Well, it's too late; he's in the elevator now.

I wandered toward the station, thinking of writing my notes early, but one of the orderlies approached me. "You better get back to Mr. Bronsky."

"What's he done now? He isn't smoking in bed, is he?"

"Not that I know, but there's money everywhere. His bed is covered with bills. Anyone could steal that cash. Money is supposed to be locked in the safe at the nurses' station."

It can't be! Where did Mr. Bronsky get money? He didn't appear to have cash when he stripped to take the shower. Certainly I'm not supposed to pat down every patient to see if they put their valuables in the safe.

I stormed down the hall and into his room.

Mr. Bronsky seemed to be sleeping, but there were twenty and hundred dollar bills all around. Shaking him would have no consequences. Calling would have no effect. I began to gather up the money. It occurred to me that I should count it, so I started over again.

Mr. Bronsky, you are a pain! For two cents I could run away, just up and go. Let Miss Westlake hunt for me. I might get drunk. Was every day going to be this challenging?

How I wished I were in England with Charlotte. She must be having a fabulous time visiting castles and … I made myself concentrate on counting the money. Eight hundred, nine hundred. I added another hundred to the pile of bills.

What if someone comes and sees me? They'll think I'm stealing from—

Before I could finish that thought, the head nurse pulled aside the curtain and I froze.

"He's a bookie," she said, when I stood trembling in front of her. "Darn! I should have told you to watch for his friend, Homer." She took the bills I offered. "He's the intermediary. Homer is not allowed on the floor, but he comes up the stairwell so he doesn't pass our station."

"I don't think Homer came onto the ward today," I said meekly. Now it would come out that I knew the patient was missing and hadn't reported it.

"No. What then?"

"Mr. Bronsky is drunk. I found a flask in his pocket."

"Homer," the head nurse said, wrinkling her face and shaking a fist in the air.

"Maybe, but I suspect that he left the floor." Hesitantly, I told her about my search and that Mr. Bronsky could have been missing for more than an hour.

"That rascal," the head nurse said. "I've tried to protect him, but he'll be moved to a locked ward when the doctors get wind of this."

"Has this happened before? He's very likeable," I said.

"A daredevil. Yeah, likeable too," the head nurse said. "He was a paratrooper, you know. Shot when he landed and kept in a German prison. Escaped twice and taken back." She laughed. "He'll probably escape our locked ward too."

I could picture this shrunken old fellow climbing into a laundry basket to get wheeled out of the locked ward, and that made me smile.

"Mr. Clements won't be back from intensive care before you're off duty. As you know, when they do a laparotomy, the doctors open the abdomen looking for what's wrong. In this case, they suspect a pancreatic tumour. When you come in tomorrow, I'll make sure he's your patient. It won't be good news and he needs a caring nurse. You established good rapport today." She tapped me on the shoulder again.

Pancreatic tumour. I'd do my homework. I was feeling better about my prospects, and I hoped Mr. Bronsky would still be my patient as well. I wanted to get to know him.

At least the head nurse gave me credit for doing a good job.

It wasn't until I was repeating what had happened to my classmates that I saw the humour of the situations and could laugh about the day. Grandma would have loved hearing those stories. She'd say ... what would she say? "Way to go, girl!"

Chapter 3
The Falls

In the first weeks of my training, I hung out at the student union with a bunch of interns and other student nurses. Bud, the athletic type, was an organizer. He tried to interest us in playing baseball, but we all demurred. Then, one Friday in October, he said, "Hey, let's take off and go to Niagara Falls." That's all it took for the six of us to head down the interstate the following day, with Jeff, Kenji, and I in the back seat of Bud's station wagon, and Jan and Norma on the bench in front with him.

We made two washroom stops for Jan *en route*, and a couple of miles before the Niagara exchange, we all agreed to stop for an early lunch at the local Keys Restaurant. Bud parked in a shady area. Since I wanted to change shoes and Jan wanted to fish in her satchel for regular glasses, Bud stayed behind with us, while Jeff, Norma, and Kenji went into the restaurant to pick a good table. When the three of us entered, the hostess put up her hand. "Sorry," she said, "the restaurant is reserved for a private party."

Our three friends were seated at a corner table. It was eleven-fifteen and only four other spots were occupied.

"What time is the party?" Bud said. "We won't be long. Our friends are already over there waiting. Put us at the bar if you like."

The peroxide-blonde hostess moved from behind her reservation stand to block our way. Her eye flicked around in a nervous tick. "I said the room is taken."

Jan cowed behind me. She knew that she was the reason for the rejection. I clenched my teeth.

It's because Jan is coloured. So unfair. I can't believe this is happening.

From across the room, Norma waved to beckon us. She seemed puzzled about why we weren't joining them.

"Doesn't look taken to me," Bud said, in his causal, self-assured manner.

The hostess held her ground. "You can order take-out," she said, faking a welcome smile.

"Okay," Bud said. "I know what this is about. Come on." He grabbed Jan's arm and pulled her toward the exit. "This is outrageous," he called back as the door closed behind them.

I glared at the rigid hostess with her bleached hair, extended eyelashes, and revolting ruby lips. In April, the U.S. Senate had passed the Civil Rights Bill. The newspapers were reporting about civil rights walks and bus boycotts and sit-ins. Dr. Martin Luther King Jr., his African American and white followers were demanding equal rights for coloured folk. I stood there alone. Apparently neither Bud nor Jan thought it appropriate to put up a fight.

What can I do? I too felt helpless.

"I'll just explain to our friends," I said, pushing past the self-appointed guard.

When we got back to our car, Bud had opened the door and was urging Jan to get back inside. She was crying. "Damn, damn, damn," he said. Then Jeff, the affable redhead, took over, hugging Jan and saying comforting words.

"Sometimes I think I should go to North Carolina and do those sit-ins," Jan said. "It might make a difference."

"No," I said. "You're going to be more effective as a nurse. Stick with it. You've got friends here."

She took the tissue I offered.

Kenji seemed not to understand what to make of the situation, or was he wondering if a Japanese person would also be rejected from some places?

Many people still feel that Japan and Germany are our enemies. I wonder if he's already met rejection. Is it any better in Norma's country? Did people of colour get better treatment in Canada? Is this going to completely ruin the day? Maybe we can have a picnic, or won't Jan be allowed to sit at one of the picnic tables either?

Then Jeff took Jan's hand momentarily, and laughed reassuringly as he ran his fingers over her frizzy hair. "Hey, you've copied my hairstyle," he said, before fluffing up his own red curls.

He's trying to lighten the sting. Good guy.

I resolved to pay more attention to Jeff. He had played darts with me several times at the student union.

He seems unattached. I should get to know him better.

Kingsley and I had parted after junior college graduation and my brothers kept saying that I should have a new steady.

Bud got into the driver's seat and slammed the door. He fumbled around until he had the toll money at hand and then turned on the radio, before starting the car and driving out of the parking lot. As we moved back onto the thruway, he concentrated on the road. Jan, sitting next to him, was as stiff as a manikin. She stared through the windshield. Jeff, now in front, tapped his knee and sang along to the country-western trio that blared over the airwaves. Norma, sitting in back with me, was fiddling with her camera. Kenji looked out the window. No one had anything to say.

Is someone going to suggest turning back? That can't happen. Jan will feel completely rejected. We've got to show that we don't approve. We've got to make her feel accepted in our crowd.

At the White Castle in Niagara Falls, New York, we huddled together with Jan in the middle as we entered the premises. No one had strategized, we just did it. Jeff joked and pretended to do an Irish jig. I think he wanted to distract the staff, but the two waitresses and the cook, talking from behind a window, paid no attention. One of the girls came, wrote our order on a pad that she carried in her checked apron, and left to fill our requests. I sighed with relief.

At least not everyone demonstrates prejudice. Keys is out from now on.

Jeff turned to Norma. "So, your dad is on sabbatical from the University of Toronto?"

"He'll be here at least two years," Norma answered.

"I've got to meet him. Eventually, I hope to get a residency in Canada, and I'll bet he could help me out."

"I suppose. It depends on your grades and recommendations," Norma said.

"Toronto might be a good place to open a dermatology clinic. What do you think?"

"We have universal medical care, you know."

"Sure, but—you do have specialists, don't you?"

"Yes, usually referred to by a GP and paid for according to a pay-scale."

I realized how little I knew about Canada.

With Norma next door, I can get to know more about her country.

"Yeah," Jeff said. "I should get more details before I make a move. Now let's see," he laughed, "Kenji could I get rich and famous in Japan?"

"What to say? Get rich might be difficult." Kenji punctuated the sentence with a merry chuckle. He put his hands on his knees and leaned into the table now that he was part of the conversation. And when no one spoke to him again, he took a sip from his water glass. I was watching his reaction and thinking about how to get him back into the discussion. He looked quite handsome—neatly turned out as usual, wearing a blue short-sleeved shirt with the collar open, and dark trousers with a leather belt that was much too long and overlapped in the front, after passing through a steel buckle. The rest of us were in jeans, but either no one had told him it would be an informal trip or he didn't own jeans.

He gets free room and board, but his stipend is only about a hundred a month. He has to be frugal.

Kenji had shaved before our trip, so that his face was as smooth as a glossy apple, and his smile appeared relaxed, as though he were enjoying the company.

"Jan, you ever been to the Falls?" Jeff asked.

I sighed.

This guy is good, always trying to make Jan feel at ease.

Jan answered in a matter-of-fact manner. "No, but I've been very interested, particularly since I read an article about the man who went over the Falls in a barrel."

"Lots did that," Bud said. "They want to be rich and famous like Jeff."

"Did I say I wanted to be rich and famous?" Jeff replied, and then shrugged.

"Last year, a coloured man did it," Norma said.

Jan got up to go to the washroom. I wondered if she was still feeling badly or if she had a bladder infection, since she'd been the one to suggest the stops we'd made earlier. I followed her. "Anything wrong?" I asked when we were inside the ladies' facility.

"Not really," Jan answered, but she didn't sound convincing.

"I had a bladder infection once, and I had to go all the time."

"It's not that. I'm on a diuretic. I'm getting so fat, I have to get rid of water, or I'll be weighing as much as my mom."

"A diuretic. Did the doctor say you have a problem with water retention?"

"I didn't ask a doctor."

"Oh, Jan. You can't play around with your health. You can't just take medication. How did you get the pills?"

"I've got my source. Don't worry about me."

"Jan, you jog, and you eat well. There's not an ounce of fat on those ribs. You're a healthy girl."

"That's easy for you to say. You don't know how obesity runs in my family. Dad doesn't seem to mind and my mom's a nice person. Her second graders love her, but she's a tub."

"Jan, please. I don't want to meddle, but I think you should see a doctor."

She laughed. "I am seeing a doctor. I've got one for a boyfriend. Bud likes thin girls, even thin coloured girls." She splashed water over her face so I wouldn't notice her tears.

Bud hasn't been very demonstrative since Keys; I wonder if she's thinking that he'll drop her after today. Maybe he's the source of her pills.

I could do little about the bigots, but I vowed to use every skill I learned to stop Jan from self-medicating.

"There's a much better view of the Falls from the Canadian side," Norma said. "From here you look down over the American Falls; from Canada, you face the American and the Horseshoe Falls. We don't need the car. We can walk across the bridge."

"Okay. Sounds good to me," Jeff said.

"Sure. Let's," Bud agreed.

We parked in a lot near the Falls and everyone got out. Jeff grabbed Jan's arm and swung it high into the air as they walked. Bud and Norma followed, laughing at Jeff's antics. Everyone was trying to make light of what had happened.

Kenji held back. "I can't cross," he said. "No passport with me, but you go. I will look from this side."

We can't just leave a guest to our country.

"I'm staying with Kenji," I called. "I've been to the Canadian side already."

"Not necessary," Kenji said, shaking his head so that a straggly lock of hair fell over one eye.

Bud turned back. "You sure?" he said to both of us.

"I want to." I jutted two fingers in the air, in a victory sign, to seal the decision.

He tossed me his car keys. "We won't be gone long. I guess there are shops you can check out."

Kenji gave me that playful look of his. I could tell that he was glad to have company. When he smiled, a tickling feeling went through my body.

For a time we stood by the railing, looking down at the water rushing over the lip of the Falls. *What are we supposed to talk about? Do I have to find something mutual? I feel so shy with new guys, and especially someone foreign.*

We wandered through the flower garden. He asked the names of the flowers. I knew some names.

"Pansy," he said, "looks like happy face."

"What about those sunflowers?"

"Big smiles."

Oh good. He's easy to talk with.

Next we discussed books. I was surprised that he'd read a lot about Madame Curie and Gandhi and Clara Schumann. Clara, he said, was a composer, but she put her husband's needs first. "A wife should develop her talent."

That's how I feel. I want to have a husband and a family and *a career.*

"Do you like music?" he asked. When we walked side by side, he stood tall, and I noticed that he adjusted his steps to my shorter strides.

"I took piano lessons, but I don't remember much. Can't even recognize many of the classics."

"I think you do." he said, waving a finger in the air like he intended to test me.

"Okay, try me."

He sang a melody. His pitch was melodious and perfect.

"Scheherazade and the composer was—don't tell me. Gee ... I'll get it." I twisted back and forth, gyrating my arms and feeling like a high school kid again. "Rimsky-Korsakov."

"You are right." Kenji lifted his clasped hands above his head to cheer my success.

He sang another.

"It's a minuet," I said, snapping my fingers. "Can't tell you the composer."

"Bach. See, you know a lot," he said.

He hummed "Twinkle, Twinkle Little Star."

"Ha, ha. Classical? You're kidding? Did your mom sing that to you when you were little?"

"Mozart," he said.

"Really? Did Mozart write that?"

"He arranged it."

I'm impressed.

We had wandered back to the railing. The wind had changed and the mist from the Falls was thick. People a few feet away were invisible. Suddenly a huge avalanche of water hit me face on. It was like an ocean wave. Water filled my mouth and nose so that I coughed and gasped for air. The deluge was over in seconds. My brown hair dripped. My white blouse stuck to my chest and water falling from my blue skirt was forming a puddle on the sidewalk. Being nearer the Falls, I had taken the brunt of the wave. Kenji's feet and lower pant-legs were wet.

"You look so ..." Kenji said, letting his voice trail off. He seemed to be holding back a grin.

I laughed. "Like a drowned rat, we would say. What am I going to do? And you, your feet are wet." I fluffed up my wet hair.

"I feel like duck," he said, as he walked in a circle, planting his feet down pigeon-toed, so that the water squirted from the soggy leather.

"Brr," I shivered, and laughed at the same time.

"It is cold. You can't stay wet."

"I know. I am thinking what to do. What about you?"

"Soon dry. I don't mind. I can fold up pant legs." He bent to roll up the wet parts.

I checked my purse. Thank goodness I'd brought more cash than I'd expected to need. "I'll buy something at that shop." I pointed to a pavilion with racks of American and Canadian flags, post cards, key chains, as well as skirts and tops. "Want to come along?"

"Sure."

The staff of the clothing boutique wouldn't let me enter. I was dripping too much. Kenji volunteered to do my shopping, and I handed him several bills.

I stood outside, flapping the bottom of my skirt while Kenji went inside. We agreed that he'd bring items to the window so I could pass judgement. First he held up a white blouse, drew a pear-shaped figure in the air, exaggerating the breasts and wiggled the garment in front.

He was alluding to my breasts, which made me blush and laugh at the same time. I shook my head and opened my arms wide. "Bigger," I mouthed. "Size 10."

He made a surprised face and held his arms out wide, still addressing the size of my breasts, and then returned with another blouse. It was made of very thin material.

"Thicker material," I said, making gestures like I was fingering the thickness.

I'm not sure that he understood, but the next time he returned with a red pullover. When he held it up, it looked just right. "Yes," I exaggerated my word by opening my mouth wide. "Red is a good colour."

Next he chose a skirt. We used the same mime gestures. "How much?" I asked, pretending to count dollar bills. He answered by flicking his fingers. I nodded. Outside he handed me the parcel and I went to the public washroom to change and fix my hair.

"I did good job," Kenji said. "You look pretty. Red shirt and blue skirt."

I pretended to pout. "Didn't I look pretty before?"

"Yes, but now you are *wow*." Kenji laughed and I laughed with him. It seemed the most natural thing that our hands touched as we walked to Bud's car with my wet clothing in the shopping bag.

The Ford parked near Bud's station wagon had a radio on and the car door was open. "Weirdo or what?" The man with a moustache leaning against his car said, as he nodded to greet us. When he saw our expressions he must have surmised that we hadn't heard the news. "Some goon is going over the Falls in a barrel. The police boat can't get to him now. He's too near the Falls."

Kenji and I stood still to listen.

The man motioned, urging us to come closer. "Those dips. He'll be the eighth daredevil to make it, *if* he survives. The dimwit."

"What does it mean?" Kenji asked.

The man answered, "The bloke told a reporter he was going to make a name for himself. In my opinion, it takes no talent to kill yourself." Measuring how big the barrel would be, he explained to Kenji that the man was in a wooden vessel like ones that hold wine.

"Why does he do it?" Kenji asked.

The man explained. "Daredevil. Those guys think they'll be in a movie and make lots of money. It's a short cut to fame. Does anyone know the names of the fools who did it in the past?" He shook his head. "Many died, you know. One man took his dog, and the dog put his nose in the air hole so the man suffocated. Downstream when the barrel came to rest, the dog walked out of the barrel okay. The man was dead." He shrugged. "Listen."

Kenji and I moved closer to the radio. I nodded a greeting to the man's wife, who was sitting on the front seat.

When the person on the radio reported that the barrel had disappeared, the man by the car exclaimed, "He's over the American Falls," and he started to run toward the nearby railing. "Hurry!" The man turned back and beckoned to us. "We might see him."

His wife didn't follow, and Kenji and I stood transfixed.

We heard the announcer say, "Too late. Too late. The Niagara Police tried, but they couldn't rope the barrel in."

Among the people crowded against the railing in the distance, we spotted the announcer, sounding breathless as he made his report on the radio. "Just seconds ago, the river took the latest daredevil over the brink. I'm at the railing overlooking the American Falls. The water is too frothy to see what is going on. There is supposed to be a police patrol boat at the base, but it is obscured by the mist at this moment. Folks, is this going to be a successful stunt? We will have the answer very soon. Does anyone know the stunt man's name? Get his name, please." He seemed to be requesting help from someone in the broadcast studio and took a moment to get a pair of binoculars from his satchel, slip the strap over his head, and then adjust the eye-pieces to his eyes. "The fog is too thick. I have to say that if he survives, the police will arrest him. It's against the law to do stunts at the Falls. Good, good … the air is clearing a bit. Let me focus these binoculars a little better."

My breathing was shallow.

I don't even know the guy but I'm worried. I hope he's okay. I don't understand why anyone puts his life in danger like this. Does he have a family? His actions are a flagrant disregard for his loved ones.

Kenji must have sensed my stress. He rested his hand on my shoulder. There was a fearful expression in his face.

The announcer was speaking excitedly. "I think, yes, it looks like there's a person on one of the boulders at the base of the Falls. Is he alive? Wait a minute, folks. Folks, the police are roping in a piece of wood." The pitch of his voice wavered and his words came more slowly. "Looks like it's part of the barrel. I think it is. Two more police boats are approaching. I see more pieces. If our daredevil smashed into the rocks, he couldn't … he can't … have survived." The announcer paused.

Kenji and I looked at each other. We were both holding our breaths.

"Can't someone find out his name? Just a minute, folks. Our researcher is getting his name. Oh yes. Yes. My producer says the reporter he spoke to before entering the barrel has left the area." The announcer sounded very frustrated. "Ladies and gentlemen …" he hesitated again. "If any of you listening know this man's story please phone in to our station." There was a sober tone to his voice. He seemed to be reading from a crib sheet, which he must have brought along. "Most of his predecessors, those who survived, travelled around the country trying to make money by selling pictures and describing their feats. Their fame was short-lived. None became rich. Only two of the survivors have different stories. One went over accidentally. That was Roger Woodward, who fell out of a boat upstream. He was only seven years old, but survived wearing only his swimming trunks and sneakers. The second was Nathan T. Boya, a coloured man. When interviewed last year, he said he did it because he had to. He doesn't know why, but he wants us to forget that daredevil adventure. He became a doctor. He wants to be remembered for saving lives. This is the kind of man we can look up to. Let's remember *that* name: Nathan T. Boya." The airway went silent. "It's bad news. I see clearly. Bad news. Bad news. There *is* a body on the rocks." After a moment of quiet, we heard another voice say, "We must pause for a word from our sponsor."

"I don't want to look," I said to Kenji and turned toward our car.

"No. I also do not wish to look," Kenji said.

"I admire that man, the one who says he wants to save lives," I said.

Apparently Kenji didn't get the gist of what I'd said, but his response pleased me. "I will try," Kenji said. He made big eyes.

"Why did you choose medicine?" I asked.

"*Nei*," Kenji said, giving himself time to think, "You believe I plan to save the world."

"Well, do you?"

"You will laugh when I tell you reason."

"Try me."

"The girl I liked had father who was surgeon. I thought she would want a doctor for boyfriend."

Was he kidding or was that the true story?

"Are you still trying to please that girl?"

"She is not in picture. I discover that I like what I study. Maybe I will do good, maybe I will keep people healthy. Maybe, but not sure. I will try."

Must be true. He's very honest. It's great that he can be honest with me when he hardly knows me. I admire him.

"So, are your parents pleased that you're a doctor?"

"I believe so. Father is Japanese history professor. They think academic life is good, but they approve my choice. I finish high school and then take exam for University of Tokyo Medical School. I fail first attempt but study and pass the following year."

He's persistent. Wow. That's good. "You can enter med school right after high school?"

Kenji laughed. "Only if you pass test. Very difficult test. Most people must study a year or two before they pass."

We were silent for a time. The experience of hearing the sequence of a man's death on the radio haunted me. I tried to think of something that could take our minds off the man in the barrel. "Want to listen to music? We can sit in Bud's car." I suggested.

We sat on the bench seat. I turned the switch, turned on the radio, and sat with my hands folded in my lap.

Kenji spun the dial until he hit a music band; then he put his hand on top of mine. "Very nice," he said. "You like music. I will invite you to hear the orchestra many times."

Our eyes met. It was perfect. I just grinned.

I can't wait to write Charlotte about my new friends, and Kenji in particular.

Chapter 4
The Shampoo

"Alice Nelson is amazing. Amazing woman." These words fell from everyone's lips. This seventy-year-old woman, who recently had broken her foot in a car accident, was in the hospital because of a lump in her breast.

"I'm doing okay," Mrs. Nelson said, when I offered to help her walk on crutches up and down the hall for exercise. "You have other things to do. I'm fine." The medication nurse was greeted like she was dispensing candy. After uncovering her lunch plate, Mrs. Nelson exclaimed that chicken soup was her favourite. She knew which patients had visitors and struggled on her crutches to the bedsides of those who didn't. No wonder her bedside table was filled with cards from well-wishers, and vases of flowers had arrived from her church and from a bridge club.

I was assigned to give Alice Nelson a bed shampoo. "With that cast on her foot she can't take a shower. Anyway, she could use a bit of pampering," the head nurse said.

I was flattered, because this was an escalation in my duties; my classmates were still only assigned bed baths. With Mrs. Nelson flat in bed, it was going to be difficult to wash and rinse her hair without getting the bed wet. I was determined to live up to the nurse's confidence in me. Furthermore, my heart went out to this brave patient.

Mrs. Nelson was an attractive woman, with snow white hair and eyebrows painted in an arch that drew attention to dark brown eyes. She was big-boned, solid. I pictured her walking like a flag bearer in a parade before the crutches slowed her down. When I approached, she was lying flat on her back in bed, with her head resting on her clasped hands.

My chance to shine.

I pulled the curtain, arranged a towel and then a rubber apron around her neck, and rolled the sides to make a trough that would direct water into a basin on the floor. Cheerfully I made her comfortable with a pillow under her knees and another against her feet as a foot rest. I was satisfied with my preparations.

"You think of everything," Mrs. Nelson said, smiling up at me.

I held her hand momentarily while explaining the procedure and reassuring her that she was in good hands. Next, I wet her shoulder-length hair with lukewarm water. "How's the temperature?" I asked, as the water trickled from the enamel pitcher.

"Fine, just fine," she said, stretching to look at me without lifting her head off the apron. "It is very kind of you to do this for me."

"My pleasure." Doing a procedure that made a patient well or made them feel good gave me instant reward. I'd experienced that feeling a few times when I put my patients' feet in basins to soak.

Mrs. Nelson is going to love the head massage. I'll offer to set her hair with curlers if she has any; style her hair just as she likes it. She's going to feel pretty.

"It could be warmer," Mrs. Nelson said.

"Of course." I added hot water from the spigot at the sink in her room. I felt like I'd won a million dollars. Some parts of nursing were okay.

"Hmm," Mrs. Nelson said with a sigh. "Very nice." If she were a cat, she'd be purring.

Charlotte would laugh if I wrote her about giving a bed shampoo—not her concept of an adventure. Oh, well, she'd introduced me to so many exciting ideas; I liked her in spite of our different attitudes. She should be in Copenhagen by now, maybe at the Tivoli. I didn't miss going to that amusement park, but I would miss visiting Karen Blixen's home in Rungsted. I was sure there would be souvenirs from her life in Kenya where she'd lived with her husband, a Baron, and fallen in love with Denys Finch-Hatton. Would Charlotte go there? I'd expected to get details about the furnishings of castles Charlotte visited and stories about the former residents, which would make me envious, but her notes were short, often only a postcard giving a new address. Her descriptions of new friends made them sound uppity, not like friends I'd choose.

I applied the shampoo to Mrs. Nelson's hair. The foam bubbled up. I swished it around, gently lifting her head with one hand to reach the back. I worked my fingers near her hair line, and then back and forth behind her ears and lower onto her neck, and then up again to her hairline. The contented sensations that washed through me when I was having a shampoo, came again. I was sure Mrs. Nelson experienced the same.

"You've got magic fingers," Mrs. Nelson said, her voice sounding mellow, like she was on the verge of a hypnotic state.

"Thanks."

She let out a long breath. "I'll cheat God again."

"Oh?"

"I didn't die in the car accident. Maybe I was supposed to, but I didn't die. I'm always positive." Her eyes were closed. The words flowed in a monotone, seeming to come effortlessly.

"That's a good way to be." I curled some of the soapy hair around my finger and let it spring back. It was pleasant to play with the soapy hair.

"I'll be remembered for my positive nature," she said.

"Yes." I nodded agreement.

"It's amazing, what some people think they will be remembered for."

"I suppose you're right."

Suddenly a man appeared around the curtain.

"Dean!" Mrs. Nelson sprang alert. As she lifted her head off the rubber, her neck stiffened. "I suppose you drove all night. How many times did I tell you not to take a chance driving eight hours straight?" Her forehead furrowed; the frown seemed uncharacteristic.

"Martha said you wanted to see me," the man said.

"Your sister always exaggerates. Of course it is good to see you, but …"

The man took off his jacket, threw it across the foot of her bed, and pulled up a chair. "Don't let me interrupt."

"Finish later," Mrs. Nelson said in a commanding tone, while shooing me away with her fingers.

I wrapped a thick Turkish towel around her head and began to look in her bedside table for a comb and brush, which we'd be needing soon.

She turned to address her son. "Did you stop to eat on the way? I suppose you only had coffee."

"Actually, the roads have been cleared and I made very good time," the son answered.

"I've heard that before. You'll be remembered for taking chances. We were just talking about how people will be remembered. How will *you* be remembered, Dean?"

He leaned forward, resting his elbow on his thigh, and propping his head on his hand. "I guess I haven't given it much thought." He was smiling and I was pleased to see that he had a sense of humour.

"Not much thought." She laughed. "That will be a good epitaph for your grave. Very appropriate!"

Dean's smile flickered a bit, and then he turned to look out the window.

"Phoned Martha yet?" Mrs. Nelson asked.

"Oh, I better do that," Dean said, and excusing himself, he stood up, getting ready to leave the room.

"Well, go and do it," Mrs. Nelson commanded. To me, she spoke in the same commanding tone. "You can resume the shampoo."

I removed the towel and started the gentle massage routine again. Circles, circles ... moving the suds, pressing lightly against her scalp and making circles. Around and around over the crown, by her temples, behind her ears, at the forehead, back to the temples.

"I have a friend in a wheelchair who lives alone," Mrs. Nelson said in a dreamy voice. "She thinks she'll be remembered for being self-sufficient in spite of her disability. It's *me* who takes her shopping and to doctor appointments. Is *that* self-sufficient?" She emphasized particular words as she spoke.

I cradled her head, while adding extra bubbly soap onto the right side of her head, and then onto the left side, hoping that the movement would bring her back to the relaxed state again.

"My friend, Susan Pritchard, is having a bronze bust of her father made, to give to the university where he once taught. Brilliant man." She raised a finger and shook it. "Bronze is appropriate. High and mighty. Too good for most of us. That hard-nosed old fart." Mrs. Nelson sneered, then laughed.

I gasped.

Did I hear her correctly? Hard-nosed...I don't want to repeat her derogatory term. That doesn't sound like the Mrs. Nelson we know.

Words flowed from her mouth like water rushing from a broken dam. "Betty Glover says she'll be remembered because she never takes the best seats at church. She's inclined to drop her handkerchief and forget to pick it up. She's like a mouse. If she doesn't leave something behind no one knows she's been there. Get it? Mouse droppings?" Mrs. Nelson laughed and then pointed to her forehead. "Scratch a little more to the left would you?"

With the ball of my fingers, I pressed hard along her hairline. I was so annoyed about the way she talked to her son, and the way she described her friends, that it was easy to apply more force to my massage, even though I realized it might not promote relaxation.

She grimaced, but I pretended not to notice.

"Could you scratch a bit by my left ear?"

Hmm. The sweet voice has returned. I'm not buying it. As Gramma would say, "Dang bust it!"

I gave the spot a cursory rub.

Thank goodness we're almost done.

I squeezed the bulk of the suds into my hands and shook a glob into the waste basin holding the used water. It splashed and spread like seaweed smothering a lake. I repeated the process, flicked my wrist with a jerk so that another glob hit the gooey waste. I dried my hands with a spare towel, flung it onto the floor and gave it a kick.

Good. It was so pleasant at first, but now it's turned sour. A quick rinse and that's the end.

"Do they ever carve 'amazing mother' on a tombstone, I wonder," Mrs. Nelson said.

Amazing! To think I used to value that word. Do I have to keep listening to all this negative talk? Is that what nursing is about?

"I have a son and daughter," Mrs. Nelson was saying. "They're grown now, but I never interfere with their lives."

I wonder.

"Dean is a sales manager and Martha is a teacher, has two of her own. One is eight, no, nine, and one is eleven, I believe. It's hard to keep track. I never forget their birthdays."

Never? You can't even remember how old they are!

The friendly reference to her grand-kids didn't soften my annoyance. I could hardly wait to get away from her.

"One of those cards is from them." She raised her arm indicating the pile of get-well wishes on her bedside table.

Wonder what they wrote.

"Little Linda and little Andrew. Andy, Martha calls him. I don't know why you name a child and then insist on calling it something else."

I poured the water from the pitcher, lifted the locks of her hair so that the water could get underneath. It wasn't easy to rinse without getting her gown wet. How tempted I was. But my conscience took over.

Patience, Claire. You're almost done.

"Dean never had a nickname. Martha calls herself Martie, but I refuse to call her that. It was my husband's choice to name her after his mother, rest her soul. Heart of gold, they say. Generous to some. Hard as a gold brick is how I saw it, but she was civil. Thank goodness we didn't have to take her in when she got old. My children will never have to ... well, they might want to take me in, but I'll tell them that I don't expect it. Martha has an extra room. She's probably aiming to invite me there after my surgery, particularly since it will soon be Christmas. They would never send me back to my apartment at Christmas."

Bet they'd like to.

Impatient to finish, I ran my fingers through her hair and then poured more water. Her neck muscles grew stiff so that I couldn't tip her head.

"Don't resist. Let me move you," I said. She couldn't see how set my lips were as I forced her head into position.

"Dear, you don't have to shout. If you tell me what it is you wish me ..."

I tipped the pitcher letting the entire contents douse her hair like a massive wave. The water splashed down the trough in a torrent. "There now. It's much easier if you let me manage things."

Good thing she can't see my face.

My smile reached from ear to ear.

"Whew, that was fast," said Mrs. Nelson.

The head nurse pushed aside the curtain and looked in. "How is it going?"

"This young lady is giving me a shampoo," Mrs. Nelson replied, without any semblance of the sweetness.

The head nurse smiled at me. "Claire is one of our best," she said and left.

I took a deep breath.

She wouldn't say that if she could read my thoughts.

The sweet tone was back. Mrs. Nelson was saying, "That head nurse is so kind. Everyone is kind, but I don't know why they gave me that coloured doctor."

"Dr. Margolius? He's chief of breast surgery," I replied.

"Really?"

I got another pitcher of water—filled mostly from the cold faucet.

Sorry God, but ... I'll pay for this. Here goes.

When I poured it though her hair, she trembled.

"Oh, that's a bit on the cool side. Maybe you didn't test it first."

"Cold washes out more shampoo," I said, matter-of-factly. I hoped a feeling of satisfaction didn't show on my face.

"Of course."

I wrapped her head in another towel, and then removed the rubber apron and carried the basin and all my paraphernalia away. When I returned, she was drying her hair. I put the brush and comb on the bedside table within her reach.

"My hair curls easily. Do you think you can do something with it?"

"Sure," I said and began to ease the comb through snarls in her hair.

I'd love to just yank it, but I'd better not.

She screwed up her face. "Oh ... oh! I guess I should do it." She took the comb from my hand.

The doctor arrived. "You look great, Mrs. Nelson. You've even had a shampoo."

He smiled at me, and then came closer to address my patient. "Your surgery is tomorrow, so I want to check your breast again. The right one, isn't it?"

Mrs. Nelson's face turned as pale as a turnip. She pressed her lips tight together and closed her eyes while the examination was taking place.

"We'll send a biopsy, a sample of the tissue, to the lab while you're in surgery," the doctor said. "It is possible that we won't have to remove your breast, but you understand that we might have to do a radical, remove lymph nodes as well."

"So you told me already," Mrs. Nelson said. After the doctor left, she pulled me close and whispered, "Do I have to let that coloured man operate? Why, he probably hasn't done much more than cut up chickens."

"He's a specialist. Been here five years. You're in good hands."

"Flowers for you," one of the nurse's aides said, approaching the chair where Mrs. Nelson sat.

"They will be from Hubert," Mrs. Nelson said. "I'm surprised he hasn't poked his nose in to see if I'm really sick. My ex, you know. All about guilt. Men suddenly get thoughtful when they are on their own." She took the card off the green wrapper and opened it while the aide got a vase of water for the flowers. "Why, it's from Dean. Now isn't he a dear son? Sometimes he surprises me."

I noticed that there were tears in her eyes. Next, I got a pan of bath water, soap and towels, and laid them out. "I'll step away while you bathe," I said.

"But aren't you going to do it?"

"It's good for you to be active. You don't need help. Here." I pinned the cord used to summon help from the nurses' station onto the bed next to her chair. "Pull if you need anything." I left.

No Claire. You don't have to feel guilty. That woman doesn't need any more fussing over.

When I returned, she was dressed in a fresh gown and robe and had pushed the table aside to stand on her crutches. "I wouldn't need these if my tire hadn't blown. I went off the road. Oh, I'm a good driver, but did you ever try to steer a car that wobbled every which way?"

Claire, don't weaken. She's getting to you. Next thing, you'll be waiting on her hand and foot.

Finally I managed to say, "Your hair looks nice. I hope it feels good."

"I guess so." She pulled a rose from the bouquet, swung the crutches so that they supported her as she stepped away from the bed and into the room, and then out into the corridor. "Hello, Mrs. Bishop. How are you doing?" I heard that artificially sweet voice, which was making me feel ill. "Here, this rose is for you."

"You are so kind," Mrs. Bishop said. "Is your surgery tomorrow?"

"Yes. What do you think? That coloured doctor is going to operate."

"He's good. Operated on my neighbour who went home already."

"I hope you'll say a prayer for me."

"I sure will. I just know you'll come through okay," Mrs. Bishop said.

As she went around the floor, Mrs. Nelson reminded everyone of her pending operation.

The next morning Mrs. Nelson's son and daughter were there before she left for surgery.

"No tears," Mrs. Nelson said. "Be brave. No tears."

Neither of them appeared to have wet eyes. Dean kept checking his watch, and Martha walked back and forth at the foot of her mother's bed.

Bet they can't wait to go for coffee.

"I'll cheat God again," Mrs. Nelson said. "I have a feeling."

I've got a feeling too. You probably will. People like you seem to survive.

The orderlies arrived. I pulled the screen and helped transfer her to the gurney.

"Wish Momma luck," she called back to her son and daughter, as she was being moved.

"Good luck, Momma," they said in unison.

After the gurney cleared the doorway, Mrs. Nelson reached out, and I took her hand to instinctively give it a squeeze.

Okay, so that's what a good nurse should do. Now say something upbeat.

"Keep the faith," I said. "We'll be waiting to look after you when you return to the floor." Slowly, I let go of her hand. In spite of wanting to resist it, a wave of compassion had swept through me, seeing this woman finally acquiesce and put her future into the hands of our medical staff. I really wanted the surgery to be successful.

The head nurse summoned me. "Mrs. Nelson left a note this morning. Let me read it to you. 'That girl you sent to wash my hair is extremely rough. She refused to give me a bath. I guess she's new at the job. Give her some pointers. I'm sure you know how best to go about giving a shampoo.'"

I felt the corners of my mouth turn down. I didn't know whether to laugh, slam my fist into the wall, or apologize for the cold water. And to think that I'd begun to think I could learn to love caring for *all* my patients.

The head nurse grinned, crumpled up the paper and tossed it into the waste can. "I overheard your conversation. You've got at least a day before she comes back from intensive care."

"Me?"

"You can handle her, Claire. I'd bet my life on it. Anyone else would have drowned her."

Well to tell the truth ...

She tapped my shoulder. "As nurses, we develop skill for dealing with all sorts of people. We're here to give them the treatment they need regardless. She's scared out of her wits, has to think she's in control, but no matter what happens in surgery, you'll manage."

Chapter 5
Escape

After the experience with Mrs. Nelson, I found nursing much more interesting.

The skill of performing procedures safely was being hammered into us in classes, but I had discovered that understanding the patient's reactions to life situations and their medical conditions was crucial to their recovery. One needed to understand the patient's history and worries. I decided that I'd learn to show empathy and help patients no matter what their attitudes might be, and that I could learn by observing full-fledged nurses and our team leaders—the doctors—whom we revered. I formed conclusions about my next patient's problem rather quickly, but it disturbed me to find that the doctor attending her didn't see the obvious problem, and being in a learning mode myself, I felt that I should help him to learn something.

It was January, 1961, and Dr. Purcell, a few months out of med school, sat in the nurses' station, legs crossed at the knee. He was casually cozying up to one of the nurses who was trying to chart notes. He had light, curly hair, dreamy blue eyes, and an engaging smile, so I could see why the nurse let him interfere with her work. When I walked by to get the cover for our new patient's chart, he beckoned me to come speak to him. "You on admissions? We'll need Mrs. Rossi's specimens right away." He gave my uniform a once over. "Did they teach you students how to get urine and stool samples? Can't have any contamination." He wagged his finger at me.

He is one of those! My friends are right.

Several of the girls had worked with him and concluded that he thought he was another Dr. Kildare, star of a brand new TV program we all liked. He was handsome yes, but had none of the insight or diplomacy that Richard Chamberlain portrayed in that series. I could feel the hair on my arms prickle.

You are full of yourself. I know the admission procedures very well, doctor. Maybe better than you.

I sighed, because this was one dilemma I hadn't envisioned—tolerating condescension or risking conflict with a superior.

I've got to find a way to deal with your condescending attitude. I'll just demonstrate that I am fully trustworthy.

With my blue eyes still focused directly at him, my answer was a bit sharp. I acknowledged that I did in fact know how and that I would, of course, fill the order as soon as the patient complied with the request. He returned to charming the nurse. It was a poor start to my work with Dr. Purcell, but I was smart enough to overcome my prejudice.

This conversation put me in an anxious state, so I trotted away to make certain that the unit was ready for Mrs. Rossi. The nurse's aide hadn't missed a thing. The bed pan, wash basin, kidney basin, pitcher, and tumbler were all accounted for. I returned to the nurses' station in time to see a short woman, less than five feet tall, getting off the elevator, and concluded that she must be Mrs. Rossi. She was lugging a huge cardboard suitcase with both hands, and was bent sideways to support a carpet bag slung over one shoulder. Rushing to help her, I noticed that under her tweed coat she wore a calf-length, shapeless, print dress. An antiquated black felt hat tilted enough to reveal her grey hair. She reminded me of photos I'd seen of refugees struggling down the gangplank when they landed at Ellis Island fifty years ago. I wondered if, like them, she had packed all her worldly possessions for this visit, otherwise why was this suitcase so heavy? Out of breath, she plunked the luggage down onto the floor, and then looked around and rubbed her nose with the back of her hand. There was a terrified look on her face. Certainly the hospital smells of medications, cleaning fluids, laundered linens, starched uniforms, and steaming water-baths to sterilize equipment, and the sounds of carts, wheelchairs, and people hurrying along the slick tile corridors would all be new to her. She was going to need my help to feel that the hospital was a safe place, and I knew what to do.

"You must be Rowena Rossi. I'm your nurse, Claire Winchester," I said, reaching out to take the suitcase.

"Pleased, I'm sure." Mrs. Rossi freed her hand and extended it, even though she looked unsure of the proper protocol.

Dr. Purcell called from the nurses' station to say that he'd be along in a few minutes.

It would have been kinder for him to have joined us, but then I'm in the mood to give him the benefit of the doubt, and rationalize that maybe he has duties to attend to first.

We started down the corridor, her steps steady and in pace with mine as I laboured with the luggage.

What's in here that's so heavy? Clothing wouldn't weigh this much. Books? Unlikely. And why didn't admissions send her up in a wheelchair? Poor soul. Didn't any family come with her?

We entered her room.

"This bed is yours," I said, swinging the case onto bed B, next to the door. The monstrous suitcase was a problem. It wouldn't fit in the small cupboard allotted to a patient, nor could it be left beside her bedside table.

She looked across the room, past bed A and out toward the parking lot, then frowned and edged forward to pat the mattress. "I thought Diana said I was to have a window."

"Diana?" I questioned.

"My daughter. She's buying flowers."

I felt more protective.

Why would a daughter stop to buy flowers before helping her mom to settle? Some people had strange priorities. I will fill the void and help this dear lady to be comfortable in the hospital. Thank heavens there is a daughter. She can lug this gigantic suitcase back home. I can't imagine that there's anything important in it that will be needed for such a short stay.

"This your first time in a hospital?" I asked.

"Yes, Miss."

"We'll try to make you comfortable."

"Oh, I won't be trouble."

"Would you please take what you need out of this case, and we'll send it home with your daughter? There's no storage space here."

Mrs. Rossi looked panic stricken. "But I need everything. I'll be here two weeks, so what's there has got to stay."

Two weeks? Just for a GI series test?

Now I was confused, but I didn't pursue that issue.

She'd discovered the drawer of her bedside table and was taking a toothbrush, soap, comb, hair brush, and pink nightie from her carpet bag and aligning things in strict order.

While some women smell like perfume, leather purses, cigarettes, new perms, or fat, and men often smell like aftershave, dry-cleaning fluid, tobacco, or sweat, this woman smelled like laundry soap, cheap nylon, and lye cleaners. It said something about her lifestyle.

A blue hospital gown had been left on her bed. "I'll pull the curtain while you change into this." I held it up for her to see.

"No, no," she said. "My nightie is new." The nylon sparked as she lifted a new gown from the drawer. "It's a gift just for the trip."

I held back my grin.

A trip! I wouldn't describe a hospital stay in those terms. She can't know how painful her GI Series is going to be. I've got to help her through the hard times. I asked for a challenge and here it is.

"First you must wear a hospital gown," I said. "Later you can change."

While eyeing the equipment above her bed, she ran her fingers through frizzy hair that looked like a fresh permanent, and then turned around and around inside her curtained space, like she was getting the feel of her surroundings.

I pointed to the suitcase. "Need anything from here?"

She shook her head, so I slid the suitcase off the bed and onto the floor, and then pushed it between the table and the bed. It couldn't stay there, but for the time being ... Dr. Purcell would be along shortly, and even though I disliked his approach, it had been etched into our training that the doctor was the head of the medical team, and I was determined to make him respect me. I offered to help her undress, but she drew in her shoulders, and I realized that she felt embarrassed, so I told her to change, and that I'd be back shortly.

When I returned, she'd hung her clothes in the closet and climbed into bed. She smiled up at me trustingly. The sight of her stained fingers, the riddled blue veins in her hands, and her skinny arms crossed over her chest made me feel more protective toward this woman, who obviously led a hard life. Her vital signs were normal, except for a fast pulse and slightly elevated blood pressure, likely due to anxiety. I helped her into her slippers and led her to the washroom. Fortunately, she could produce the samples we needed. The dark urine meant that I should give her plenty of liquid. There were no outward signs of clotted or fresh blood in the stool. I explained that the doctor was coming to do a physical. She didn't understand, so I said, "He'll listen to your heart and—"

Her eyes sprung open wide. "Nothing wrong with my heart."

"Just a ritual. The doctor checks everything." I removed her felt slippers and helped her back into bed.

"It's my belly that's been acting up."

"You tell him everything. He'll look you over, and I'll stay right here." I adjusted the spread across her chest.

"Thank you, Miss."

A lady wearing a mink coat over a royal blue suit stuck her head inside the curtains. "Mom, you didn't wait by the elevator as I asked," she said, with an air of exasperation in her voice. The intruder carried an enormous vase of mums. She looked right and left, like she didn't know what to do with the flowers. "I'm Diana Aberfield," she said, eyeing my student uniform.

The daughter. Hmm. At least she has family.

I didn't know what to do with the flowers either, but I took them and was headed toward the window ledge when the woman commanded, "Just a minute." She crowded the water pitcher, glass, and box of tissues closer together on the bedside table and gestured for me to put the flowers there. I complied—for the time being at least.

"You must be her daughter." I managed a smile for her benefit, and introduced myself.

"Yes. Mrs. Aberfield," she replied. "I can't stay. I just want to see that Mom's settled." She gave me a polite nod. "Mother, you know that I've got to pick up the twins at school." She kissed her mom on the cheek. "You look all cozy, but my goodness, brush your hair. That old hat has … And you aren't wearing your new gown." She turned to look at me. "Help her put on the new gown I bought, will you?"

"She can change after the doctor does his examination," I said, confirming the agreement Mrs. Rossi and I had made.

Mrs. Aberfield tapped the bedside table. "My husband and I are supposed to fly to New York tonight. I wonder if we should."

The question seemed aimed at me, so I answered, "The doctor," I had been about to say intern, but noting the way she'd reacted to my student uniform, I had altered my word, "will be along shortly. He might have some questions."

However, Mrs. Rossi spoke up, "No, no. You go off with Ralph; it's okay." She smoothed the spread with her hands. "The nurse is very nice."

The daughter seemed to weigh a decision and then said, looking directly into my eyes, "I've left a number. They'll call about the results, won't they?"

Results?

I checked Mrs. Rossi's chart. "We've got a New York number, but is there anyone who could come in before you get back? The tests will be very stressful for your mom and—"

"I'll phone in," Mrs. Aberfield interrupted, and after giving her mom's hand a pat, she pulled open the curtain. Pausing at the doorway, she waved, and then disappeared down the corridor.

Damn. I forgot the suitcase. Some family. Can't that daughter stay and meet the doctor? That woman couldn't wait to get rid of her mother's care. Okay, so I'll stand in for her. I'll make sure this dear lady gets the attention she needs from our medical staff. Maybe I won't wind up being a nurse, but I know what is expected of me in this situation. Charlotte would be surprised. I'm getting better and better at this job. And what's with Charlotte? She wrote from Denmark and she didn't even visit Hans Christian Anderson's house or go to Isaac Dennison's place like we discussed. She's just hanging around universities.

Dr. Purcell arrived and I stayed to assist with the physical. Did he introduce himself? No, he left that for me to do. He barked orders. "Open your mouth. Tilt your head. Hands out of the way so I can listen to your heart." I mimed what she was to do, and she seemed reassured by my help. "Pulse is fast," he said.

"Of course. Everything here is strange," I said.

He should have noticed her cold hands. What kinds of people are allowed to intern these days?

"Hurt here? How about here?" he asked, listening to areas across her abdomen. She denied any pains. "So what brought you to the hospital? What are your symptoms?" Dr. Purcell stepped back and scribbled some notes on her chart. Not once had he looked her in the eye.

"What bothers you, Mrs. Rossi?" I asked. "Where do you hurt?"

"Well, sometimes I don't have enough breath. That's when I carry the washing out to the line. The basket is heavy, you know. But it's my belly that hurts most. Don't think I digest the way I used to."

"Poor digestion," Dr. Purcell wrote. He stretched and squared his shoulders like he was bored. "What do you eat?"

"I get up at five. For breakfast I cook eggs for Dad and Mom. Oats. Dad wants his oats and black coffee."

"Your parents? How old are they?" Dr. Purcell looked amazed that a woman her age would have parents.

He must think people should die before seventy. Leave the planet to the young. His attitude is hard to take.

"It's my husband's folks. Dad is 95 and Mom is 92. She's in a wheelchair, so I help her get out of bed and put her down for a nap, and at bedtime, too. My back goes out sometimes." Her right hand rubbed the lumbar area of her spine. "Bacon has got to be crisp. A pound stretches for a week. An egg is enough breakfast for me. Lunch is usually soup. Vegetables. He wants chicken or fish at night. Seems I'm always busy cooking something or washing up."

"Yes, yes, yes." Dr. Purcell tapped his pen against the chart. "Anything else?"

She looked back and forth from the doctor to me, like I should tell her what to say. "My head. I think I have a headache over here sometimes." She pointed to her temple, and when Dr. Purcell wrote nothing, she grunted a laugh and said, "My belly swells. Minnie Spiro had an ulcer. Maybe that's it. Maybe it's my kidney. Does it hurt here when you got a kidney?" She punched her side. "No, that's appendix. Maybe it's appendix. Or my ankles. I can't stand the cold like I used to." An anxious look covered her face. I could see that she felt she wasn't giving the answers the doctor expected. She eyed me like a frightened child asking Mother for help.

Dr. Purcell snapped shut the chart. "We'll run a gastrointestinal series." With that pronouncement, he left.

I was really perturbed. This doctor gave our patient no reassurance whatsoever. He didn't even explain what was going to happen in words she could understand.

Okay, I will explain.

I tapped Mrs. Rossi's hand, indicating that I'd be back, and followed Dr. Purcell into the corridor carrying the specimens.

"Oh, you got them," Dr. Purcell said. "She's just a hypochondriac. Why do the GPs send us people like her?"

I don't know where the gumption came from, but I stepped in front of him so that he had to stop to face me. "Because she *has* a problem." I fixed him with unblinking eyes, but tried to make my voice sound understanding. "Didn't you get the clue?"

He stared back. "And is it your duty to tell me how to do my job?" He raised an index finger and slashed it though the air, then pushed me aside. "The x-ray and tomorrow's tests will give the answer, Miss … Miss …?"

"Claire Winchester," I said, then clamped my lips tight.

How could I defend my stance? Let him report me for insubordination.

He hastened away. Luckily he didn't see the sneer I gave him.

Mrs. Rossi was full of stories about her daughter, a clever girl, who sang in the church choir, was president of this and that, and about her son, who had been a minor hockey star, and had a degree in business. She also told me how she lived with her husband's parents because they had taken her and her kids in when her husband had been killed in a construction accident. She wished she could buy things for her grandchildren, but she'd had to quit her cleaning job, and her in-laws only gave her money for essentials.

A nurse's aide brought the list of menu options. I noticed that Mrs. Rossi squinted and held the sheet close up.

"Shall I read your choices?" I asked, and she handed over the list.

"Isn't this grand? Somebody else going to cook." Her face relaxed.

After I read the items, she said, "No roast. Maybe roasts cost extra. Well, never mind. At least I don't have to sweat at the stove."

The bland choices were because of her stomach complaints, but I didn't try to explain.

"Hope they don't have brown bread. I like white. Pancakes would be good for breakfast. Sausage. I like sausage, but Dad don't. The house has got to run the way he wants it. I hate it that he still uses a pot. He could get up to the toilet. I do, but he won't. Winter is hard. He has gas heat in his room, but keeps the furnace turned down so my room is cold. Now how did I get onto that when we was talking about food?"

It's good that she has enough confidence in me to tell me about her life. Makes me feel more protective.

"Let me get your glasses. Are they in your carpet bag?" I said.

"I like your sound when you read," she said. "I'm pretty tired."

It occurred to me that she might not be able to read English or any language.

"Is anyone having ice cream tonight?" she asked.

"I'll see what I can do." I made a mental note to phone the dietitian.

"I'd be obliged." Mrs. Rossi seemed to be looking at what her room-mates were doing, now that her curtain was open. "What goes on here in the evening?"

"You're going to be rather busy, but after your tests, you could go down to the visitor's lounge and watch TV.

"TV! Diana has TV, but I seldom go there. Dad doesn't want one. Are the pictures full of colour?"

"Afraid not. Just black and white. Don't think any hospital has colour TV yet, but I'm sure it will come."

"What are the tests going to be?"

"Well, the technician is going to give you an EKG—that's a heart test—and then later this evening, you'll have an enema."

She drew back. "Enema?"

"They're going to x-ray your intestine tomorrow. You know the place where the food goes after you eat?"

"Because of what I told them?"

"We want to find the cause of all your belly problems."

"I wish I'd shut up. Now what have I done?"

"You've done nothing wrong. We just want to check and find out what is making you feel bad."

I'd been assigned to follow Mrs. Rossi until her bedtime. Her son arrived before she'd finished the dinner on her tray. He carried a huge box, plopped it on the bed, and then bent to kiss his mother.

"You shouldn't be buying me things." Mrs. Rossi blushed like a young girl. "Whatever did you do this time?"

"Finish eating, and then you can open it."

"I'll just have the ice cream. They don't cook fish the way I'm used to."

I took the tray away and put the box in front of her.

"My, my," she said, looking radiant. "Just look what you brought." She peeled aside the tissue and held up a quilted, pink bathrobe. It's the best I ever had." Her eyes were teary.

"Well, Mom, you deserve it. You'll be up flirting with all the doctors in no time." He turned to me. "When is her operation? She says she'll be here a couple of weeks."

I must have looked surprised.

"I don't suppose you know," he said to me, and then turning to look at his mom, he said, "Think of it as a vacation."

Vacation indeed! No one in her family understands what tests she's having. I suppose Dr. Purcell would have told the daughter if she'd stayed to listen.

"Is her surgery tomorrow?" he asked.

"There's a battery of tests," I shook my head, "but no surgery is planned so far."

The son looked perplexed. "I thought ... well, Mom thought ... she said that her ulcer was going to be repaired. We hired someone to look after my grandparents for two weeks."

"Good idea," I said emphatically.

Well, now someone is going to see what is expected of this woman. She's got a hard life and she's too old for that responsibility. What's this about an ulcer? Where did that spring from?

The next day, when I reported to work for the afternoon shift, Mrs. Rossi was back from her tests and resting in bed. Dr. Purcell was standing by as Dr. Peters, the Chief of Internal Medicine, sat at her bedside describing the results. His voice sounded kind. He must have been about sixty, short, almost bald with just a bit of grey hair over his ears, and wore black-rimmed glasses. "And so," Dr. Peters concluded, "you can go home this evening." He removed the specs, and put them in his breast pocket. "I'll get the nurse to phone your daughter or son."

"No," Mrs. Rossi wailed. "I can't go home." Her lips twitched and she turned her head away.

Dr. Peters seemed flustered. "You're amazingly healthy. We find nothing the matter." He stood. "For a woman of sixty-five, I have to say you take good care of yourself."

Dr. Purcell eyed me with an air of superiority that made me furious.

"Don't you think I need to be operated on?" Mrs. Rossi said. "I think it might be my liver."

"You're as healthy as a forty year old."

"Please, doctor, don't send me home."

"We can't keep you here. You're a healthy woman."

"Please let me stay. Can't I stay just a little longer?"

Dr. Purcell appeared ready to chime in, but Dr. Peters held up his hand and turned to me like I might have an explanation.

"She needs an escape," I said. "She's exhausted." I described her daily routine, looking after two ninety year olds, seven days a week, year after year with no time off.

"Why don't you have a vacation?" Dr. Peters asked. "Your father should hire someone."

"My family wouldn't take to that. Besides I owe them cause of all they done."

"Your debt has been well paid." Dr. Peters shook his head. "I'll talk to the social worker and to your son and daughter. We can make things better for you." He looked to Dr. Purcell for confirmation, and the young doctor nodded enthusiastic agreement, though I doubted if he had a clue about the role of social services. "If you'll excuse me," Dr. Peters said. "I have to make some calls and I'll be back." He swished out of the room, with Dr. Purcell in pursuit.

"Don't you get government checks because of your age?" I asked, when we were alone again. I was about to suggest that she give herself a vacation.

She grinned. "I got my first check this month. Know what I bought?"

"I can't guess."

"Can you boost that suitcase up on the bed? I'll show you."

When the case opened and the lid fell back, I gasped.

"Look at the frames I got for my kid's pictures. There's Rose, age two. She calls herself Diana. There she's three, well ... maybe four. George, he's playing hockey. And that's me and my husband. I was an office cleaner, and he came to make some repairs. That's how we met. He was a good man."

"You brought all those pictures to the hospital?"

"They'd be smiling at me from everywhere in those pretty frames. Those were happy days."

"Well, now you can take them home and have them smiling at you inside your room or maybe all over the house."

Dr. Peters was back, with Dr. Purcell in tow. "We're going to let you stay until Monday. My secretary will make an appointment for me to meet with your son and daughter. I'm sure something can be arranged to get some help at home."

So, Dr. Purcell, do you now get the idea that medicine is about the total needs of a patient? It's not just about some infection or the failure of a body part. The symptoms may indicate another need and then we call in another department to help.

After the doctors left, I said, "Well now, want to change into your pink nightie? You can walk around in the new robe too."

She held the robe and nightie to her nose, inhaled, and giggled. The robe and nightie smelled like the sizing in all new garments. "It's hard for me to get away, you know. Dad and Mom depend on me. But Diana said I'd better get a checkup. She picked this place. Wait till I tell her and Ralph how nice it is."

Maybe I've been hasty in my appraisal of Diana. Maybe she did see that her mother needed time off and this was the only way she knew to help her escape. We never know what is behind a person's action. Hmm, in future I must be less quick to form judgements.

We passed Dr. Purcell gliding along merrily in the corridor. He stopped short and threw out his hands in awe. "Well now, Mrs. Rossi, aren't you a sight for sore eyes? All pretty in that robe. Pink is your colour," he said, winking at me.

His flirtatious manner worked this time. It made Mrs. Rossi happy, and it made me laugh.

Dr. Peters is going to teach this young upstart that medicine is about total care. Seems possible that Dr. Purcell got the message. It's great that he doesn't bear grudges. Things can work out if we are patient.

I sighed contentedly. All was right with the world. Nursing was turning out to be very different from the bed pan, and pill-pushing routine I had imagined.

After dinner that evening, I opened my pharmacology text book, but I couldn't concentrate. Something was gnawing at me. Maybe it was because notices that tuition for the next term would be going out soon, and Mom would open any notice that came from the university. I had to make a decision.

Scenes from my nursing experiences flicked through my mind and made me smile. On behalf of Mrs. Rossi, I heard myself speaking up to Dr. Purcell—the doctor who was in charge of my patient. Was Dr. Purcell ever surprised when I challenged his assumptions about that dear, little old lady? How much I'd changed in just those few months. Who could believe that shy Claire Winchester felt so self-assured these days? I was making a difference in the lives of my patients, and I was learning to recognize my prejudices about some of their actions—Mrs. Nelson and her rejection of coloured people and the grandiose picture she had of herself. I might have been more help to her if I'd realized that her attitudes covered up her fears, but I could forgive myself; I was learning. Charlotte once said that I took life too seriously, meaning that I had no sense of humour. Mr. Bronsky's smoking chair and gambling money together with Kenji's teasing was making me see the amusing side of life. I liked the feeling that every day brought new challenges. I could always stay one more term and meet Charlotte in Chile, if that was still her agenda. But, did I really want to quit the program?

Charlotte was acting like a lost soul. Her compass needle was spinning all over the place tying to find a direction. Okay, I understood her wish for love. Being in love was a super feeling. I was sizing up Kenji every time we met to see if he was my soul mate. He made me so happy. I hoped Charlotte would find someone as interesting and caring as Kenji was to me. But I needed a profession too. Didn't Charlotte? Maybe she would find one later. In many ways I had the feeling that I'd moved on more than Charlotte had. I'd been such a dependent person and so eager to please others in the past. I was growing up.

I reread the few letters that she had written. They disappointed me. When she wrote it was always about the guys she'd met, and she had a new girl friend, Beatrice, granddaughter of Lord somebody from England, and their pedigree horses. Never had she commented about my new friends or my amusing or poignant experiences in nurses' training, which I detailed when I wrote to her. She was considering enrolling at some European university for the spring term—reason to meet boys, I surmised. Art interested her after enrolling in a short drawing course at the University of Copenhagen. She'd suggested that I make an effort to see the Degas exhibition at the Cleveland Museum. At least that bore some resemblance to the dreams we used to have. I wasn't jealous. If I compared my life to the one Charlotte was living I felt I was on top. I was learning, feeling needed, mastering a profession, I had a swell boy friend, and many more close friends.

I lifted my packed suitcase down from the top shelf in my clothes closet and opened it. On top was the black and pink bathing suit with the ruffled skirt and polka-dot halter top. It looked so childish. I'd picked it following Charlotte's idea of what would be sexy on me. It made me laugh to recall how I looked parading around our city pool in that outfit. No wonder my brothers' friends whistled and called to me, "Hey, little sister." I must have looked like a freshman kid ready to start high school. I decided there and then to drop it in the box for clothing going to the Salvation Army Shelter. Other halter tops and towels could go too. For a moment I panicked when I couldn't find my Honolulu ticket wrapped in the towel. Then I remembered that I'd moved it into a pink draw-string purse. Onto the Sally Ann pile went the purse, but first I recovered the ticket and put it on my desk. That reminded me of the tuition payment. Dad thought the tuition was already paid. How could I explain that I hadn't made the payment? I glanced up at my calendar on the wall. Time for a decision. I sighed and smiled. I was learning so much about myself as well as about medicine and how to care for patients. And I couldn't imagine leaving my friends, especially Kenji, and Norma and Jan and Jeff and Bud. Tomorrow I would get a refund for my flight ticket to Honolulu, and then I would pay the tuition. It was a surprise that the decision was so easy to make.

I tried on two pairs of shorts—green and brown. They still fit and would be useful here in summer. I set them aside with the pale blue tailored summer dress to take home when I returned the suit case to its spot in my bedroom closet. I remembered Teddy's quizzical look when I packed that suit case. My dog might think that I was returning home to stay, but I'd explain to him what was happening.

Charlotte had mentioned that she was toying with the idea of coming home for Christmas. Could I wait and explain my decision to her? No, I had better put my plans in writing. I didn't think that she would be surprised. The letter wasn't the hardest one I would ever have to write. I tried to be tactful.

Chapter 6
Physiotherapy

My dear, dear five-year-old pet, Teddy—the Border Collie I'd chosen and named when I was fifteen—had recently been hit by a car. Five weeks had passed, but his hind quarters were still paralysed. The vet told Dad that, with Teddy's sort of spinal cord injury, we'd just have to wait and see.

No dogs were allowed in the dorm, so when I'd left to start nursing school, Ted had stayed behind with my folks. That meant Dad or Mom had to walk him, and on one of their outings, Ted had broken away and crossed the road to check out another dog. That's when the car had hit him. Dad blamed himself for the accident, but maybe I hadn't trained Ted to obey commands properly. I wanted Ted to walk again. I wanted Dad to feel better. I went home as often as I could. I taught Mom how to give him passive exercise. Dad learned to hold Ted up by the tail, hoping that eventually he'd be able to bear weight on his back legs when he walked. My nurse friends agreed that those measures weren't enough. Exercise in a whirlpool could make a difference, and there was a perfectly good whirlpool right there in our hospital. The Physiotherapy Department would never give permission. The discussion progressed. If we acted on the quiet, we could treat Ted in our hospital whirlpool, make him better, and no one need know.

Kenji was loaning me his car for the trip to pick up Teddy. The old Plymouth sputtered and choked down the dorm driveway. "Girls always have trouble with a stick shift," my brothers had said, but I was determined

to get the hang of it, and Kenji had been patiently giving me some pointers, practising in the parking lot down by Lake Erie. Signalling to my
classmates, who were seeing me off, that I would be okay, I kept going and
drove away.

*It's just getting the rhythm between the clutch and the gas to change gears. It'll
take a few miles, but I can do it.*

Ahead of me was an hour and a half drive into the country. The roads
had been cleared of snow, and the weather man predicated a cool but clear
day and evening.

Mom would have made a special snack and muffins for me to bring back
to my classmates. Dad would have bought a bag of apples. I knew I'd get a
great greeting from Teddy. I really hoped that even one whirlpool treatment
in the hospital physiotherapy pool would improve Ted's chance of recovery.

The traffic was terrible. It took longer than expected to get home. I
couldn't spend any time with Mom and Dad, but they understood. They
just handed me a box full of goodies. Dad carried Ted to the front seat of
Kenji's car. "How will you get a 40-pound dog from the car to the pool?"
Dad asked.

"We've got a plan," I said, settling myself into the driver's seat. I asked
Mom to call Norma and tell her that we should still arrive at 9:15, the time
we'd agreed to meet. Ted was resting his head on my hip. Mom had put a
blanket over his rear quarters. I wondered if that was too hot for the long-
haired dog, but left it. I turned on the ignition.

Dad pounded on my window. "One of your tail lights is out. Did
you know?"

I rolled down the window enough to tell him that I'd be careful, and off
we went. The non-functioning light was a surprise, but the highway was
lit up, so I didn't give it much thought. Ted snuggled beside me. He didn't
seem to be in pain.

The carefully concocted plans involved three of my classmates. Jan had
been hanging around the Physiotherapy Department, saying that she was
thinking of changing from nursing and wanted to know what physiothera-
pists did. She was actually there to case the joint—to see how we could get
into the whirlpool secretly. She'd discovered that the cleaning staff arrived
around 8:00 p.m., that the key to the pool hung behind the receptionist's
desk in the waiting room, and that the cleaners went in and out with the
door unlocked during the hour they cleaned. She intended to slip in while
the cleaners worked, hide in a closet, and then open the door for us when
we arrived. When closed, the door to the clinic locked automatically, so
there'd be no problem about leaving. Norma, my best friend, was the clear
thinker, so her job was to work out the details of the move. To have a
fourth pair of hands, we'd asked Flo, who was good with dogs.

Friday evening had been chosen because the hospital staff were in a hurry to start the weekend and wouldn't hang around doing extra things. We had another scheme to get Ted from the car to the third-floor Physiotherapy Department. By 9:30, Ted's treatment in the whirlpool could begin.

As I sped back to the hospital, I hoped to stay just ahead of a car that was going my speed and would have both back lights working, but cars behind got impatient and whizzed past me. After a while, I concluded that it didn't seem to matter that one light was out. With lights piercing down from the high poles, cars seemed very visible. Ted stirred from time to time, and I patted him for reassurance. Once he tried to turn on his side, but realized that the seat was too narrow. I thought of pulling over and helping him get into a different position but remembered that cars might not see me, so using one hand, I helped him resettle as best I could. I found soothing music on the radio, adjusted the heater, and checked my watch, which showed that it was 8:15. I was right on schedule. Hypnotically, I drove between the white lines on the pavement, thinking only of my objective.

Suddenly, I heard a siren, and saw flashing lights! *My back lights! Are they after me?* One police car shot past. All traffic was slowing down. Ted tried to sit up. With one hand I bunched the blanket around him so that it supported him in a half-sitting position. The officer, who was directing all cars into the fast lane, nodded for me to pass, and I nodded back. There had been an accident. Three cars had collided and the middle car was smashed like an accordion at both ends. Apparently the people involved had been taken away.

Hope no one was seriously hurt. Thank goodness our car wasn't hit!

My heart was pounding. Already all three cars were being hooked to tow trucks. As I rounded the third car, an officer directed me off the road and onto the berm. I was bewildered.

He must think that I was part of the accident.

As he approached, I put down the window. "Your tail light is out, did you know?" he asked. I decided to play innocent and replied, "Must be a short or something. Thanks. I'll get it checked." I smiled. Thank goodness I had my driver's license in my purse, but I had no idea where Kenji kept the car registration.

Why didn't I think to ask him? I'll have to get rid of that cop before he thinks to ask for the documents. Stay calm, talk sweet, be friendly.

Ted barked, not an angry bark, just one to tell the stranger that he should be acknowledged.

"Okay, Teddy, this man is our friend," I said, but I was worried.

If this policeman comes any closer, to look inside the car, Ted will think I'm being threatened and defend me with his teeth, but if I ask him not to come closer, it will look suspicious. What a dilemma!

I gripped Ted's collar to hold onto him, just in case he charged. The cop made no aggressive moves, but Ted tried to edge across my lap to sniff at him, and I clenched my teeth behind my grinning lips, as I struggled with all my might to hold Ted back.

"Is something the matter with your dog?" the cop said.

"He was hit by a car. I'm taking him to get treatment so that he can walk again. I'm a nurse," I said.

"I have a dog looks like him. Border Collie, is he?"

"Yes. He's a great pet."

"I hope the treatment works. You can't drive with your back light out though. Can you call someone?" the cop asked.

"Oh, gee, no. And we've got an appointment for 9:15." My brain raced, trying to think who could come to meet us.

Some of Kenji's friends have cars, but I can't bother them. Oh God, as a last resort I'll have to take a taxi. Do taxis allow dogs? Anyway, I don't have much money.

The officer tapped his foot on the gravel.

Since he was a dog lover, I pinned my hopes on the likelihood that he would let us go with a promise to have the light fixed right away, but instead he said, "Hang around a few minutes."

I mentally calculated the money I had in my purse. Often Dad slipped me a ten or a twenty when I went home, but this hadn't happened.

I've got the five dollars I brought for gasoline, which I didn't need because Kenji had filled the tank. Damn. Am I going to get a ticket? What am I waiting for? If I have to call a taxi, I need to get to a phone booth.

I wound up the window and began to search the glove compartment for the car title. It wasn't there.

Where else can it be? More than likely in Kenji's wallet. Darn, darn!

I sat there tapping my fingers on the dashboard. Dear sensitive Ted licked my arm. I cuddled him and told him that somehow we'd get him to that whirlpool and get him able to walk again.

The officer returned. "You work at East General?" He sounded friendly. I nodded.

"I'm finished here. So this is the plan," he said. "I'll follow you to the hospital parking lot. You can get a pal to take you to the vets. You'll have to leave the car there overnight, and I want you to *promise* to get all lights working first thing tomorrow."

"Oh sure," I said. "Ted and I thank you. Gee, that's terrific." I could feel the muscles in my face relax.

I'm just lucky that the cop didn't ask to see the title, not yet anyway.

At the hospital, I headed to the back of the lot. My friends were there with a wheelchair. They started to wave and run toward me until they noticed the cruiser following in my wake and saw that it was stopping beside me. Then they backed into the shadows. The officer approached my window to give me a last warning, and then left.

When my friends heard what had happened, they thought I was very lucky not to have been in the accident, and to have gotten away without showing the car's title and insurance paper.

Norma was dressed in a long coat with a hood over her head. She'd brought a baby blanket, and the plan was for her to hold Ted as she sat in the wheelchair, but Ted didn't want to sit on Norma's lap. He barked.

"He can't bark," Flo said, sounding anxious. "He'll attract the guards. Can't you stop him?"

"He doesn't know Norma," I said. "I'd better hold him. I know how to scratch his chin to comfort him."

Norma removed her disguise, and I put it on. Ted seemed to approve of sitting on my lap, all wrapped in baby blankets so that only his snout peeked out, as I held him close to my chest. He growled when Flo adjusted the blanket, but was reassured when I put my head against his and whispered, "Hush, hush. You're all right."

We had agreed to make a dash past the information desk, and that the two girls would crowd around Ted and me in the wheelchair while waiting for the elevator. They would make goo-goo sounds and talk like they were admiring a new baby. If only we could keep from giggling.

When we were about to exit the elevator at the third floor, the girls spotted Dr. Blake, head of the orthopaedic clinic. He was dashing down the corridor but hesitated long enough to say, "Wrong floor, girls. This is Physio. Nothing open here. Aren't you student nurses? Where did you want to go?"

Norma stammered something about Pediatrics, and hurried back into the elevator.

Dr. Blake called out, "Fifth floor."

We didn't think that Dr. Blake saw Ted and me.

The elevator took off and stopped at the fifth floor. Several visitors had stayed overtime and were waiting to get on. We were so close that they couldn't help but notice me in my funny costume holding a dog like an infant. Someone teased, "How's your baby?" and the other passengers turned and laughed. They must have thought that we were smuggling in somebody's pet, and they approved.

Norma quickly punched third floor and in seconds the elevator stopped for us. We went out single file, accompanied by calls from the departing visitors. "Bye, bye. Take care of that little one."

The corridor was dimly lit and gave me an eerie feeling. We paused to get our bearings. No one spoke. A motor was running in one of the rooms. There was a swish as the elevator went up and down, but otherwise the corridor was quiet. When we resumed our mission, the creaking wheels of the chair and the girls' footsteps on the grey tile floor resounded so that anyone working in one of the rooms could have heard us. I shrank from the thought of what we would do if we were challenged. Sensing the change of scene, Ted tried to draw himself up to sit straighter. I blew into his fur and held him close.

"Which is the door?" Norma whispered. "It looks so different at night."

"There aren't any signs, just numbers on the doors. Did Jan tell us the number?"

"Don't think so. Keep the wheelchair back. I'll tap on this one and see if Jan answers."

We all gave a start when we heard the sound of someone running down the stairwell and sighed relief when they didn't stop at the third floor.

Norma knocked on three doors until she found the right one; Jan let us in, and we used the key hanging behind the reception desk to unlock the door to the whirlpool room. She and Flo lifted Ted off my lap and put him on the tile floor. It must have seemed cold and hard to him. He stretched out his front paws. I guess we all felt ill-at-ease, afraid of the consequences of being caught, because we coordinated our tasks without communication. I got down and moved Ted's hind legs as a warm-up. He bent over the sides of the pool to sniff the water.

It appeared that Ted was receptive to our plan.

Jan clasped her hands together in a gesture that meant our plan was working.

"Won't he pee in the pool?" Flo asked.

We hadn't thought of that.

"Would you know if he pees?" she asked.

"It's been over three hours since he went," I said. "We should have taken him into the bushes before we brought him inside."

"It's too late for that now. What do we do?" Jan asked.

"Pee is sterile," Norma said.

Jan spoke up, "To be on the safe side, we'll drain out all the water after his bath. I can stay, and make sure we don't leave any hairs, and fill the tub up again after you're gone."

"That complicates things, but we have no choice," Norma said.

I changed into the swim suit I'd brought and climbed into the pool. Flo and Norma handed Ted to me. He got water on his face and shook it so that the girls got sprinkled. As I'd hoped, the water buoyed up his body, and it was easier to move his hind quarters. Following Jan's suggestions, I gave him a good workout. His hind legs began to move freely like he was swimming. I supported his middle and let him paddle. After half an hour, we invented a strategy to lift him out. The girls took two huge towels and made a sling. Ted shook water all over when he was put down on the poolside, but no one cared that they got wet. The treatment really seemed to be beneficial.

A new problem arose. What could we do with the towels we'd used as a sling, as well as to dry Ted? Jan solved that problem. She planned to drop them down the chute. A bundle of loose, wet towels would bewilder the laundry staff, who could probably smell the chlorine, but no one would be able to prove how they got to the laundry at that late hour.

The last trick was to get Ted out of the hospital and back to my parent's home. I couldn't use the car. We decided to smuggle him into our dorm, which was connected to the hospital by a tunnel. He could spend the night in my room, and Mom could come for him in the morning. I'd have to phone home and tell Mom and Dad about our change of plans. With the major hurdles passed, I was feeling proud that we'd pulled it off. The other girls looked cheerful; I knew they agreed.

Jan was letting out the water; we'd dried Ted, and wrapped him in blankets. I'd dressed, and he was sitting on my lap in the wheelchair, ready for our exit from the pool room. We weren't talking in hushed voices any more, but were laughing and imagining how soon we could brag to our classmates about our feat.

Then there was the sound of keys turning in the door from the reception area to the hallway. Everyone froze. Jan switched off the lights in the pool room, but it was too late to switch off lights in the reception area.

"What's going on here?" I recognized Dr. Blake's voice calling from the adjoining room.

Jan, Ted, and I were still in the whirlpool room, but Norma and Flo were caught.

"Well? What are you girls doing?" Dr. Blake's voice was terse.

"Sorry," Norma said.

"Sorry? For what?"

I could tell that he was standing right beside the pool room door. Jan gently pushed it shut and the lock clicked. Ted let out a feeble bark, and I clamped my hands around his snout.

Dr. Blair sounded friendlier. "Okay. I think I know what you're up to. You girls decided to have a swim, right?"

Jan and I listened, and I clasped Ted tightly to my chest while still holding his snout, even though he seemed to understand that he wasn't on guard duty and should be quiet.

Dr. Blake laughed. "Let's check the whirlpool. I hope you were smart enough to leave it in order."

"Yes, yes, we did," Norma said.

"I should have a look just the same. Well, I don't have a key. How did you get in? I bet you got in as the cleaners were leaving." He tried the door. Jan and I tensed. The door wouldn't open. Ted didn't make a sound. "Well, I've got to hand it to you." Dr. Blake chuckled again. "You're not very original though; I pulled the same trick when I was in med school." His voice sounded far away, like he'd walked to the corridor door. "Better go now. Keep this hush, hush." He laughed again. "Go on, off you go. If I catch you in here again though, I'll . . ."

I heard a kerfuffle of laughing girls and hurrying feet, and the door to the hallway open and close. Jan and I waited quietly for a few minutes. The water had drained, and Jan decided to leave the tub empty. We hoped that this was done occasionally. Using another towel, Jan swished up the hairs Ted had shed. When sufficient time had elapsed, she opened the whirlpool door so that Ted, sitting on my lap, could be wheeled through reception and into the hallway. The door shut and locked behind us. Jan dumped the wet towels down the chute and pushed us to the elevator. Norma and Flo appeared from the stairwell.

"We've got to get you back to the dorm before the door to the tunnel is locked for the night," Norma said. Everyone was in agreement and fortunately the elevator was empty when we got in and journeyed to the basement.

Back in my dorm room, we began to giggle.

"We did it! We did it!" Jan shouted. "High five everyone."

Ted barked.

"Quiet, quiet. Dogs aren't allowed to sleep in our rooms. We still have to hide you." I cuddled him.

"You have to recover now, Teddy," Jan said. "Look at what we've done to help you. Are you feeling better?" She scratched his chin.

Norma and Flo gathered around to rub his ears and scratch his tummy.

Ted had no trouble making himself comfortable. He sighed and stretched out in the middle of my bed. I got into my blue flannel pyjamas and managed to curl up in the remaining space. I think Mom was amused, but she appeared anxious when we smuggled Ted to her car the next morning.

Word got around that the plumbers had been called in to identify why the whirlpool had emptied itself. Dear Dr. Blake. He said it was a mystery, but since the mechanism was working again, no one need worry. We four avoided the Physiotherapy Department and Dr. Blake for weeks.

Chapter 7
The Best Cure

It was June, 1961. Time passed so quickly; before I realized it, my second year of nurses' training had begun. Kenji and I'd been dating often throughout the fall, winter, and spring—going to movies, concerts, taking drives into the countryside, cooking in our dorm kitchen, or eating Japanese sushi at the home of his Japanese friends, the Yamadas.

This particular evening capped off a fabulous day of wandering through a woodland and picnicking at the top of a bluff overlooking the river, with a small fire made from branches we gathered together. I'd inhaled a bit of smoke, and lost the clip to hold back that lock of my hair that always wanted to fall over my eye. My blue pants were all wrinkly, and my white Polo shirt had a mustard stain, but who cared?

The sun had set; the sky was darkening as Kenji parked his Plymouth in front of the nurses' dorm, and turned off the ignition, a few minutes before curfew. His black hair was ruffled from the wind, his cheeks pink because of the outdoor exposure, and his beard showed signs of a day's growth. When he pulled me close, I could feel his ribs through his blue t-shirt; he was so skinny. The kissing, which I knew would end this wonderful day, was about to begin. But suddenly, he leaned back, looking and sounding alarmed. "Claire, what's the matter with your face?"

"Why? Do I look strange?" I said, patting my cheeks, which felt flushed, and then I started furiously rubbing my bare arms. I must have had too much sun. This was our first hot day and maybe …"

This itching is terrible, but I'm not going to complain and make a bad impression on Kenji. Oh, but something is dreadfully wrong.

"I don't know, but my lips feel funny and my arms itch something awful." I began to have trouble getting air. I gripped my neck, and pulled myself tall to stretch it, gasping.

"Can't you breathe?"

My mouth was open wide. I shook my head while labouring to take a breath.

"I'm taking you to emergency." Kenji started the engine, turned on the headlights, and spun the car out onto the street. He drove around the corner to the emergency entrance of the hospital, patted my knee for reassurance, left his door ajar, and ran inside to the admissions desk.

In seconds, an intern in white was at our car, pressing an oxygen mask against my face.

"She needs an airway," Kenji said.

Orderlies lifted me onto a gurney, while the young doctor held the mask in place.

I struggled to expand my rib cage, trying to inhale through the mask.

Breathe, breathe.

I was aware that the swelling had spread throughout my face and eyes, because I could barely see.

How can this happen?

Several people fussed over me in the examining room. Someone said, "Her temp is up. Blood pressure is falling. You haven't much time. Look how blue her lips are."

"Get the trach tray," someone else shouted. "Do you know this woman? Is she on any medication?" he asked.

I can't speak. Oh, God I want to yell. "No tracheotomy! Please, no tracheotomy! I don't want a hole in my neck!"

I tried to wave my arms in protest, but didn't have the energy to lift them. I was desperate to breathe.

Air, air!

Nothing else mattered.

Okay, maybe a hole is okay.

I closed my eyelids. Red and blue lights registered on my brain. *Where am I?* I laboured.

Suck in. Suck in.

It was as though I were floating ... floating ... floating, but I strained and, through blurred vision, I saw a nurse preparing a syringe and felt a needle piercing my shoulder. Then I felt a tube being threaded into my nose, and knew it was going down my trachea and into my lungs. Within moments the struggle to breathe abated.

Sweet, sweet oxygen.

My chest moved up and down fast, but without any extra effort from me.

"Airway's in," I heard someone say. "We won't need a trach."

Though I was getting air, the itching on my face and arms was worse. I checked.

Red blotches.

My inclination was to dig with my fingernails, but I controlled myself, rubbing them with my fingertips instead.

Where is Kenji? Did they send him away?

Then I heard his melodious voice, sounding hesitant, and betraying his anxiety. "My girlfriend is a student nurse. I don't know about medications."

"Looks like an anaphylactic reaction. Is she allergic to nuts or something she could have eaten?"

"We were on a picnic, and had a fire. We didn't eat nuts," Kenji said. "Maybe something in the woods?"

"Poison ivy," a male voice replied. "She could have inhaled some in the smoke, and got it on her skin too. Careful! Don't touch her clothing. Might be coated with resin and you'll pick it up. Even a mild case of poison ivy is very unpleasant, believe me." And then the person added, "She needs the breathing tube; we'll keep her overnight."

Where is Kenji?

He had moved and was standing right beside my gurney. I could just make out his blue shirt and dark trousers, and tried to make sad eyes at him, but with the swelling, he probably couldn't read my message. I wanted to reach out for his hand, but knew that I shouldn't. Maybe my hands were still covered with the poison ivy resin. I tried to sit up. "What about you?" My lips moved, but with the breathing tube, no sound came out. He was able to read my lips.

"I'm okay. I worry for you."

"I can breathe," I mouthed, weakly giving him a thumbs up. "Thank you for—"

"Don't try to talk."

I was sure he was smiling even though my vision was still blurry. I imagined I could see the wave in his black hair and his brown eyes staring at me. I must look a sorry sight—all red and puffed out.

The orderlies were there to wheel me to a room. "Wash your clothes," I heard them say to Kenji. "You mustn't get poisoned." I nodded to him, as I was being wheeled away, and made a telephoning gesture. Again he understood and I was happy to be seeing someone as intelligent as Kenji.

"Do not worry, I will call the dorm and tell them where you are," Kenji said.

In the hospital room that I was to share with another patient, the nurse gave me an injection. "A steroid," she said. She wore gloves, and helped me strip off my clothes and drop them into a plastic bag, which she tucked into my bedside stand. "Wash them as soon as you get home," she advised.

Next she prepared cool bath water and washed me all over, and then put cortisone cream on my face. Blisters were beginning to form. I could have screamed; the itching was so severe.

You've got to concentrate on something soothing. Swimming, imagine you're swimming in a cool lake. Feel the waves washing up and over you. Think of rain. Feel the cool drops hitting your face and arms.

A doctor pushed aside the curtain. "What's her temp?" he asked.

The nurse put the thermometer into my mouth, and then in good time, showed him the results. I couldn't tell whether he was satisfied.

"This itching is terrible," I managed to communicate to them, gesturing and silently forming the words.

"We're giving you a sedative," the doctor said to me, and told the nurse to monitor me closely.

The nurse followed him out of the room, but was back within minutes. She cleaned my arm with a cotton swab, and I felt the needle.

If only this shot puts me out.

I was burning. The itching was ... unbearable. I could no longer form words even in my head, but if I strained I could make myself remember Kenji's voice telling me all about himself: he helped his father garden; he liked to fish with his friend Makoto; they caught butterflies, and captured insects.

In a half-drugged state, I awoke to the sounds of metal clashing.

Where am I? Did Mom drop something in the kitchen?

I was confused, and it took a moment to figure out my location. My eyes were open enough for me to see the faint glow of light coming through the door-way from the nurses' station, and a low-powered bulb had been fitted into a goose-neck lamp in our room.

The night nurse must be sterilizing equipment. That's what the banging is about.

Breathing was no problem, with the tube still feeding my lungs, but my bed was wet. I'd perspired enough to make my gown damp and clinging.

My temperature must have dropped, but this itching is still driving me crazy.

"Are you awake?" a voice said, from the bed across from me.

I hadn't noticed that there was another person in my room. I gestured an affirmative at her, which she seemed to understand.

"I can't sleep either." It was the voice of a girl, maybe my age. "You looked terrible last night. Were you in a car accident?"

I wanted to laugh when I thought about how I must look—like a blown-up balloon, with skin stretched too tight. I mouthed the words "Poison ivy," and mimed scratching desperately. She nodded, and bounded out of bed. "Poison Ivy! Well, I know what to do!" She turned on her bedside lamp. The light was too bright and hurt my eyes; I winced and quickly brought my arms up to cover them.

"Sorry." She understood and switched it back off. I could tell that she was headed for our washroom and, in moments, she was back by my bedside putting something under my pillow.

"Don't you worry," she said, still standing beside me. "This is a home remedy for itching. My grandmother taught me."

I cocked my head at her, inquisitively.

"A bar of soap. If you carry soap with you, you will have no more itches. It works for mosquitoes, bees, and poison ivy. I put some in your bed."

I laughed to myself.

Voodoo. Who is this creature?

"Do you want to talk? We might as well since we can't sleep."

I shook my head.

"If you've got something on your mind that's keeping you awake, just tell me."

I shook my head again, and pointed to my breathing tube, expecting that she'd understand. I turned my face to the wall, and hoping that the itching would bother me less, I got into a fetal position.

"Well, I'm going back to my bed, but you can call me if you need anything," my roommate said. Her feet tapped on the tile floor as she left my bedside.

It's no use. I can't stand this itching. I've got to get another sedative.

But before I could act, I heard the night nurse scurry past our door and heard several more footsteps belonging to the aides and orderlies following her. There must have been some emergency down the hall.

Darn it. No one will answer my call now. I have to wait until the emergency's over. I made another effort to find a comfortable position.

"Are you better?" the girl asked. And it seemed to me that she was sitting up. I nodded, lying, but didn't turn to face her. The last thing I wanted was to make idle conversation in the middle of the night when this damn itching was driving me nuts.

"You don't seem better," she said.

Oh God. This creature thinks she can read minds!

I wanted to send her off into oblivion, and shut her up. I opened my eyes and found her bent over me, so close that her breath bounced off my face. In the dark, the white of her eyes shone like a cat caught by a flashlight. Her breathing was audible and she smelled of an odd perfume.

I tensed, clamped my eyes shut, and pulled my arms close to my sides.

"Your face is like a pumpkin." She laughed.

I decided to ignore her, but she reached out and ran her fingers through my hair. "Your face is like a pumpkin," she repeated.

Disgusted with her insensitivity, I gestured toward the skin on my arms. "Swelling," she nodded. "I can fix that," she said, calling back as she left to go to the washroom again, "Is it okay if I make your swelling go down?"

What am I supposed to do? I can't call out to the nurse. This itching is unbearable, and I do not want this roommate hanging over me. Maybe if she goes to get another bar of soap or something, she'll leave me alone.

What I want to say is that if you're so smart, just do it. Get another bar of soap, toothpaste, whatever you want to do. Then just stay away. Leave me alone.

Next thing I knew I heard what might have been a purse snapping shut and then the roommate was back. "This will feel cool," she said. I clenched my teeth because I really didn't like having her near.

"What did you say?" I mouthed and lay still, resigned and waiting, almost hoping that she was onto something.

I heard her spit and then felt something hard being massaged onto my forehead by her finger. I tried to see what she was doing, worried that I was encouraging her to do something dangerous.

Strange high-pitched sounds came from her mouth.

Is that a chant? What did I get myself into?

The rubbing continued.

In some respects this is amusing.

I licked my lips. Air from her nostrils hit my face and it was so uncomfortable it made me shiver. The sing-song went on and on. The amusement soon wore off and I tried to reposition myself farther away, but she grabbed my arm with her free hand and held me firmly.

Oh, God. She's got a strong grip.

I squirmed. She released the hold she had on my arm and began to massage my throat. *She's a witch! She could pull the breathing tube out of my nose. She could strangle me, and I can't even reach the cord to summon help.*

I could feel the hair on the top of my head and on my arms reacting. I was scared. I started struggling frantically, not caring that my desperation showed.

"Shush," she said, and continued her chant, still massaging my throat. "This is how my grandmother did it."

I lay there paralysed with fear. *Even if I could call out, who would hear?*

"Maybe you think this is weird," she said.

My muscles tensed, and perspiration formed on my upper lip. She was dangerous. How I wished for someone to rescue me!

The hand that had been on my neck reached across me to get my right wrist.

Such a strange fragrance. It's like nuts ... walnuts, maybe. I tried to smile, in an effort to appear friendly.

She replied with firm assurance, "You like my perfume? Keeps germs away."

I could see that she was grinning in the dim room, with the awareness that she had me in her power.

It seemed imperative that I free myself, but how?

I'm connected to the oxygen outlet above my bed, and the swelling restricts my joint movements. Darn, darn! I can't make my brain focus.

She began to rub my wrist with the object.

What can it be? Some medication that I'll react to? Are there any poisons that kill through the skin?

I tried to think what it could be, and then something fell onto my bed.

"Oh, the penny!" she explained.

A penny. I chuckled inside, I was so relieved.

She's been rubbing my wrist with a penny. A penny! If only I could laugh.

"One, two, three ... One, two, three," she said. Having retrieved the penny, she continued her treatment for another minute or two. "Now, we're done. I never did this before, but I'm sure I got the sequence right." She was patting my arm when the centre light flicked on.

"Hilda, what are you doing?" The night nurse stood in our doorway. "Are you keeping Miss Winchester awake?"

With the light on, I could see the girl. She was tall but was really only a child—maybe fourteen or fifteen.

"Hilda, get your robe," the nurse commanded. "I'm going to let you sleep in the vacant room across from the nurses' station tonight. If you can't sleep, then read or do something else, but don't wake the other patients."

"I just wanted to help." Hilda sounded peeved. "I remember how Grandma got my swelling to go down when I had a bee sting."

"Room 712. Go ahead and put yourself to bed. I'll check on you shortly."

Hilda stared back at the nurse, while rearranging her pyjamas.

The nurse handed Hilda her robe and walked with her to the doorway. "Bed B is free. See you in a minute."

"Pediatrics was full so Hilda was sent to us," the nurse said. "She's a handful—been hospitalized a lot. Her grandmother believes in some sort of sorcery. I hope she didn't keep you awake long."

"Not long," I mouthed. I had to laugh at myself.

"It's time you can have another steroid injection, and another sedative to make you sleep."

I nodded gratefully at her, and tried to smile.

In the morning, the nurse removed the breathing tube, helped me to the washroom and then back into bed, gave me a fresh white hospital gown, straightened the sheets and pulled one over my chest. Then she gave me the injection in my arm. "One of the doctors is waiting to see you," she said, turning to nod toward the doorway.

I turned. Kenji, in his white coat, came forward and looked down at me. I could smell my favourite aftershave. He was smiling, so that the dimple in his right cheek was accentuated, but I read concern in his eyes.

"Oh, my," I said, feeling the elation one gets when you see someone special.

Below the sleeves of his coat, his arms were painted white.

He had followed my eyes and said, "Calamine lotion. Just my arms." He laughed. "The picnic was worth it, but I missed the sweet hug at the end." He wiggled his shoulders. His face burst into a wide grin, as he assured me that I looked almost normal again. His eyes sparkled.

"I am sorry. So sorry," I said. "The flowers or when I gathered wood for the fire."

He squared his shoulders, like one in charge, and used a deep voice to allay my anxiety. "I will be okay."

Hilda sauntered back into our room to get a toothbrush she had left behind. She was about to use our washroom when she noticed Kenji's arms. "What happened?" she asked.

"Poison ivy. " I replied as I tried to warn Kenji with a shake of my head not to get involved.

"We can fix it, can't we?" She addressed me and then Kenji. "We can fix swelling and itching. The nurses say I should be a nurse. I like to help people."

It dawned on me that my swelling was down, and even though the rash was still as red as ever, the itching was tolerable.

Could it be that Hilda's treatment … No, no way.

Hilda sashayed in our direction, but Kenji interceded and blocked her way.

"It's okay," Kenji said, "I have the remedy."

With that, Hilda retreated a bit, and Kenji bent to kiss my lips. "Must kiss a sweet girl." Just our lips touched, but it was heavenly.

"Well, if you don't want to be cured." Hilda shrugged her shoulders. "Western medicine doesn't fix everything."

I agree, but I like Kenji's remedy. Kisses and more kisses.

Chapter 8
A Day in the Clinic

I was still panting from running up the driveway in time to get to the student nurses' dorm before the front door locked for the night. After closing time I'd have to ring the bell to be let in, and if that happened often, I'd be called before the Dean and lectured about being responsible. Once inside, I ran through the lounge, down the hallway, and barged into Jan's room. Still trying to catch my breath, I threw myself onto Jan's single bed, beside Norma, under the window facing the courtyard. Norma, in pink pyjamas, lay back on Jan's pillow and was reading from the notes she'd taken during Dr. Vanger's lecture.

"Where have you been?" Jan asked. She wore striped pyjamas and sat at the maple knee-hole desk, the standard furnishing supplied to each of our dorm rooms. "We were worried. I thought you were going to study dermatology with us."

"I've been over at the path lab with Kenji. Sometimes he needs me to check the English in reports he writes about his patients. He's finished working with Dr. Williams in the polio wing and now he has patients with endocrine problems. He offered to show me pancreatic tissue under the microscope. Do you know you can actually see the Islets of Langerhans, the cell clusters that make insulin?"

"How is that going to help you tomorrow?" Jan asked.

"I think she's sweet on Kenji," Norma said, while rearranging one of the metal curlers that she wore to bed, so that her brown hair would be wavy by morning. "She'll be okay."

"Can you name the thirty-nine types of skin conditions a dermatologist deals with?" Jan asked.

"Jan, she's only going to work in the clinic." Norma sat up. "She'll be helping patients undress and get into hospital gowns. She is just supposed to make them feel comfortable about the examination and reinforce the importance of treatment."

Jan nervously tapped the tip of her pen on the desk. "She's also supposed to answer questions about their condition, you know."

Norma was never flustered. She was the brightest girl in our class, and she was practical. "If she can't, she'll just say, 'You should ask the doctor,' or else she'll repeat their question to the doctor. No big deal." Norma picked up the textbook that was next to where she was resting, and thumbed through the pages, looking at the illustrations of skin conditions.

"No big deal for you, Norma," Jan said. "You know everything. Where does a measles rash begin? What does it look like?"

"Jan, for goodness sake," Norma said. "No matter which doctor is working tomorrow, that question won't come up."

"I don't agree," Jan said. "When Dr. Vanger lectured, he asked if we could recognize a malignant melanoma. I think we're supposed to. What do you know about warts? What about psoriasis?"

"Oh my gosh," I said, "psoriasis." I counted out the things I knew on my fingers. "Isn't infectious. Hits whites, seldom the coloured. Often on the elbows, knees, and abdomen. Damn. I can't recognize any of the conditions, just from pictures in our book."

"Why are you so afraid of Dr. Vanger?" Norma asked. "He reminds me of a big teddy bear. He badgers us because he's enthusiastic." When no one commented, she continued. "I'll bet every one of you has a crush on him."

"Maybe," Jan said, wiggling her shoulders like she was embarrassed.

"He's got freckles too. Curly red hair and freckles." Norma's voice dropped several octaves. "Such masculine hands." She laughed. Norma was teasingly repeating a phrase she had often heard Jan use to describe our psychology prof when he outlined his lecture on the blackboard.

Jan blushed.

Norma slammed shut her textbook. "Well, I'm going to bed, or maybe I'll fix something to eat first. No more room in my brain."

"Geez. My arm itches." Jan pushed up her sleeve so that she could use her nails. "Look, it's all red. What the ...? I've got some effing rash. Am I allergic?" She shook her fists in the air as though she were angry at the world. "Oh, my God."

"It's from your scratching," Norma said. "Just nerves. Come on, I'll make tea for us, and we can forget about dermatology."

"I better not," I said. "I think you're right. I have to study the pictures in our text." I stood and thumbed through the book Norma had left behind. *There's tons of detail but every picture looks just like the last one to me. Heavens, I can't tell them apart.* All the excitement of spending the time with Kenji was gone. Even if I stayed up all night, I couldn't make a dent in all we were supposed to know.

"Don't worry," Norma said. "The derm clinic is only a fraction of your grade."

Her words weren't encouraging. "My first year average is good, but gosh, if I start failing halfway through our three years ..."

Norma turned to give me a harsh look. She thought I worried too much.

When we girls walked down the hall toward the kitchen, Jan was rubbing her arm through the cloth. *It's her nerves. I agree with Norma.* I was about to scratch my arm too, but stopped short. I left my friends at the doorway to the kitchen. *Now back to work.* I went to my room, got into my pyjamas, and sat down at my desk. The book illustrations reminded me of the slides Dr. Vanger had projected during class, and that reminded me of Kenji sitting beside me, pointing out what I was to look at under the microscope. *Useless.* The wonderful sensation of Kenji's kisses came back, and all I wanted to do was hug myself and dream.

The clinic was short-staffed when I arrived the next morning. "Do me a favour?" the head nurse asked. "Before you assist Dr. Vanger, shake down these thermometers for me. The practical nurse took temperatures yesterday, but I see she didn't shake down the mercury. They're soaking in disinfectant in the lab."

Dr. Vanger.

My heart sank.

Why couldn't one of the other dermatologists be working today?

I not only wanted to impress our favourite teacher, but also worried about my average. In the lab, I began to shake the thermometers. One, two, three. My arm was tired after the first three, and there were 30 or 40 more soaking.

This job is going to take all morning, if my arm holds out.

I shook some more. Four, five, six. It helped to count. Then I noticed the centrifuge.

Could I? Why not?

I opened it, distributed the thermometers evenly, shut the lid, and turned on the machine.

A minute should do it.

I left them in for only a minute. When I checked them one by one the mercury was down, way down, almost into the bulb.

Good thinking.

I complimented myself.

Why hasn't someone used this method before?

My first patient was young, only 17. He had tousled brown hair, and was trim and muscular—likely into sports. After he changed into a hospital gown for the examination, I took his temperature. Only 36.3 degrees. Not 37? I put the thermometer back into his mouth. A minute later it still registered below normal. I carried it to the window to check. Yes, only 36.3 degrees.

Some people do have a lower than average temperature.

After taking his pulse and blood pressure, I recorded the findings.

Dr. Vanger bounced into the room like he'd just returned from jogging. I managed not to blush as I again noticed how solid he was, his blue eyes, his curly red hair, and freckles.

Bet he was a mischievous kid, and kept his family hopping.

Dr. Vanger's white coat was pushed back and he stood with his hands in his pockets. His manner emanated confidence. He nodded to greet me and asked the patient, "What brought you here today?"

"I've got acne on my butt." The patient laughed nervously and glanced to see what my reaction would be.

I tried to look serious, concerned only for his discomfort in having to undress in front of a young girl. Behinds weren't new to me, but the young man seemed embarrassed about my presence, so I made sure he saw me step behind the screen before the doctor had him bend over the examining table to expose the redness.

Dr. Vanger called me back. "What would you call this acne?"

I had to step forward to look. My mind was blank.

Say something, anything. Don't just stand here looking dumb!

"I'll bet you're a swimmer," Dr. Vanger said to the patient. "Nurse, here's an example of a rash. No eruption of papules or pustules."

He addressed the young man, "I bet you sit around in a wet swimsuit."

"Sure."

"Get that wet suit off. That's what is causing your itching and redness. Dry yourself. Meantime I'll prescribe something to clear this up."

"That's all?" the young man said, sounding relieved.

"That's it," Dr. Vanger said. "You're free to go." He addressed me. "Now, I did all the work this time. See how you make out on the next patient." He winked.

I tried to smile.

But I'll be so embarrassed if I fail.

The next patient was a large white woman, forty-three. She wore a blue print dress with a navy sweater buttoned to the neck. "My trouble keeps coming back," she said. She was behind the screen changing into the hospital gown. "My ass gets real sore." When she stood in front of me, she pointed to her bottom, and I thought of the young man we'd just treated.

Well this one isn't a bathing suit rash. But what is it?

The bright red patches on her bottom were laminated with silvery scales. Those were important clues.

Darn, darn. What …

I could think of nothing I remembered from the pictures. Then a ploy came to me. "What does the doctor call it?" I asked.

"Sir Assus." She laughed. "That's what the doctor calls it. Sir Assus. Isn't that something? Calling a trouble after your ass?"

Ah, psoriasis.

I was tingling with pride that I'd contrived a way to get the right answer. My elation didn't last. Her temperature reading baffled me.

Only 36.3!

I asked her not to talk, and reinserted the thermometer into her mouth while I checked her blood pressure and pulse. The thermometer reading didn't change. Before I had time to ponder this unusual circumstance, Dr. Vanger came into the room. He greeted our patient and turned to me. "Well, nurse?"

A cotton blanket covered the patient's buttocks as she lay on her abdomen on the examining table. I pulled the blanket down enough to uncover the area.

"I believe it's psoriasis," I said.

"No, no, nurse," the patient called out. "You got it wrong. I told you it's Sir Assus, Isn't it, Doc?"

"We can call it that," Dr. Vanger said with a grin. He lifted his eyebrows like he'd caught onto my trick. "Now, Mrs. Thomas, I'm giving you a prescription for medication and an ultraviolet light treatment. The nurse out front will make arrangements. Wish I could say that would cure it, but sometimes those macules come back." He scribbled on the requisition pad.

"It's okay, Doc. I know you do the best you can," the patient said.

The next patient was dressed in a fashionable navy suit with a frilly white blouse. Blue pumps matched her outfit. She was of average height, with broad shoulders, narrow hips, and carried herself quite erect. Her hair was light brown, cut with bangs that fell onto her forehead, and golden-highlighted waves that cascaded onto her shoulders. Her make-up was attractive. She gave her particulars—Sandra Smith, age thirty-three—and sat looking nervous as I took her blood pressure, pulse, and temperature, which was uncannily below normal. Remembering my success with the last patient, I asked her what the doctor had called her skin problem. She began to cry. "It could be skin cancer. I have a black mole on my back."

Serious. What's the name of the cancer that comes from too much sun? Maybe that's her problem. Didn't Dr. Vanger tell us in class that by physical examination you could usually tell whether a condition was malignant? What were the clues? What was the name of that cancer?"

I looked around the examining room hoping that there were some textbooks I could skim through, but there weren't any.

Didn't he say that malignant ones usually had uneven edges and are multicoloured? How could I ever learn to differentiate between types just from pictures? Oh God, I will fail this course.

"Let Dr. Vanger have a look," I said, then asked her to change into a gown.

She shook her head and didn't move from the stool where she'd been sitting, so I told her that we couldn't do the examination unless she changed. Still she sat there whimpering. Finally I guessed that she wanted me to leave.

Well, I don't like undressing in front of a doctor, but I'm another woman, for heaven's sake.

I gestured for her to go behind a screen, and waved that I was leaving the room.

After a few minutes, I knocked; she called, "Okay," so I went inside and found that she was already on the table, back-side up, ready for the examination but with a cotton blanket covering her back.

Wait until the doctor peels back that blanket.

So much for modesty.

When Dr. Vanger entered the room he said to the patient. "We'll hope for the best," and he patted her hand. "Nurse, I'm going to biopsy the mole. Would you please get the set up and prepare a local aesthetic for me to administer?"

I was in a quandary.

We are supposed to assist with procedures, but we also have to remain in the room at all times so that we can attest that there had been no hanky-panky.

Some unscrupulous women tried to sue doctors for misconduct.

Should I go and leave them alone, or suggest that he step outside while I get the equipment? Do I risk offending the doctor, seeming not to trust him not to molest a patient, or trust him not to molest a patient and be proven wrong? Do I risk allowing a situation that could get the doctor in trouble, if the patient were to make a false accusation, or risk getting myself in trouble by overstepping my bounds? Darn, I have too many dilemmas to resolve.

I opted for the simplest approach and just did as I was asked. When I got back, the two were talking in low tones.

Her position is the same. Nothing out of line has happened.

The conversation stopped as soon as I arrived with the tray holding the syringe and equipment.

Dr. Vanger checked and nodded that everything was in order.

I uncovered the area on her back. Dr. Vanger washed his hands, and injected the local aesthetic. Then both of us washed our hands again at the basin. I held the sterile gloves for him, donned gloves, and then used forceps to paint the area with antiseptic.

After the biopsy was completed, and the wound bandaged, I left the room carrying the tray of instruments, and used sponges, and the tissue in a sterile container. The mole would be rushed to pathology.

The head nurse tapped me on the shoulder. "Good job, Miss Winchester."

Back in the room, I found Dr. Vanger holding Miss Smith in his arms. Furthermore, she was crying, and he was wiping the tears with his finger and saying sweet things like, "It's going to be okay, sweetheart. We found it in time."

I wasn't prepared for this. Was this just comforting a patient or something a nurse should report?

What a playboy! And to think we nurses hold Dr. Vanger in such high regard!

"It's okay," Dr. Vanger said again to Miss Smith. "We'll get the report back in a day or two. With luck we won't have to do anything else. But there are other procedures. Okay, honey. Okay. Do you think you can get dressed now?"

If only he hadn't called her sweetheart and honey, I could believe that the embrace was his way of comforting.

But they look so intimate.

My back stiffened.

Okay. Just do your job. If he tries to give me a high grade just to keep me quiet, well, I'll tell him I don't take bribes. Truth is, I didn't recognize any of the skin conditions and I am prepared to fail this clinical rotation.

Miss Smith took the Kleenex he offered and started to walk behind the screen. Her gown fell open in back, and as she turned to the side a bit, I couldn't help noticing something. Fortunately Dr. Vanger had left the room, because I must have looked shocked when I noticed that Miss Smith was really Mr. Smith.

"He's great, isn't he?" Smith said between sniffles from behind the screen.

"A ... a good doctor," I stammered, hating that I had to cover up my real feelings.

"He's my partner, did you know?"

"N ... no," I said.

Oh my, how do I reply? Do any of my friends know? We all have a crush on him. "Dr. Vanger is right," I stammered, finding it difficult to speak after the shock of the discovery. "The report may be favourable. Anyway, there are further things that can be done if ..."

"You are very understanding. I dreaded this day, but you made it easier," the patient said.

"Me?" I grimaced behind the patient's back. Thank goodness Smith didn't know what I'd been thinking.

On the way to the waiting room to get our next patient, the head nurse smiled. "That wasn't easy. Dr. Vanger looking after his own partner. We wanted him to let someone else do the biopsy, but he insisted." She shrugged as if to say that the doctor is the boss.

I wonder if she knows. I'll bet I'm not the only one that's so naive. Yes, she must know. She referred to Smith as his partner.

The delivery man handed the head nurse a package.

"Our new thermometers," she said. "Never knew thermometers wore out, but would you believe it? Every patient this morning had a temperature reading of 36.3. Even the little girl in Room 2, and I know she has a fever."

"Geez," I said, as she brushed past me into the examining rooms to distribute the new thermometers. "You never know."

At least you could say that I had good intentions. I still wonder why that happened.

Chapter 9
Halloween

Some of the interns proposed having a Halloween party in the pathology lab—on the hush, of course. It was an ideal setting, with jars of organs sitting around, beakers of coloured liquids and Bunsen burners we could light in the dark room. The party would start at midnight.

Over the past months, Kenji and I had been seeing each other as often as possible, in particular we'd spent a lot of time with Kenji's friends. Fred Yamada was born in the States, his parents having immigrated to the U.S. when they were young, and he'd married Yoshiko, a bride sent by his aunt from Japan to be his wife. Kenji helped Fred dig up a stump in their suburban backyard, and mowed their lawn when Fred was busy. He'd visit with Fred in Japanese or romp with their poodle while Yoshiko taught me Japanese cooking, how to write Hiragana, or how to make origami cranes.

Kenji was a great tease—had given me several playful nicknames. When I had to summon his help to get something from the second shelf in Yoshiko's kitchen, and when I needed a pillow at my back in order to reach the brake and clutch while driving his Plymouth, he called me Pewee. On occasion I put my hair up on rollers. The result was a Shirley Temple-like hair style. He gave me the moniker Golden-locks. But his favourite tease was about my breasts, saying that they jiggled as I walked. He liked for me to wear my blue sweater that fit snuggly over the curves. If a letter came from his brother, Kenji would translate what was happening at Tokyo University, the university, where his brother studied. There would be details about their neighbours: who passed a test to attend Keiô University, and who would be going to England to study. Mostly, he read tales about friends, with little comment about his parents except for excerpts about visiting maternal grandparents in Hokkaido. I understood that the Tokyo home they had shared with his paternal grandparents had been destroyed by American incendiary bombing, and his father, a university professor, had been saving to rebuild a dwelling on the same site. At times, when we took a drive, we'd discuss what kind of marriage we each wanted. He said he wanted to bring his med students home to discuss their studies and have his wife there to cook for them and listen to their love life problems. I liked that picture. I wondered if Kenji wrote to his parents about our dates.

Kenji had lost much of his reserve and agreed to do a skit with me at the party. We'd brainstormed together about making it funny, with gestures and pigeon English. His English was pretty good by that time, but he didn't mind being teased because of his accent and rare stereotypical mannerisms. I always smiled when I heard him saying "So. So desu ka?" in a bass voice, when we would likely just nod and say, "I see." I suggested that we be cartoon characters in the skit, but he didn't read Superman or Tin Tin as a kid. "I thought Hergé's Tintin books were translated into many languages."

"Maybe," he said, "but my mother didn't allow me to read comics. She was very strict. She thought cartoons were a waste of time, even though many were historical tales; I should be studying. I used to go to Makoto's house to read his animation books." He laughed. "Want me to be a black dog? Norakuro was an army dog, one of my favourite comics."

For Halloween, Kenji wanted to look like Einstein with a shaggy wig, beard, and black-framed glasses, and so that was the skit we wrote. All that day I bounced merrily along, going from class to class, my thoughts preoccupied with rehearsing my part instead of paying attention to the lectures.

Between classes, Jan, Norma, and I talked about costumes. Norma was dressing like a kid and acting out nursery rhymes with her partner. Jan had borrowed her mom's back evening dress, but she wouldn't tell us who she was going to impersonate. "It would spoil the surprise," she said. I would wear green scrubs to impersonate an operating room nurse.

Anatomy was our last class of the day. Miss Freeman handed back our exam papers. When I saw my grade, I let out a frustrated sigh.

Leave it to this old biddy to ruin everything.

I stared at the answers she'd marked as wrong, and then clamped my lips shut and slammed my fist on the arm of my desk chair. Norma looked at me, anger written on her face too. She hammered her feet against the floor. Many of our classmates were crowding up to question the professor about the test, but Norma and I hurriedly left the classroom.

In the hallway, we stopped. "What's wrong with this?" I pointed to the question about where to give a spinal puncture. I'd written "between the fourth and fifth lumbar vertebrae," and Miss Freeman had put an X though my writing and inserted, "into the subarachnoid space between."

"Doesn't between *mean* 'into the space'? And this one." I read my answer, "'Haemoglobin is in the red corpuscles,' and she's written 'in the erythrocytes.' Red corpuscles and erythrocytes are the same thing!" I puffed out my cheeks and blew a long breath. "G...gosh darn it!" I said, catching myself before I used the swear word. Neither Grandma nor Mom would believe I could swear, but I was about to.

Jan had joined us and heard my rant. "She wants us to parrot the exact wording that she uses in her lectures. Look at me. I don't know half of what either of you know, but I got an A. What did you get?" She looked at me, and then at Norma.

"C," Norma said.

"Same with me," I answered, still furious.

Jan continued, "Miss Freeman likes it when we stay after class to ask her questions. You have to play her games."

"Memorize the crappy way that that *old woman* explains things?" Norma flinched in a manner that indicated she would die first. Like me, Norma had studied anatomy and histology in junior college. We knew more details than the nursing course taught, and Miss Freeman was always restating our comments as though we were wrong. It made us feel stupid in front of our classmates, though I think they probably weren't as gullible as we feared.

The term "Old woman" was as derogatory as any reference we dared use, though I could think of a dozen more I would have *liked* to use to describe Miss Freeman. She was nearing sixty-five, stood five foot one or two. The skin sagged from her bony arms; the lines on her face arched down, and her thin grey hair was frizzed out to disguise the lack of it. True, she smiled a lot, but her look bore a condescending element. Her knobbly fingers were always jittering about, like she didn't know exactly what to do next. Many of our classmates liked her, because she reminded them of their grandmothers who'd always had supplies of fresh-baked cookies or cakes when they visited. To them, she was quaint.

Quaint? No way; she's unfair—just a wizened, fussbudget, in no way like my grandmother.

"I could write better lectures than the ones she gives," Norma said.

"You could," I agreed. "The only reason the girls stay to ask questions is because she doesn't explain well in the first place."

Norma shrugged. "It doesn't matter in the long run. We'll graduate with good averages, and get good jobs, but my dad won't understand how I could almost fail this course."

"Come on, girls." Jan wrapped her arms around Norma on one side and me on the other. "Party time. Let's get back to the dorm and get ready."

Our skit involved the use of Adam, Norma's skeleton. Adam was a big brute, so Keith, an African American friend of ours with amazing physical endurance, wound up carrying him, while Kenji, Norma, and I took the props. Kenji also made himself useful by running ahead to open doors. Keith was dressed as a sorcerer in a black robe. When we were outside in the dark quadrangle, crossing to the education building, his skin was so black that I couldn't make out his features, or even see him really in the black robe. Looking back, it appeared that the white skeleton was loping along the path under its own power. Unfortunately, Miss Freeman also saw Adam moving at that fast pace through the dark garden. She swooned and grabbed the branch of a spruce tree to steady herself. She was looking at her hand, and in the dim light from a nearby window, we could make out that it was scratched and oozing blood. We stopped to apologize.

"You've hurt yourself," I said. "I'll take you to emergency. Someone had better look at that hand."

It would happen to someone like her—the old, old so and so.

Miss Freeman tossed her head, "I'll manage. It's nothing."

In the dark, I couldn't see her face clearly, but she sounded peeved. I offered to walk with her back to her lodgings in the nurses' residence, but she refused vehemently.

Okay, I offered, so have it your way.

Adam was getting heavy, and it seemed best to end the encounter with more words of apology, and proceed.

We were arriving early to do some arranging. Some of the guys were supposed to be there to unpack the beer and drape work tables with Halloween paper, but the door was still locked. We could hear music and soft voices. We knocked and called, yet no one answered.

"Listen," I said. "Who's that? Are we at the right room?"

Keith leaned Adam against the wall, and we all froze in the silence of the hallway, listening to the sounds coming from within the room—music and voices.

A man's voice said, "Reach," and a girl's voice responded, "I'm trying."

The man said, "I'll do you first and then you do me."

"I can't find your leg."

"Is this too much for you?" the man asked.

"No, no. I'm enjoying it," the girl said.

"Spread your legs," the man said.

"You want me to open up more?" the girl replied.

"You're almost there," the man said.

"Oh, oh, I think I'm doing it." The girl sounded elated. "Wonderful."

I felt my face getting redder and redder.

How embarrassing! How could they? It's such a public place.

Keith and Norma couldn't contain their laughter. I didn't think Kenji understood, and I wasn't going to explain in front of the others. Then Kenji grinned, so maybe he did understand after all.

The music stopped then, and we heard footsteps coming toward the door. Keith raised his eyebrows, like he was asking who the couple could be.

Should we pretend we haven't heard them?

The lock clicked, the door handle turned, and then the door opened. It was Bud and Jan. Before any of us could speak, Bud said, "We're doing the tango for our skit. I've just taught Jan the leg crawl! She's *really* good!"

I was bent double, laughing as I walked into the room. Keith was laughing too, so hard that he had trouble managing Adam.

"Hey, guys what's so funny?" Bud asked. He looked perplexed. "Here, I'll give you a hand." He lifted Adam's legs onto the table. "So? Let us in on the joke. What's so funny?"

Keith explained, and then *everyone* was laughing.

"Adam will fall off the table if you leave him lying so crooked," Bud said. "Oh, I see; it's just scoliosis. Look at that lumbar spine."

"Don't talk about lumbar spine to us," Norma said. She explained our anger over Miss Freeman's test. "Where would you give a spinal puncture?" she asked.

Bud screwed up his face, implying that the question was simplistic. "Between the fourth and fifth lumbar vertebrae."

"Yeah," I said. "That was my answer too."

The fellows sympathized and agreed that Miss Freeman wasn't much of a teacher.

In minutes, the rest of the gang arrived. The pizza man came with our food. Beer cooled in a tub of ice. We laughed and repeated our assumptions about the dance lesson until Bud insisted that we all learn to tango. Tables were pushed aside. Since no one else knew the steps, our versions were quite entertaining.

Then Kenji's and my skit began. Adam lay covered with a blanket on a table. Kenji was the surgeon, and I was the scrub nurse, dressed in green with only a few wisps of hair sticking out from under my green cap.

"I most noted Japanese diagnostician," said Kenji, also dressed in green, and wiggling his torso with exaggerated pride. "This patient, very sick." He spoke as though he were delivering a lecture to a learned group. His face was nearly covered by the mask and oversized cap, which slipped down over his thick eyebrows.

Some fellows whistled. One shouted, "Yeah, lumbar scoliosis."

"What are the symptoms?" I asked, trying to act coy while keeping a straight face.

Now I'm supposed to wiggle my hips close to Kenji, but I feel so self-conscious.

"We must check body. Most certainly I can fix," Kenji said. He was whole-heartedly into the acting, pulling chunks of cauliflower from the skull and tossing them into the air. "Brain normal. I'll put it back." We both mashed pieces of the raw vegetable between the teeth and into the nasal cavities. "Next ... heart." Kenji withdrew a red, heart-shaped cushion I'd made. "Too soft." He was enjoying himself, not a bit self-conscious like I felt.

"Love," Bud called. "Someone's in love," and the others laughed.

I blushed. Kenji stiffened and said, "Very serious disease." Next he pulled a long chain of linked sausage out of Adam's thoracic area. "Intestine. Too long. Could be the trouble."

"Sure is," Keith said. "Hey guys, intestines where the lungs should be?"

Bud said. "That guy has so much scoliosis anything is possible."

Kenji bowed and continued, "Let me see what else." He retrieved a can of kidney beans from the cavity. "Too many kidneys." He passed the can of beans to me, and I rolled it down the floor toward Keith who caught it and whistled.

"This case baffles," Kenji said. Pretending to look carefully around the pelvic area, he pulled out a plastic bag. "I got it," he said, triumphantly. "Floating pancreas out of place." Kenji held up the bag, which had Norma's goldfish swimming inside. "I think the patient is cured."

When we planned the skit, we hadn't thought of all the ramifications.

"Tadpoles. You should have brought tadpoles, right guys?" Bud laughed. Everyone joined in and started to applaud.

Kenji held my hand as we took our bows. He grinned at me with approval.

He's really a good sport.

Then he stripped off his mask and cap, and let his green gown fall to the floor. He used his fingers to comb his messed-up hair. To me, he was handsome in the black trousers and white shirt he often wore, with the collar open. The rest of the guys were in jeans, but I didn't think Kenji owned jeans. I'd never seen him wearing them.

The music was turned up, and we were opening the box of pizza when there was a loud knocking on the door.

"Quiet," Bud said, putting his finger to his lips. He turned off the recording.

Keith extinguished the burners. We froze; no one made a sound. Kenji crouched beside me. The private hospital rooms weren't far, so I thought someone must be objecting to the noise. If we were quiet, we thought that whoever it was might go away, but the knocking was repeated even louder.

"Police. Open up!" The shouts grew louder.

Fortunately, Bud wore a white shirt and he and Kenji could have been mistaken for professors staying late at work. When Bud opened the door, he and Kenji each held test-tubes in their hands, as though they were doing an experiment, while the rest of us stayed hidden.

Miss Freeman led the troop. She looked like a determined reformer leading a band of protestors. One of the two officers following her found the light switch and turned on the overheads.

Really, is this about her scratch? Why wait until now?

"We've a complaint that someone stole a skeleton from the nursing school." Seeing Adam, the officer exclaimed, "There! Who is responsible?"

Miss Freeman stood with arms crossed over her chest, looking prissy and smug.

"No, no," Norma said. "Adam is mine."

"Which one is Adam?" The officer looked from one fellow to another. "Speak up or we'll arrest the lot of you." He was hefty, and when he rattled the handcuffs, he appeared ready to waylay anyone who tried to leave.

This was overkill, but it must be Miss Freeman's doing.

"Adam is the sk-skeleton," Norma stammered. "He belongs to my father. My dad's a surgeon, but I keep him in my room to study the bones. Adam, I mean. The skeleton. I loaned Adam for the party tonight."

Miss Freeman looked startled. She wrung her hands.

"You sleep with a skeleton?" The officer laughed, probably having guessed what had happened and trying to lighten the mood.

Bud spoke up. "If a skeleton has been stolen from the school, we don't have it."

One of the officers looked at Miss Freeman. "You're sure your skeleton is missing?"

"Well, er …" She bowed her head. "I saw them carrying … I followed them … I thought they would damage our school skeleton!"

"We'd better check. See if your bones are gone. Come on." One officer nodded for Miss Freeman to lead the way to her classroom.

"This a party?" The other cop asked.

"Halloween," Bud answered.

The officer made big eyes and nodded like he approved, before turning to follow. "Don't go away."

I put my hands on my hips. "What's that woman got against us?"

"She's getting back at us for frightening her," Norma said. "Prepare for a D on the next exam. Can't we report her or something?"

Bud hugged Norma, and Kenji squeezed my hand, saying, "You'll be okay. I think she's going to be surprised when she gets to her classroom."

Everyone was enjoying the pizza when the officers and Miss Freeman returned. The merriment stopped as Miss Freeman began to speak. "I-I am so sorry." She covered the scratches on her wrist with her uninjured hand. "My skeleton i-is still there." Her fingers covered her face. "How embarrassing."

"Problem solved," one officer said, eyeing our food.

Bud passed the pizza box and each officer took a piece. They declined the beer.

Bud pressed Miss Freeman to accept a slice but she was reluctant.

"I'm sorry officers," she said. "I called you out when you have more important things to do. And I've interrupted their party."

Keith apologized again for frightening her.

I put a slice of pizza on a plate and handed it to her. She rested the paper plate on the counter and reached to take my hand, and Norma's. Addressing the policemen and the interns, she said, "These two girls are the bright ones in my class. I've been very hard on them, because they will one day be teaching anatomy, and I want them to be as thorough with details as I am."

Hmm. Is this an apology or what?

Reluctantly, I let her squeeze my fingers, while she also squeezed Norma's.

"I wish I'd gone to parties when I was your age." Her voice was subdued. Our hands were dropped. "I hope you'll come to visit me when I retire at the end of term. It would be nice to hear about your careers ... and the parties."

Norma and I looked at each other. Almost in unison, we said we'd like to drop by and hear what she was doing; it seemed like the polite response.

"I invite all of you." Miss Freeman gestured with open arms to the others. "Maybe I'll try baking cookies. I suppose you all like cookies. And beer. Yes, I'll get in some beer too."

Everyone nodded appreciation for the offer, but I imagine that only Norma and I seriously considered keeping the date. The whole affair left me feeling glum, not because Miss Freeman had almost ruined the party, but because she seemed like such an unhappy person.

"Here, have a beer," Bud said, putting one in front of Miss Freemen as she took a dainty bite of the pizza.

The officer in charge announced that they'd be off. "I suppose you have permission to use this lab." We could tell from his face that he was teasing and didn't want us to answer. "There's always some hanky-panky on Halloween."

Bud reached to take Miss Freeman's hand. "How about a dance?" he said, leading her onto the dance space, as she turned to wave a dismissal to the policemen.

She blushed and let herself be whirled around. A half hour later, and after a few more beers, she stopped, pounded on the counter with her fist, and said, "G-girls," the words seemed hard for her to form, "tomorrow I w-want you to know that I'm giving you a quiz." She giggled.

"Disgusting," Norma mouthed.

We looked at each other, but I didn't want to say the word that came to my mind. *Even drunk, she's the same old biddy.*

I thought of walking out but didn't want to leave the party.

"Listen up," Miss Freeman said, lifting her glass of beer and waving it unsteadily. "I'm pie-eyed." She began to giggle. "Just joking about the quiz, you know." She reached for my hand to steady herself and whispered, "Can someone take me home? I don't know whether I can make it on my own."

Kenji and I escorted her to her lodgings. When she'd unlocked the door, she hesitated, brushed aside a lock of my hair and said. "You're one of my girls. That was a wonderful Halloween."

Even though I felt an aversion to her touch, I understood.

Just a lonely soul. I hope I don't come to that!

The door closed. Kenji and I locked hands.

"You will visit her when she retires, won't you?" Kenji asked, and I nodded in the affirmative, glad that he too could show sympathy for this old lady.

Chapter 10
Baby Johnson

"Caroline! Caroline!" That was my patient, Marla Johnson, screaming from her room.

I'm fed up with her howling. Everyone is. Ye Gods, when will she stop?

One of the nurses passed me in the corridor and said, "Where on earth is that nurse, Caroline." I cringed and avoided her angry eyes.

Thank goodness Mrs. Johnson hasn't remembered my name correctly. Claire doesn't sound like Caroline, but ... She doesn't want me to leave her bedside, even for a moment. I can't even go to get water or to go to the washroom.

The other nurses were justly concerned about the effect of those shouts on the expectant mothers they attended. Probably none would understand why the medical staff, and a nurse in particular, would let someone suffer so much.

We student nurses were required to follow fifteen expectant mothers through their deliveries and afterwards, but I hadn't yet had a patient deliver. Only one week left in Obstetrics before moving on.

It's going to be terrible if I don't get to attend at least one natural birth.

My instructor was sure that Marla Johnson would have her baby that day, since she'd already been in labour for seven hours. "Encourage her; show her how to breathe. Hold her hand and mop her brow," my instructor said. Early in the day, I'd been allowed to give her a whiff of nitrous oxide through a mask, at the height of her pain, but then the doctor decided that any relief was only delaying the delivery and forbade the use of the mask.

I returned to the vigil. "Caroline, Caroline, do something." Marla reached her arm out to me, still huffing from the last contraction. "I can't take it. I can't. Get Dr. Morgan to give me a shot, the mask ... anything!" She panted.

"Squeeze my hand and shallow breathe. The contraction will be over soon," I said. When the contraction ended, I freed myself and replaced the cool cloth on her forehead.

"I know, I know, but I can't. I can't. I don't want a baby. I can't take it. Mother didn't tell me it would be like this. Oh, oh, here it goes!"

"Good. Pant, pant, pant. That baby is moving. Any time now. Any time."

I'm tired of my own voice. Not sure I believe what I'm saying, either.

What good was I doing? None.

There were sounds of a gurney being wheeled out of the next room.

"Is that coloured Johnson woman going ahead of me?" Marla asked. "I know her. Her husband looked in when they arrived. It's only been a few hours. They used to get us mixed up at the clinic. She's Arla and I'm Marla. Why can't I … My God, my God!" She gasped and held her breath.

"Okay, take my hand. Pant. You've got to relax between contractions."

Here we go again for the umpteenth time.

"Pant when they come so you don't push on the baby before it's farther into the birth canal. You can do it," I coached. My watch said twelve noon.

Five hours. I've been here since seven a.m.. I'm as weary as Marla. Weary, discouraged, and getting angry.

This was a hopeless situation for me, too. Even though it wasn't my fault, I felt I was letting down the school if I had to move on from Obstetrics without observing a birth. Between contractions, which were still five minutes apart, Marla liked to tell me about the outfits she'd bought for the baby boy she expected. His name was going to be Kenneth, after her husband. I hoped she'd be just as happy if the baby was a girl and brought up that point once or twice.

"Why do I have to suffer so? Why? Why? Every woman doesn't have such a hard time, do they?" Marla whined.

Dr. Morgan walked though the doorway. "How you doing, Marla?" He was in greens, apparently fresh from delivering someone else's baby.

"Miserable. This is my first and last kid, doctor," Marla said.

Frowning, Dr. Morgan used his stethoscope to listen to the baby's heart rate. He checked my patient's heart also, and then put on gloves and had me position the patient so he could check the cervical dilation.

Marla complied with the procedure.

"Not good, Marla. You're still only seven inches." Dr. Morgan shook his head.

"Why? Why? Can't you give me something?" she pleaded.

"Inducing you might be dangerous, and I don't want to do a C-section. You've got to deliver that baby yourself." Dr. Morgan ripped off his gloves and threw them into the bag I held for his use.

"Are you punishing me, doctor? I know you told me I shouldn't gain so much weight," Marla said.

"I want you to deliver a healthy baby." Dr. Morgan tapped his fists on the foot board of the bed. "Could be hours yet," he said to me, as he left the room.

He's discouraged too. Wonder what the options are. Has he ruled out a Caesarean? Would I get to scrub for that? I'd rather attend a natural birth. Come on Marla.

After the doctor left, Marla began to cry. "I'm so sorry I gained all that weight. He told me I'd have trouble. God, I wish I'd listened. I wish Kenny was here. Oh Kenny, I need you. God, you're never here when I need you." Marla's face grimaced. She squeezed my hand until I thought the knuckles would break.

I checked my watch again for the hundredth time.

If ever I get pregnant, I'm not going to gain so much weight. Okay, now find something positive to say ... even if you don't mean it.

"With luck the baby will be born before your husband gets off that plane from Chicago. Come on, Marla." I tried to sound like a cheerleader at a football match.

She grunted, clenched her teeth, and cried out, "Caroline, Caroline!" Then she fell back against the pillow, spent.

She may be tired but she can still talk, talk, talk.

And I was tired of her voice, tired of trying to stay interested.

"Kenny's visiting his mom. She's always getting some ache or pain. I didn't want him to go when I was due, but it sounded like she could be having a heart attack. She doesn't like my clothes, or me either. Fatso. That's what I've become." Marla's eyes teared, and I handed her a tissue. "I was once a beauty queen. You wouldn't recognize me. In those days I had lots of beaus. Before I met Kenny. Now, I hardly see him. There's work and visits to his mom. Oh, but you should see what he bought me. The cutest dress to wear when I go home. It's blue cotton, the colour of my eyes. He says I have the bluest eyes."

I stepped aside to wet the cloth to bathe her head with again.

Well, I hope it fits. You're still overweight, you know.

She raised her voice to carry across the room. "He says with my golden hair I should always wear blue. I've got a closet full of swell evening dresses." The smile disappeared from her face and her eyes began to water again.

"What is it, Marla, a contraction?"

Hurrah! Three minutes apart. Good sign. Some progress, at last.

"I just realize that I'll still be fifty-five pounds heavier, won't I? I gained seventy-five and the baby and placenta weigh about twenty pounds."

I nodded.

She was sobbing in earnest. "I won't be able to fit into my size eight dresses." She held out her hand for another tissue. "I told Kenny that a pregnant woman has got to eat what she's got to eat. He believed me. I am so sorry. Doctor Morgan said the baby couldn't make it around all that fat. Damn, damn, damn. Oh, Caroline, help me!"

I wiped her tears.

For pete's sake. What else can I do?

The head nurse stuck her head in the doorway and motioned for me to approach. "How is it going? She'll be exhausted if things don't happen soon."

"I know," I said.

And here's me focusing on how I felt. Can she tell that I've about had it with all that incessant talking, screaming, and waiting?

The head nurse patted me on the shoulder.

She knows. She's been through this before.

When the next contraction began, Marla said, "Kid, this is it. Come on out. Come on out!"

It was likely that there was progress, but I didn't like to keep measuring her dilation. It wasn't that reassuring, and she needed to rest between.

Best to make her comfortable and wait, wait, wait.

At least the talking had diminished.

At two o'clock the head nurse came to check again. She listened to the baby's heart and checked the dilation, then smiled. "Marla. Good for you. We'll move you to delivery. It's almost time." She brushed by me and went out the door, and in minutes the orderlies were there transferring Marla to a gurney.

"How is she?" a sandy haired man was shouting as he ran to the room.

"It's Kenny. Oh, Kenny!" Marla called as she was being wheeled toward the delivery suite.

"Mr. Johnson?" I asked, but didn't wait for his answer. "The baby is coming. Go to the head nurse." I kept pace with the gurney but gestured with my arm. "Thank God you're here. The nurse will get you a gown and help you scrub so you can attend the birth."

The man just stood there, frozen.

Is this guy going to be able to handle seeing a birth? Some fathers fainted. But then he said, "I better call Mother. She wants to know."

Darn. Can't he see that his wife needs him now—not his mom? I'm too judgemental, I know, but ...

Marla was calling his name as we entered the delivery room.

The baby was born at 2:16. For the first time, I got to see a wee head emerge, and then shoulders, and then a baby girl was in Dr. Morgan's hands. The doctor rubbed her back and the baby opened her wee mouth, wiggled her head from side to side, and let out a loud whoop as she took her first breath. The doctor handed the baby to me to check. This wee individual had balled up her fists and screeched almost as loudly as her mom had been doing. I had to smile when I thought about it, and I pictured how it might be when I had my first baby.

My whole body seemed to be smiling and it was Kenji's face I was imagining, as the two of us looked at our new baby. Lately, he had been calling me his girl, and was even jealous when he saw me playing darts with Jeff at the student union. He spent a lot of money on presents too, though it wasn't necessary. I laughed to myself. He had such a fun sense of humour. The gifts he bought were so original. He'd gone to the Japanese grocery and bought Japanese pickles. The next gift was a translation of a Japanese novel, and the next was a four-leaf clover that he'd picked on the front lawn. How long did he spend hunting for that gift?

Dr. Morgan stopped what he was doing and looked up. "I've delivered a few hundred babies, but it always seems like a miracle."

I felt the same way.

Every baby is a miracle.

After wiping off baby Johnson, I put her on her mom's chest.

"A girl! Oh, she is beautiful." Marla bent to see the baby's face. "She is! I think she's got Kenny's nose. Look at her. She is so sweet. Your daddy is going to love you," Marla said. "Where is Kenny?"

Yes, where was that husband?

"Your husband went to make a phone call." Though I wished to sound matter-of-fact, I know my voice had a hard edge.

That guy was such a wimp. Chickening out of seeing his own baby born.

"He'll be here shortly," I said, adding under my breath, "I hope."

"We'll take the baby to the nursery so you can get some rest." I cuddled the squirming little girl, her arms and legs flailing about, wrapped her in a blanket, and put her into the crib to move to the nursery. Then we helped Marla off the delivery table and onto a gurney. In her room, the head nurse and I lowered the shades.

With luck Marla can get some sleep. She's drained. Where in the heck is her husband?

I was supposed to be off duty, but I asked to stay on. I wanted to witness the family reunion: Mom, Dad, and a brand new baby girl. It would be a picture-perfect memory. I was sitting quietly in the private room beside Marla when Mr. Johnson burst through the door.

"Shush, she's asleep," I said, my finger over my lips. "I'll take you to the nursery to see the baby." I nodded toward the doorway and got to my feet, thankful that the wayward husband had at last appeared.

"I've been to the nursery," he said, his teeth clenched and looking like he could bite through an iron spike.

What the ...?

"She's beautiful," I said.

"Beautiful," he scowled. "She's not mine." With an angry frowning face, he strode up to the bed and looked down at Marla but didn't wake her. His eyes narrowed with something akin to hate.

I was aghast. "I know you wanted a boy, but you're going to love this little girl."

"Boy or girl, it doesn't matter. That baby isn't mine." He wrung his hands and paced back and forth just outside our door.

I could see that he didn't know whether to walk away or stay. I too was confused and started to pace beside him. "How was your flight?"

"Don't make small talk. Mother was right. Things she told me I didn't want to believe. It's Marla I've got to confront. "God damn it!" He started spouting more serious profanity, repeating a few choice words over and over before stopping suddenly and turning to face me. "How soon can I wake her up?"

"She was in labour fourteen hours. She's exhausted, but I know she was eager to see you."

"Really? That's hard to believe."

"Well, it's true. And she's looking forward to wearing the blue dress you bought. You made her very happy."

"Blue dress. I should have bought a stripper outfit, a red one at that."

"I don't understand."

"Have you seen that baby?"

"Of course. I helped with the delivery."

"What did the kid look like?"

"Not different from any newborn. All wrinkly."

"Wrinkly ... and *black!*" He shook his fists and stomped back to his wife's bedside. "Marla, wake up Marla! Wake up."

Marla opened her eyes and threw her arms up. "Kenny, Kenny! It's a girl! Isn't it wonderful?"

"I'm away a lot, but I never thought you'd—Did you think that I wouldn't know? Who you been screwing, Marla?"

Marla drew back. "Kenny, what is wrong with you? I'm your wife. I've never ..." She began to cry.

What in heavens is going on? This should be the happiest day in their lives. Do something!

I spoke up. "Mr. Johnson, I'm going to bring your daughter to this room."

"I never want to see that kid again."

"Kenny! What are you talking about?" Marla wailed. "Oh, Kenny, what are you saying? Kenny. Kenny!"

I could hear her screaming his name all the way to the nursery and back.

Mr. Johnson was at the door, on the verge of leaving, when I wheeled the crib in front of him.

The baby was bellowing at the top of her lungs.

Well, like mother like daughter.

"She's perfect," I said. "I want you to look her in the eye. I don't know what is going on, but she is your daughter and you have got to welcome her to this world."

Marla was still calling his name.

I was so determined, that he reluctantly obeyed and glanced down at the wee baby who was still protesting in loud cries.

"What?" Mr. Johnson said. "That's not the baby I was shown."

The nurse from the nursery came running down the hall. She must have got word of what was happening. "Sorry," she said. "You asked to see the Johnson baby. We have one that belongs to A. Johnson and this one belongs to M. Johnson. Maybe …"

Mr. Johnson, still solemn, turned to stare at his daughter.

"Here," I said, picking up the baby and handing the little girl to him.

Reluctantly, he let me place the baby into his arms. At first he looked uncomfortable, then the baby stopped crying and he turned the baby enough to see its face and little arms.

I sighed. "Okay, make up with your wife and get her to stop shouting too. She's been shouting for hours."

My attempt at humour had no effect. Marla turned her face toward the wall.

With the baby in his arms, Kenneth Johnson stood beside the bed, looking helpless.

"Okay," I said, reaching to take the child.

No one with that much bitterness should infect this precious baby.

Mr Johnson drew back and didn't relinquish the child. "Mother kept implying … I thought that being a good provider meant long hours."

Between sobs, Marla said, "You're the only one, Kenny."

"I know, honey. I'm so sorry." He reached over to kiss her, but she reached behind her back to push him away.

He turned to me. "How am I going to get her to know that I do love and trust her?"

I'm so angry, but I've got to come up with some good advice.

"She and this baby girl have got to be the priority in your life. It's going to take time. Marla says you travel a lot. Are you leaving again soon?"

"No. No. Maybe I should transfer back to a desk job here, even though it's less money." He pulled up a straight chair and sat down with the sleeping baby against his chest. With bowed head, he sat still for a long time as though he were waiting for Marla to reach out for him. Finally, he put one hand on the bed close to her back. "Marla, I love you. I love you, sweetheart," he pleaded.

She glanced over her shoulder. A slight smile came as she saw her husband gently rocking the baby in his arms. "Don't just buy me things," she said coolly. "Talk to me."

"Oh God. I don't want to lose you—or our daughter." He held the baby out so he could look into her sleepy eyes.

I tiptoed out of the room, stopping only to wave when Marla noticed me leaving. My part of the mission was accomplished.

Well, that wasn't easy, but now they look the the kind of family I hope to have.

Chapter 11
Introducing my Beau

In robust form, Mom was singing "God Rest Ye Merry, Gentlemen" when I threw open the back door from the carport, hastily stomping the snow off my boots and rushing into the kitchen to give her a kiss. She stopped slicing the quarter of butter, which would dot the Pyrex dish of crackers and oysters, and wiped her hands on a tea towel that hung from her apron, before giving me a hug. The morning sun beamed through the windows over the sink, and lit up my mother—who was wearing a print apron over her navy blue dress—and her shiny pots, which sat simmering on the stovetop. Between the roasting turkey, the rolls, and fresh coffee, our kitchen smelled like a heavenly paradise.

Kenji, standing on the welcome mat, quietly took off his jacket, and hung it on one of the wall pegs next to my parents' winter wear. He was about to remove his boots. I'd told him that my folks would be rather formal at Christmas; my dad would dress in a dark suit, though he might take off the jacket if the house got too hot. Kenji had understood. He looked handsome in a white shirt and striped tie, plus a blue cardigan and dark pants. I noticed that he'd had a haircut for the occasion, but fortunately, the wavy lock of black hair I liked so much was not touched. I was very proud of him.

"Claire, you're tracking snow onto my clean floor," Mom said, with no bite in her scolding. She turned to get her first impression of Kenji. "Your Dr. Akiyama's got more sense." She nodded a greeting to Kenji, and he smiled, then aligned his boots next to theirs.

Mom, please, please make a good impression and don't scold.

"Oh gosh, sorry," I said. "Mom, this is Kenji."

Mom seemed uncertain about what to do, then she reached out to shake his hand. Kenji too appeared unsure of what was expected. He bowed and then took Mom's hand.

Dad burst through the outside door carrying split logs for the fireplace. Mom would have told him that I was bringing Kenji, and he must have seen the Plymouth parked in front of our extended bungalow, but he looked startled and stopped whistling immediately.

Kenji was quick. "Let me help." He reached to take some of the wood.

"Hello there, young man," Dad said, as he handed over a few logs, and then stepped out of his boots.

Kenji repeated his rehearsed phrase, "I am glad to meet you."

Mom must have been apprehensive about Dad's next comment. She was quick to say, "You are welcome here."

Oh God, let this meeting work. Let my family make Kenji feel at ease, and please, please, they've got to see what a great guy he is.

"It is good that you invite me for Christmas dinner," Kenji said. In stocking feet, he followed my dad across the kitchen and into our family room.

"His English is pretty good," Mom whispered. "Can he eat our food?"

"Mom, don't be silly. He's lived here a year and a half. I've told you how clever he is. And call him Kenji. Don't be so formal."

"Your dad wasn't happy that you were bringing him, you know."

"Dad never liked any of my boyfriends." I pulled off my jacket, and hung it on the peg next to the others. I'd worn a red sweater and dark blue skirt. Carrying a pair of slippers for Kenji's use, I hurried to join the men.

Dad was saying. "I guess you don't celebrate Christmas where you come from."

"Not the same as here, but the department stores all have Santa Clauses."

"Hmm," my father said, scratching the top of his head, which was his way of showing disapproval. "That's not the message I'd hope a heathen nation would get about Christmas."

For heaven's sake, Dad. Japan isn't a heathen nation.

Dad was arranging logs in the basket beside our stone fireplace, while Kenji stood looking on.

"Whose side are you on?" Dad confronted Kenji.

Oh my, what's Dad getting at? Can't you just be the pleasant host you are with all your friends?

I listened for a while, as my dad went on, and on, not really giving Kenji the opportunity to respond to his initial question, or any others for that matter. "Too bad the Bay of Pigs invasion of Cuba failed," he was saying. "Guess we didn't give those ex-Cubans enough help." He added another log to the fire. "Your country worried about Russia? Well you should be, what with the Berlin Wall put up in August and Russia launching the bomb in October. Then too, you've got to worry about China—split with Russia last year, but they've got so many people. It will be no sacrifice to those Chinese communists to start a war; losing thousands of men won't faze them a bit, not with their population."

I suppose Dad is trying to think of a subject that will interest Kenji, but he's way out of order. This day could be a disaster. Kenji would likely agree with Dad's concerns, but I didn't want to put him on the spot by talking about international politics. I'd better take control of the conversation. What, oh what, can we talk about?

I stepped up to sweep away some ashes that had spread onto Mom's hooked mat. "Isn't it cozy in here Kenji? Sit wherever you like," I said, but my Dad's deep voice drowned me out.

"We don't drink in this house, but I can get you a glass of orange juice or ice tea."

"Thank you," Kenji replied as he cautiously sat down on the chintz-covered sofa facing the glowing fire.

"Well, young man, which is it you like? Juice or tea?" Dad was still standing, so he towered over Kenji on the sofa. With his broad shoulders, accentuated by a white shirt that had been formally buttoned to the neck, and neatly adorned with a festive tie, he managed to look quite menacing.

I bit my lips.

Dad, Dad, please don't be so testy.

"Orange juice, please," Kenji said, as he tightened his knees together and crossed his arms over his chest.

I was torn.

What should I do? Help Mom and leave Kenji alone with Dad, or stay. I'd better stay. Kenji doesn't look very comfortable.

I bounced down on the sofa beside him and reached out to take his hand, but he quietly pulled it aside.

Mom stuck her head around the corner. "Claire, show your beau the family album. He'll see the people he'll be meeting. Tommy's on his way. He's got some news to tell us."

Thanks, Mom. Great idea—a neutral subject. I remembered how, in earlier days, Kenji and I had looked at the Yamadas' albums, and though we didn't know any of the people in the pictures, he'd told me about the sites, such as Nikko, where his parents went in summer—where one could pull a fish right out of the lake and eat it five minutes later.

"Tommy is my younger brother. He's always late." I gestured with open palms extended, asking Kenji if he was interested in the album, and he nodded affirmation. I went to get the leather binder from the bookshelf next to the fireplace, sat down and opened it on our laps.

Should I warm him about Uncle Harry? If Dad's comments were out of line, what would happen when Uncle Harry recited his opinions?

Before I could explain about the pictures on the first page, which had been taken at Mom and Dad's wedding, there was a commotion in the front part of our house. My older brother, John, and his wife and baby, had arrived. Kenji stood when they entered the family room.

Dad will be impressed that Kenji knows Western etiquette. I've got to learn Japanese etiquette and Japanese, so I don't make a fool of myself when I meet Kenji's folks.

After the ritual of removing coats and introductions, Heidi, my sister-in-law, left the baby with my brother and went to help Mom, who was making coleslaw. Years back, when Heidi had first offered, Mom had relinquished that task with some reluctance, because Heidi's recipe was different from ours, but after two years of having Heidi in our family, Mom's attitude had changed. Now we often heard Mom say, "Some German things are just fine."

I was glad that hatred toward German people was fading, but disappointed that too often Americans still bore dislike of Japanese people, without even knowing any Japanese or knowing much about the culture.

Lately, if anyone was critical of Germany, Mom was inclined to say, "Well, I think we have German blood in our family way back," or "Heidi's people are a lot like us." Now Heidi was so well accepted that she could come into Mom's house, and Mom would listen to her suggestions, even when they were counter to Mom's ways.

My brother handed little James to me. He was only four months old. The baby batted his wee eyes for a moment and then went back to sleep in my arms.

Heaven. It's heaven holding a little baby. It would be even more heavenly if he were Kenji's and mine. What would he look like—or she? Probably have Kenji's Asian eyes and black hair.

I remembered some of the conversations we'd had about marriage and family. Kenji said his children could become whatever they wanted to be. But once he asked, "What would we do if our daughter wants to marry an Indian?" And I said, "We'll tell her that international marriages aren't easy, but if you love each other and want to overcome the hurdles, it's grand," I said. "You always want to get to understand each other better and to accommodate. You make each other feel secure and content." He'd just laughed, the happy laugh that meant he agreed.

Dad bent down to look at James. "The baby's really fair, isn't he? Got Heidi's blue eyes and blonde hair. And look at those arms? Going to be a big, strapping football player."

At least Dad didn't say an architect, which had been his goal before he married my mom and got strapped into supporting a family. But Dad seemed like a person content with his life. He'd risen to become bank manager, sent the two older kids through university, and was paying for my nursing course. He'd pleased Mom by building an extension on our house for a family room. I wondered if he had any regrets. Maybe. He'd tried to direct both of my brothers into architecture, though in the long run it seemed as though he'd accepted the choices my brothers had made. John had met Heidi during his tour of army duty in Germany, and then went back to marry her after he was mustered out of service. He was managing one of Mom's brothers' small shoe stores, and my younger brother, Tom, taught high school English.

Tommy will be on my side. We've always seen eye to eye. He'll approve of my decision to marry Kenji.

After coming out of the oven, the turkey was moved to Mom's Flow Blue platter and left on the counter for the appropriate time; then Dad was summoned to do the carving. We all gathered around the kitchen table to watch. Uncle Harry, Dad's brother, and his wife, Aunt Louise, were as late as Tommy.

I dread hearing the usual comments Uncle Harry makes about Japan. If we're in luck, those two won't show up.

But the back door opened with a bang. "Let the party begin," Uncle Harry said as he and Aunt Louise stomped off their shoes and then left them on the rubber drain mat. They peeled off their coats and hung them up. "Where's that newest Winchester? Bet he takes after his Uncle Harry." My uncle adjusted his trousers over his plump belly and snapped the red suspenders he wore.

"Shush," Mom said. "The baby's sleeping."

But Uncle Harry was bounding past my Dad to where Kenji and I were standing. "Howdy," he said. "So you're—"

Mom nudged him. "Let me introduce Dr. Akiyama. He's studying medicine. Very talented."

Uncle Harry wrinkled his nose, like he had his own opinions about foreigners.

Kenji bowed slightly and shook hands with Uncle Harry. "My name is Kenji," he said.

"Okay, we'll call you Ken. Hard to pronounce those Jap names."

Uncle Harry still referred to the Japanese by the derogatory wartime terms.

Oh God. What's he going to say next? How can I keep him from bringing up his war service against Japan? My family will probably railroad any of Kenji's thoughts about marrying me. I bring a lot of baggage into our relationship—none I can't handle, but can he?

We took our places at the walnut table in the dining room, with Dad at the head and Mom at the foot—when she wasn't running back and forth to the kitchen to get something that was needed. The table was a heritage piece from Mom's parents, one Mom took pride in, and for this occasion it had been extended to its full length. She had covered it with a lace cloth and had arranged a centrepiece of candles and evergreens, with fake red berries, in a silver-plated bowl.

Remember to compliment Mom on her arrangement.

As long as I can remember, Mom enjoyed decorating our house for every occasion. Not only did we have a Christmas tree in the family room, the windows were decorated with electric candles that glowed though the glass into the night. Garlands of holly were draped from picture to picture down the front hall, and every room had some Christmassy arrangement. She even changed the pillows in the family room to go with the seasons. They were red now—the orange ones, marking Thanksgiving, had been put away. Her idea of a perfect house came from reading *Good Housekeeping,* and the generous allowance Dad gave her to run the house allowed her to buy or make what she needed to keep up with the trends.

One thing about Uncle Harry, he kept conversations going, with talk about the Rose Bowl, the death of Senator somebody—whom I didn't know—who would run against the incumbent Governor, and who (according to Uncle Harry) was "a dog" and not to be trusted. Uncle Harry was sitting in front of the family portrait, which decorated the floral wallpaper. In the picture, Dad must have been about eight and Harry would have been ten. Dad was unsmiling, with his wee tie askew. He looked timid, whereas Harry sat on the edge of his chair ready to cause some mischief.

Granddad presided over his flock in a staunch army manner, like the Major he'd been during World War I. Our family were proud Americans. Grandmother liked to boast that she was the ninth generation of our ancestors who had come to America and could claim a right to belong to the Daughters of the Republic, having descended from a soldier who was a private in George Washington's army.

Dad had long ago given up debating with Harry. I think he'd felt like an underling from the time they were growing up. Their positions were finally fixed when Uncle Harry made the Navy his career during World War II. Dad was always apologetic about having weak eyes, which deferred him from military service. It irked me that Mom was constantly explaining to her friends that, no, her husband hadn't been a conscientious objector, who refused to fight for our country—that the poor man had bad eyes.

The only conscientious objector I knew was the brother of one of my high school friends. Once, a long time ago, when I was at their house, I'd overheard him arguing with his mom. It puzzled me how that woman could be so mean to her son. She'd told him to take off, that she was ashamed to have him around when their neighbours had lost two sons fighting for our country. And he'd said, "You would rather have me dead. You would be proud of me if I were dead? Well I don't have anything against those German or Italian or Japanese boys and I don't want to kill people. Besides I'm not sure that we had reason enough to go to war. Do you realize that the U.S. fluctuated about whether to join Britain or Germany? What the hell!"

I remember wanting to see what he looked like, because I pictured him to be a skinny, effeminate boy, but when he stormed out past my friend and me, he looked like a star quarterback—tall and husky. I remember thinking that it took a lot of courage to express opinions contrary to those of your family.

"Where's Tommy?" Uncle Harry asked. "Couldn't you raise a kid to be on time?"

Mom's offended, but she'll hold her tongue. Heaven knows she tried, but Tom has his own sense of timing.

"He'll be here. He has an announcement to make. You know he has farther to drive than you, Harry, and the roads are in bad shape."

"Announcement? Is he marrying that Mexican can-can dancer? That bimbo? She would loosen up this family." Uncle Harry did a shimmy with his shoulders.

"No, he hasn't seen her for ages," Mom said, lifting her chin to show that she resented his comment.

"At least Claire is bringing a doctor into the family. We could always use some medical advice." Uncle Harry winked at me and chuckled.

Oh God. Uncle Harry you're going to spoil everything.

I wanted to crawl under the table. Kenji and I weren't engaged. What would he think I'd told my family?

Uncle Harry, if looks could kill, you'd be a goner.

"Claire, thanks for bringing your friend," Heidi said. "We should make everyone who comes here to study feel at home. Christmas dinner is the best time to get to see family life." She smiled at Kenji and then I thought she was directing the next comment to me. "Even though some family members don't behave themselves. But, I suppose it happens everywhere. It did in my family back in Germany when I brought John to meet them." She gave me an understanding look.

Mom kept offering seconds of turkey, chive dressing, mashed potatoes, squash, beets, and succotash to Kenji and me, rounds of foods we had to refuse. She'd eye me to see if I thought Kenji didn't like her cooking.

"Mom, Mom. We can't eat so much. Look at the turkey and dressing we've put away," I tried to reassure her.

With his usual frown, Dad directed Mom to sit down.

"I was in the Pacific during the war," Uncle Harry said. He was standing and passing his plate around us to Dad for more turkey.

Here it comes. I know the story he's going to tell, but how can I stop him? "You in the war?" he asked Kenji.

"I was too young."

Kenji would have been a young student, and like all students, working in a factory. He'd said he helped make airplanes, but thank goodness he didn't tell Uncle Harry that.

"Sure. Sure you were. Well, you guys bombed my destroyer once."

I wanted to hold Kenji's hand, or better still, make some excuse for us to leave the room, but that would have ended the Christmas dinner. Everyone would be mad and blame someone else. The day would end unhappily for the entire family.

If only Tommy would arrive. Where is he? Always late, but not this late. He would know how to turn the remarks around, but his place at the table is still empty.

It was Heidi who stood, tapped on her goblet to get attention, and said, "Harry, you always want to fight the war all over again. Sit down. Our countries are trying to make peace. For God's sake, *shut up.*"

I smiled. Kenji seemed to be trying to keep from smiling, and John stood to salute with his glass.

Mom took the lead in joining the two of them, and we all lifted our glasses of ice tea—even Uncle Harry. For the moment, he'd lost the spotlight and the chance to pursue his favourite topic: the number of Japanese ships they'd sunk and the number of Japanese sailors he'd watched jump overboard and drown in the cold Pacific. On the occasions when he related that story, he always called those Japanese sailors, the ones who didn't go down with their ship, cowards. But he told another story about being one of the few to crowd into the lifeboats and get rescued after his own ship was hit, even though most of his shipmates had drowned. He never thought of himself as being a coward when he'd crowded into a life boat and abandoned some of his crewmates.

Dad complimented Mom on the scalloped oysters, his favourite, and about how prefect the turkey had been roasted. Mom beamed. He stepped around the table and stood with his arm around her. "To think, I married a great cook and a pretty woman to boot." Those were the lines he repeated often, but they were the compliments my mom wanted to hear. No wonder they'd been together all those years. He'd bought her the new broadloom she's yearned for, and bought a grand piano to grace the living room, even though no one played it any more. I was proud to have parents who knew how to support each other.

Kenji and I will know how to support each other too.

After the apple pie and ice cream, we all carried dishes into the kitchen. Dad scraped the plates and put them in the dishwasher. Aunt Louise put the bread and butter away and Mom covered the leftovers. There seemed nothing more for us to do, so I suggested to Kenji that we check on little James, who was in the crib Mom had set up in the guest room.

Kenji admired the baby, and watched me bounce him up and down as I sat on the side of the bed. He played with the baby's wee hand and then let me settle James in the crib while he looked at prints of floral works by Van Gogh and Monet, which Mom had hung on the wall, and at old family photos. There was one of Charlotte and me. I pointed to the picture. "Charlotte was my best pal all through school and junior college," I said. "We always said that we'd travel together through Europe and Asia, winding up in Japan. She started on a world tour, but she's in Germany now, and she wrote that she's met a guy from Boston. They're coming back, getting married and she's going to enroll at Wellesley to study art history. Her husband is going to study law."

I could be the one winding up in Japan.

The piano sounded from the front room, and I nodded that we should go out there.

Heidi was a music teacher. She beckoned to all of us, wanting us to sing along as she played the piano. I got out a book of carols, which Kenji could follow, and we all chimed in. Aunt Louise, wearing a fashionable white, woollen dress, sat beside Heidi to turn the pages on the sheet music. Uncle Harry led the pack with his booming voice, but no one minded. The Christmas tree flashed coloured lights; the electric candles hanging in the windows glowed, and the aroma of apple pie and coffee still wafted through the air.

This is just the kind of Christmas I wanted Kenji to remember.

While Heidi nursed James, we played charades. Kenji got paired with Dad. I was anxious that there could be some disaster, but they impersonated great scientists and entertained us all with their exaggerations. Kenji borrowed Mom's scarf and played the part of Madame Curie, while Dad posed as Pierre. We laughed and laughed as they tended the imaginary beakers and backed away from pretend explosions. Kenji was the one who guessed that Uncle Harry and I were impersonating Anthony and Cleopatra. Everyone clapped.

Tommy arrived with his usual fanfare, and a Santa bag over his shoulder. He distributed presents to each of us. A bracelet for me. A Beethoven record for Kenji.

Wonderful! He followed my suggestion.

Tom ate while we admired our gifts. Dad gave Mom a bed jacket and Mom gave him the 1961 Pulitzer Prize winning novel, *To Kill a Mockingbird*, by Harper Lee.

I expected Tom to say that he had to pick up someone at the train station and then produce a new girlfriend, but when he got around to telling us his news, we were all stunned. "I'm going to Africa to teach. I'm going to Kenya. Leave January 15. Now you can all come and see Africa."

Mom's face was white. Dad's was red. "You can't up and quit to traipse off like that. What are you thinking?" Dad scolded.

"I gave my notice before school started in September. It's taken months to work out the details."

"You could have told us," Mom said. She had wilted back onto her chair.

Tom, to his credit, didn't argue this time.

"It's what I've wanted to do. Now I've got the chance."

I was proud of my brother and stood to give him a hug. "Good going, Tom."

Kenji smiled and nodded, and Dad said, "Well, it's your life." But he got up, banged the back of his chair with his fist, and paced into the front hall and back.

"Howard and I are going out there together," Tom said.

I knew what that meant. Mom probably didn't, and I wasn't sure about Dad.

Too bad that my brother can't tell them that he and Howard have been lovers since high school.

The exotic girls he brought around were distractions from his serious relationship.

Heidi obliged Tom's demand for some classical music and played a little Mozart. We bid goodbyes with hugs and promises.

The snow had stopped; the roads were cleared and the sky was dark, with a few twinkling stars and a big moon. The whole earth seemed at peace. Families reconciled to differences, emotions satiated. I was filled with the sense that love could conquer all. I was happy—cuddled up to Kenji as we drove back to the city.

"What will I cook when your parents come to dinner?" I asked.

"I haven't made up my mind yet," Kenji said.

"I know, but we can pretend."

"You have a nice family," he said.

"Pretty average, but we manage to get along—most of the time."

"Your uncle Henry is very funny." Kenji laughed.

"Offensive is the word I'd use," I said.

"My uncle was very proud colonel. He suicided."

"What do you mean? Why?" I asked.

"When war ended, and he came home, people hated him. People said the military made bad mistakes. I don't think he was a bad man, but political and military men got blamed for losing war."

"I didn't know."

"It happened. Many soldiers suicided, because no one was their friend anymore. Even their children were shunned."

"My dad says we had to drop the bomb to stop the war."

"That is what your side says."

"Isn't it true?"

"That uncle wrote in his diary six months before Aug. 6. He said that the war was lost. He said that Japan would surrender very soon and he would come home."

"Oh. I don't know what to believe."

"You just follow your leaders. That's the way war happens."

"Right. Right," I said, and after some moments of silence, my mind went on to the subject of affection. "My brother is in love with a man."

"To love and be loved by another human is highest privilege."

"Will Tommy and Howard be safe in Africa? I mean, can they be open about their feelings?"

"I wonder."

"Should I warn him? What can I do?"

"Maybe say you worry, but do they have to be secret?"

My guy is so reasonable.

I leaned to kiss his cheek.

He concentrated on driving for a moment before answering his own question. "I haven't decided," he said.

It isn't that complicated for us, is it?

I knew that 1962 would be a decisive year in our relationship.

Chapter 12
Operating Room Experience

During the final year of nursing education, students spent three months at a time in several different specialties. Training to work in the operating room was the most daunting in my opinion. The first day I was to report to the O.R. was terrifying. I would be standing beside the surgeon, and expected to know every step of the operation—what tissue would be cut first, and which second, and what complications might be expected. With no verbal command, I had to be able to look into the wound and see when to hand the surgeon a scalpel or a hemostat or a retractor. I was expected to know what suture material would be used for each tissue being repaired, and to have threaded needles, clamped to hemostats, ready for use when the surgeon put out his hand.

Oh God. I'm not ready.

My nerves were on edge. I'd awakened early, gone to breakfast, but found the food disagreeable. I avoided my classmates because I didn't want to talk about what was ahead of me that day. I didn't even notice that a young man was riding in the elevator with me to the surgical floor until he spoke.

"This the operating room?" the redheaded man asked.

I'd never seen him before. He wore casual street clothes, so I assumed that he was a new med student. In our hospital, we call the operating theatre "the surgical floor," not the operating room, but his use of this misnomer didn't particularly register with me until later, when I reviewed what had happened that day. "Yes. Are you observing Dr. Alexander's gall-bladder?" I asked.

"I'm just …" he didn't finish because the elevator door opened abruptly and we each stepped off.

Since the young man appeared bewildered about what to do next, I said, "Use the doctor's change room," and pointed down the hall. "Says 'DOCTOR' on the door."

If he's observing Dr. Alexander, it's no surprise that he's edgy.

Dr. Alexander had a reputation for being the most irascible doctor in our hospital. Edgy wasn't strong enough to describe what I was going through. Some luck. My first O.R. assignment was to be his scrub nurse. I could sympathize with the lost young man. Reason prevailed over my urge to tell the supervising nurse that I was sick and needed to be excused. I wasn't a girl who could renege on a duty.

Well, Jane's the circulating nurse on the case. She'll be looking over my shoulder and drop anything I'm going to need onto my sterile tray. She'll whisper what I should be doing if she notices that I'm frozen.

My fingers felt numb and my heart was palpitating.

Dr. Anderson performed fifteen or more cholecystectomies a week at our hospital. There were many fair (light complexioned), fat, and forty-year-old people around, and those were the typical people who got gall-stones, which were removed surgically. It was the same routine with every suspected case: blood tests, x-rays, and eventually surgery. The procedures must have been old hat to him and his usual assistants, but they weren't familiar to me. When something is new to me, I need to think through the process slowly, but I expected that Dr. Anderson would be impatient.

God help me to stay calm, and not freeze up and bungle the whole operation.

I changed to greens in the nurses' dressing room, locked my day clothes in the locker, and stood in front of the mirror to tuck every hair under the green cap.

At least I'm properly gowned. Won't be scolded for that.

The pause gave me time to take deep breaths and calm the queasy feeling in my stomach. When I emerged, the young man I'd met in the elevator, having changed into operating room attire, was casually approaching the nurses' station.

In the scrub room, I put on a mask, stood in front of the basin to lather my arms and hands, and scrubbed. Then I stepped through swinging doors into the operating theatre. Jane, the circulating nurse, held the gown for me to put on and then gloved me. Around me everything was white tile and cold steel. According to the clock, high on the wall, I was fifteen minutes early. Hidden under green from head to foot, with my hands hugging my elbows, I watched the second hand moving, almost imperceptibly, from dot to dot.

Oh God, don't let my eyes above my mask betray how scared I am. I've got to look confident.

From time to time, I watched for the corridor door to open, and at last the patient was wheeled in through that door and was lifted onto the operating table by the orderlies. The anaesthetist busied herself. Her metal equipment screeched on the tile floor as she positioned it, and slid her stool so she could sit at the patient's head. After taping the patient's arm to the supporting board, she started the IV drip, containing electrolytes. Eventually she would add the anaesthesia. The drip was adjusted so that the fluid entered the patient's vein at just the right speed. Next she hooked the oxygen mask into place over the patient's nose and mouth.

So far, it's going just as we've been taught.

The corridor door opened, and the redheaded man stuck his head inside momentarily, and then quickly withdrew. I whispered to Jane that we had a new med student who must be lost. She followed his retreat to the corridor and then shook her head. Apparently he'd disappeared.

From the scrub room, Dr. Alexander burst through the swinging doors and was gowned in green by Jane. He stood with hands folded to his chest, rocking up and down in his sneakers, eyeing the clock.

His resident assistant had better not be late. Was it the redhead after all? No, there's Bob Foster coming through the door.

Dr. Foster was gowned, and joined Dr. Alexander in waiting for the anaesthetist to give the signal.

Jane painted the incision area with the antiseptic, draped the patient with sterile green sheets, undraped my table full of steel instruments, and slid it into place next to where Dr. A. would stand. I mounted the stool, making me tall enough to be able to see inside the abdominal cavity. Jane adjusted the overhead light, which spot-lit the area to be incised, but also diffused light onto the arrangement on my tray. Jane and I counted the sponges and forceps I'd been allotted. We'd verify that the number of used and unused clamps and sponges added up to the number of each that I'd been given, before the abdomen was closed, to be sure that none were left inside the patient. My hands shook, but I squared my shoulders, took a deep breath, and was ready for the greatest test of my life.

What's Dr. Alexander going to want first? The scalpel.

I remembered how our instructor had taught us to slap the scalpel into the surgeon's right hand so that he felt it was secure.

Sponging up the blood will be next.

I readied several folds of gauze and clamped them into forceps. My mind raced through the steps of the procedure that would follow, and I felt more confident.

The operation began. Just under the skin I saw something that hadn't been listed in the steps. I felt panic.

What's that? It looks like chicken fat. What's Dr. A. going to need in order to deal with that blubbery stuff?

"We'll do her a favour," Dr. Alexander said. "Lighten her load. Should charge her extra." With his finger, he severed the minute blood vessels until the fat was loose, then he lifted the mass and handed it to me.

Is this the omentum? Can't be. It's fat—just buttery, slimy, people fat. What in heavens am I supposed to do with it? It won't fit into the kidney basin I have ready for the gallbladder.

The fat oozed between my gloved fingers.

Jane hurriedly arrived with a wash bowl and motioned that I should drop the greasy, yellow mass into it, being careful not to get too close and touch the bowl with my gloved hand. A depression in the fat for the belly button looked revolting. Blood didn't bother me, but this lard-smelling blob made me gag. It was so slippery that I couldn't get a grip, and I let the fat drop from my gloves. It missed the basin, fell onto the floor, and then skidded, like a curling stone, across the tile. Bile belched into my mouth. I swallowed and swallowed, trying not to regurgitate.

Dr. Alexander was shaking his hand impatiently. "Sponge. Sponge."

I came to and fed the forceps clamped with gauze into his hand.

"Retractor. Retractor. What the hell is keeping you? Pay attention."

Where's Jane? Jane, I need you!

Then I remembered the sequence: clamp, scissors. I handed them over in succession and accepted the returns. Now the operation seemed to be on course.

I think I'm getting the hang of it.

I could actually see the purplish gallbladder nestled under the liver.

Amazing.

After Dr. Alexander severed the gallbladder, he passed it to me and I put it in the readied kidney basin. But the slippery sac with its stony contents reminded me of the fat. I froze.

"Suture," Dr. Alexander bellowed. "Suture, suture, suture." His hand jerked in my direction.

I slapped the clamp with the threaded needle into his outstretched hand.

"Is this double O or O?"

"A-a-ah," I stammered.

Have I mixed up the threaded needles?

"Who teaches you girls, anyway? Next thing I know you'll be handing me silk."

"No, sir, it's cat gut," I said.

"I know *this* is cat gut," he held up the needle for me to see. "Do you have the right size of cat gut, is what I'm asking?"

My voice quivered. "I hope so, Sir."

"You hope so. What kind of answer is that?" He worked away inside the cavity. "You're supposed to tell me jokes. Keep me entertained."

I said nothing.

God, help me. Someone help me.

"Well, come on. Tell me something juicy."

I bit my lip and concentrated on threading another needle.

Bang. The corridor door flew open and the redhead I'd seen in the elevator dashed past us toward the scrub room. Two policemen were in pursuit. "Can he get out through that door?" one officer asked, pointing across the room to the door to the scrub room.

"Yes," Jane said. "From there he can get back into the corridor."

"Head him off," the officer called to his assistants, and they retreated back into the corridor.

The head nurse appeared. "Sorry. That guy's been posing as a doctor and stealing billfolds from the doctor's change room."

"God, I never lock mine up." Dr. Alexander said. "Someone get my wallet and put it away."

"Will do," the head nurse responded, as she followed in pursuit of the thief and policeman.

We heard a scuffle in the scrub room, heard one officer making a pronouncement, and heard the back door close.

I held my breath. I couldn't believe what was happening.

"Where were we?" Dr. Anderson said as he continued with the operation. "You aren't entertaining me, so I'll entertain you. There was—" He stopped. "Jane ... Jane!" he called.

What's the matter? Is he so angry that he's asking to have me replaced?

I felt an urge to throw down the clamp, and bolt for the door.

There must be something I'm good at, but it's not being a scrub nurse.

Jane casually approached. "Need a wipe?" She held a towel ready to mop his sweaty brow.

"Not now. Not now. Get around here." He jerked his head for her to come close. "Closer," he whispered, and she leaned in. We could still hear. "Jane, pull up my shorts. The damn rubber's let go. Get inside my gown and pull them up, girl."

I was about to put my gloved hand over my mouth to hide my grin before I remembered where I was.

"Briefs or boxers?" Dr. Foster asked with a chuckle.

"Never mind," Dr. Alexander said sternly.

"I'll bet they've got polka dots," Dr. Foster said.

"Lay off," Dr. Alexander said emphatically, but I could see from his eyes that he was smiling.

Dr. Foster wouldn't let go. "Ladybugs. I'll bet he's wearing red ladybugs."

"Close," Jane said. She'd been around a long time and could hold her own with any of the surgeons. I think they liked her because of it. She knew her job and told them off when necessary. "Ants. Red and black ants."

The anaesthetist began to sing, "Itsy, bitsy, anty climbed up the water spout. Down came ..." She raised her eyebrows.

Dr. Foster chimed in. "Antsie pantsie. How did your wife let you out of the house wearing those?"

"Damn," Dr. Alexander said. "Shut up, will you. Christmas present. My sister has a strange sense of humour. Damn it. Drain. I'm going to put in a drain."

Does he mean it? I don't have one with my sterile supplies. Is this just a distraction? Where's Jane? Oh, she's gone to wash her hands.

Jane had heard the request as she returned from the scrub room. She glanced to see whether I had rubber tubing, and then used forceps to transfer a sterile hollow cylinder from the disinfecting solution onto my tray. I quickly grasped the tube with forceps from my tray and when Dr. Alexander shouted, "Gimme, gimme," I passed the readied instrument to him. He stuck the end of the tube into the incision and held up the tail for me to cut off the excess.

I readied the scissors and cut. Somehow, I managed to sever not only the tube but also one fingertip of his glove, which fell onto the floor.

I gasped. At least I had only cut the glove and not his finger, but if a crevice had opened up in the room I would have gladly disappeared into it.

"My God, girl," Dr. Anderson shouted. "You'll never be a nurse!" Turning to his assistant, he said, "Okay, Foster. You take over. My finger is exposed. I'm not sterile anymore." He stepped off the stool and started to strip off his gloves, ready to leave the room, but as he neared the corridor door, he skidded on the slippery fat residue and landed on his bottom. "Damn, damn, damn," he said, pulling himself up off the floor and exposing his slipping boxers. "Close your eyes. Damn it."

With his right hand holding his hospital gown and underclothing tight, Dr. Alexander stepped up beside me and whispered, "I won't tell what a bungler you are if you don't mention this scene to anyone." Winking and smiling at us all, he went to the door, peeked up and down the corridor, and exited the room.

As Dr. Foster tied the last stitch, he said, "You missed a good chance, Jane."

"Hush, boy," Jane said. "Get your dirty mind on something else. Mum's the word." She bent double laughing. "Fair is fair, Nurse Winchester. Don't tell on him. So, how much do you want to bet that Dr. A. is going be a lot more agreeable from now on?"

He won't terrify me either. He's got a sense of humour, and I think he means to be entertaining when he acts so gruff. I'll learn his mannerisms.

Chapter 13
Josh and His Parents

"Claire, I'm sending you to the ER," my nursing instructor said. "They're swamped with emergencies. You're to monitor a child who needs special attention."

The emergency ward! Real drama! Gunshot wounds, bloody accident victims, burst appendixes, and heart attacks!

My imagination bounced from scene to scene: handsome constables in stiff blue uniforms, with guns on their hips; interns in white lab coats shouting orders; nurses in various peak caps flashing in and out of the cubicles. Heroes. I guess I thought of them as life savers, and though I wouldn't presume to put myself in that category, I must have felt that I was at least being given a *chance* to do something heroic. I hurried through the tunnel to my assignment, panting in haste and anticipation.

"Room 4," the head nurse in Emergency said as she led the way.

A boy of about four or five, in his white hospital gown, lay looking up at us and gasping for breath. He seemed so small and vulnerable in that adult-sized bed. "Nurse," he moaned. His hands sought the source of the pain, which was a bloody dressing on his abdomen. Anguish was written all over his face.

Thoughts of heroic acts vanished fast. By instinct I wanted to take him in my arms and comfort him, but emotions had to be put aside.

Concentrate, Claire. To save him, you've got to focus on measures to ease his pain and stop that bleeding.

As we stood by his bedside, the head nurse took the little fellow's hand and passed it to me. "Okay Josh, Claire's going to stay with you." And to me she said, "His name his Joshua Shumaker. Do what you can to make him comfortable."

What about the bleeding? What about the pain?

"Has he had medication for the pain?" I asked, puzzled why the drug wasn't working.

"Nothing yet. Prop him up, keep wiping his forehead, and talk to him. It'll help."

For heavens sake. That's not enough. What is she waiting for?

A student nurse couldn't tell the head nurse what to do, but that nurse should be getting the needed medication.

The boy looked so helpless, trying to smile at me. "Nurse," he said again, squeezing my hand hard, as if that would relieve the torment.

With my free hand, I wiped his forehead with the damp cloth someone had left in a basin on his bedside table.

"He fell on a broken beer bottle. It's a nasty abdominal wound," the nurse said, as she refolded the extra cotton blanket that had been left at the foot of his bed.

"Oh dear," I said, smoothing a lock of the child's brown hair.

"He and his brother were playing in a vacant lot next to the school. His brother had the presence of mind to shout. One of the teachers called the ambulance."

I couldn't control my voice, which must have betrayed how annoyed I felt. "Shouldn't he have something for the pain? What about fluids? Haven't the doctors ordered an IV?"

"Can't. We don't have consent. His parents are on their way."

Consent!

I hadn't thought of that. My tone became more sympathetic. "Should I get him ready for the O.R.? The surgeon will want to act quickly, won't he?"

"I don't know what to tell you." The head nurse let out a big sigh and shook her head. Frustrated resignation registered on her face. Before she left, she put her hand on the little fellow's brow. "Hold on, sweetheart. Your mommy and daddy and are coming. Then we'll get you upstairs where the doctors can fix your tummy."

That wound is still bleeding. Precious minutes are creeping by. At least I can rearrange his pillows for better support.

But when I attempted to lift his head, he grimaced. The slightest movement caused horrific pain.

Never have I felt so helpless. Vital signs. The doctor will want the most recent vital signs.

I took his blood pressure, took his pulse, counted his laboured respirations, and wrote down the figures.

What else? What else? I need a lot more training to know what to do. Hero indeed! Damn it. Why did they choose me when I am so unprepared? Where are his parents?

Slowly, I sat down on the chair next to the bed, without letting go of Josh's hand. My foot tapped the floor.

Couldn't they have given permission over the phone? If the ambulance got here so quickly, what is holding them up?

I visualized them waiting for a bus.

Oh, God, do they realize what an emergency this is? The boy could bleed to death. He's already on the verge of shock because of lack of fluids.

I began to shallow breathe myself.

Shall I get some dextrose and saline so we can start the intravenous as soon as the parents come? No, I'd better not leave him.

Talk. I should talk to distract him.

"I'll bet your daddy and mommy are on the road," I said as calmly as I could.

"Where do you usually sit in the car? Let's see. I'll bet you and your brother sit in the back seat. Right? Am I right? And I'll bet you count the cows you see. Or red barns or filling stations. Do you play that game? My brother and I used to count red barns."

The boy's hand tightened its grip.

Does he want me to stop my incessant talking? How about singing? Would singing be better?

I heard screams coming from the next compartment. Someone else was in trouble. Those sounds would terrify an adult let alone a little boy who didn't really understand where he was or what was happening. I let go of his hand, got up, and was closing the door when a woman in a black bonnet pushed on it from the hallway.

"Let us in," she said, stepping inside, and rushing to the bedside. She wore an ankle-length black skirt, a dark patterned blouse, and a shawl. Though her hands were red and stained, her face was blanched white.

The head nurse and a bearded man, carrying a very old-fashioned, wide-brimmed, black hat, followed. "Get them to sign." The nurse pressed the consent form into my hands. "I'll start things rolling." She left.

"Joshua, honey," the woman said, trying to lift the boy into her arms.

The child flinched and called out with pain.

Oh, no.

I grabbed her arm and pulled her back. "He can't move. Please, just let him lie quietly." I waved the paper at her. "Sign this consent, please. Please take a moment and sign before doing anything else."

The boy's breathing was laboured. His eyes were rolling around in his head, his vision apparently going in and out of focus. There was little response to his mother's presence.

Does he recognize her voice? Already, he is ebbing away.

The mother accepted a cloth handkerchief from her husband to wipe her tears. They looked like they belonged to some group that definitely did not embrace modern life or technology.

I'm supposed to make the parents comfortable too, but how? This room, with all our apparatus must be very strange to these people.

My eyes quickly surveyed the room, picking out things that might horrify them: the blood pressure cuff on his bedside table; the hook attached to the head of his bed for an IV; the white sheets and curtains, and uniforms; the smell of disinfectants; the sounds of carts rolling across tile floors; the announcements over the loud speaker. And then there was their boy: his tiny face against the oversized white pillow; his curly hair tousled and sticking to his wet forehead; his laboured breathing.

I'll give them a moment to get composed, and take his blood pressure in the meantime.

I began to wrap the cuff around his wee arm.

"Don't touch him." The mother grabbed my arm to push me aside.

Her body trembled. She was more confused than I was about how to be helpful, and she was acting instinctively to protect her son, but she was also a hindrance that I'd have to deal with.

The father had dropped to his knee and was mumbling a prayer.

Precious time is passing.

The head nurse stuck her head through the door. When she observed what was happening she shook her head. "Not signed yet? Well, hurry them. Pull the buzzer the minute it's done. The technician is standing by to get the blood sample to cross-match."

Please, I wish you'd take over. No one has taught me how to handle a situation like this. Is nursing going to continually require me to make decisions and act without the proper training?

I'd assumed there would always be rituals to follow, procedures dictated by the patient's diagnosis, but that wasn't the case. Nurses had to be a lot smarter than I'd guessed. If every day brought unexpected challenges, this profession was going to call for ingenuity; it was never going to be boring.

Do I still feel like this is a dilemma? Choosing between disappointing my parents or pursuing nursing? Maybe they aren't equally unpleasant alternatives. I've wished for challenges, and so far I've had plenty.

Joshua's mother's wide eyes darted around the room and fixed on a pile of flannel blankets. "Aaron," she said to her husband, "get a couple of covers."

When the father stood, I pressed the consent form at him. "Please sir ... please sign so we can stop the bleeding and begin treatment. Josh doesn't need more blankets just now."

The mother had edged herself between me and the boy. "Aaron, help me get him wrapped up so you can carry him."

What? What is she doing?

She was attempting to roll the boy onto his side.

The little boy screamed, "No! No!"

I yanked at the mother's sleeve.

Her arms flailed in the air toward me.

I grabbed for them and held her firmly. "Can't you see you're hurting him?"

"*You* are hurting him." Though she soon quit trying to free her hands, she glared at me with vehemence.

I released her hands slowly, and she didn't object when I pulled back the blanket cover and pointed to the boy's blood-soaked dressing. "He's still bleeding. He needs a transfusion. If he doesn't get one, he'll go into shock."

She ignored me or probably didn't know what I was talking about. I realized that I had a lot to learn about how to translate medical jargon to people unfamiliar with hospitals. The mother motioned for her husband to pick up the boy. "It's the work of the devil. The Lord is letting the devil out," she said.

I forgot about giving the mother a better explanation of what needed to be done or finishing with the blood pressure reading. I was furious. I shook my fist at her and said, "What devil? He's a little boy! He's never done a sinful thing in his life!" My hands were clammy. I turned my back on her, and faced the father, who seemed frozen with uncertainty. "Weren't you sent here by God, because the doctors could help your boy? Pray for the doctors, but *sign* so they can get *started!*" I tried handing him the consent form again.

The mother began to stroke her son's face, and I didn't interfere.

I hope she is coming to the conclusion that they need our help.

Again, I waved the paper. "Mr. and Mrs. Shumaker, please ... you have to sign." My voice trailed off into a whisper.

I'm just a non-entity. They don't hear a word I'm saying. They can't even speculate as to what to do with the pen I keep pushing at them.

I said my own prayer.

The father took his wife's arm as he addressed me. "May we have a moment alone with our boy and the Lord?" he said.

What are they planning? Absconding with the boy? Maybe I have to take a chance though, and leave them alone as they're requesting.

"Sure. Anything." I stepped out into the hall and waited until the second hand on my nurse's watch had made two full rounds. Then I tried to re-enter, but the door seemed jammed; they'd wedged something against it so that it couldn't open.

I pounded with my fists. "Let me in," I called.

That child is going to die right there in that room, when we could have saved him. Stepping back, I threw myself at the door. The effort wasn't enough. I banged on the door more desperately.

"Open up! Open up!"

Two orderlies came running. "What's going on?" the tall one asked, and I explained. When they understood what was happening, they too began to shout, "Open this door! Open it immediately!"

The door wouldn't budge. There were no sounds from inside.

What can they be doing inside that room?

One orderly shouted. "Okay, let's go." Both of the men backed up and ran against the door with such force that it snapped open and the wedged chair flew across the room.

All of this commotion attracted attention from the head nurse and Dr. Schmidt, who arrived in a flash. "Stand back," the doctor said, pushing the mother and me aside. "Mr. Shumaker, Mrs. Shumaker, let me check his condition." He spoke calmly, with such authority that the parents retreated. "The boy's pulse is weak," Dr. Schmidt said and he turned to face the parents. "Time is running out."

I didn't think this couple would understand the significance of a weak pulse, but certainly they could tell by the look on Dr. Schmidt's face, and the tone of his voice, that things were critical for their son. Again, I pressed the form at them. "Please sign, right now."

"Rachael," Mr. Shumaker said. He put his hand on his wife's shoulder. "Let them try. The Lord brought him here. We have got to let them try."

The woman's lips were moving, maybe praying. Her eyes were closed.

Mr. Shumaker took the pen I offered, rested the paper on the bedside table, and signed.

"Okay," Dr. Schmidt said, facing both parents, "this is what we must do. Your boy needs fluids. The nurse will start an IV; we are going to need to replace some of the blood he's lost. So we'll take a sample of blood to cross-match, and then we're taking him to the operating room to remove any shards of glass, check for internal injuries, clean up the wound, and close it. Time is of the essence, so if you'll excuse me ... Oh, and if you have any questions, the nurse can explain."

The head nurse dashed out to get the IV bottle, Dr. Schmidt left, and I was delegated to explain.

Explain! These people are so ignorant and so damn superstitious.

My patience had all but expired. Before I could decide how to begin, the technician came to draw blood, and the defensive mother was at it again. She was blocking any attempt to get near her son.

"Look, Mrs. Shumaker," I said, making my voice sound calm but authoritative. "You saw his bandage. He's lost a lot of blood. Stand aside and let us get our job done. Look, here's what will happen: We will take a sample of his blood and test it to be sure that we give him blood that is compatible—agreeable to him—from the blood we have in storage. Then—" I didn't have a chance to explain further. Mrs. Shumaker was pounding her fists against the arm of the bewildered technician.

"No. No," she gasped. "You can't give him someone else's blood!"

The little boy attempted to sit. "Mommy, Daddy," he said, as if this was a final effort. He swooned back onto his pillow then and was deathly still.

Oh God no, don't let him expire! We're so close to saving him!

"Joshua, Joshua!" The mother moved again, ready to clasp him to her arms, but her husband held her back.

"You are letting him die. Do you hear me?" I said. *"You!"* I looked from one parent to the other.

I don't have the voice to command confidence like Dr. Schmidt's. There's a demeanour I need to cultivate. So far I've done a horrible job. I've screamed, and wrestled. I need wisdom and luck.

"This little fellow was sent here by God as you've said. Everything is new to you, I understand that, but you trust your God. Ask him to guide us. We can help your son, but you've got to give us the chance."

The father took his wife's arm. "Come away, Rachael," he said. He pulled back the chair I had used, and tapped it, directing her to sit down.

Immediately, the technician took the samples, and it seemed that the parents were reconciled to letting us go ahead, but that wasn't what happened.

As I was about to insert the needle to start the IV, in order to replace some of the fluid, the mother jumped to her feet again and came at me, causing me to miss the vein. The fluid began to drain into the boy's soft tissue, which swelled quickly.

At once, the mother saw the bulging infusion. "What did you do?" she shouted. Again she wrestled with me.

I turned to face them. "Hold your wife, will you?" I said to the father, with newly found confidence. "It's edema—fluid in the tissue. You grabbed me, so I missed the vein. It is only saline though—salt and water—and will dissipate. Your son *must* have this fluid or ..." I let my voice trail off ominously. "I am starting over. Step outside, and let me do my job." I moved toward Joshua again, dismissing them. When the needle was in place, and the IV running well, I breathed a sigh of relief.

The orderlies had arrived and were wheeling a gurney into the room.

Looking stunned, both parents had backed away and watched while the orderlies and I lifted Josh onto the narrow stretcher and raised the guard rails. I explained that Josh was going to the operating room, where Dr. Schmidt was waiting to clean and close the wound.

"Go and stay with him, Claire," the head nurse said, when she joined us as we followed the gurney. "Josh will have someone familiar when he comes to." Turning to Mr. and Mrs. Shumaker, she said, "Come with me. You can stay in the waiting room. We'll tell you when there's a change. Just pray that ... well, just pray."

I think she meant to say, "that we aren't too late." Thank goodness she stopped herself.

She took the mother's arm.

The gurney was wheeled into the elevator, with me following.

Josh seemed concerned about the IV. He attempted to look at the arm that was taped to the board, and mumbled something.

It probably feels cold.

"That's edema—some salt water got into your skin, but it will go away," I said. "You're going to the operating room, and while you sleep, the doctor is going to fix everything. I'll be waiting when you wake up."

An hour passed, then an hour and a half. I stayed in the waiting area, looked at magazines, and paced the floor. What if the boy died?

How can this happen in an age when we have all the tools to save him? Those stupid parents. Stupid! The parents will blame me, the persuader, and the doctor. Do people sue for things like this?

Those two certainly would call upon the Lord for vengeance. I hoped never to meet them again. What was the use of talking about brotherly love?

There's so much ignorance in the world. And me? I'm ignorant of how to do my job. Claire, you've got a lot of psychology to learn if you're going to make it as a good nurse.

At last, the call came for me to go to the intensive care unit. There, I held Josh's hand and watched him breathe easier, now that the pain was under control. In another hour, he opened his eyes, and seeing me, he smiled.

"Gosh," I said. "I missed that grin. You're in a special care unit. Now you'll get better and better."

Thank you, God. Thank you.

"You'll want to sleep, and I'm going to tell your mommy and daddy that you're doing fine. Tomorrow, when you feel better, you'll be moved back to the ward. Your mommy and daddy can be there, and I'll be your nurse again. Hope that's okay."

He grinned and then closed his eyes. His breathing was normal. He drifted off, and I slipped away.

Though I dreaded the confrontation, my next duty was to the parents. They'd been in the waiting room for nearly four hours, and would be frantic with worry, and maybe with guilt also. I supposed they hadn't eaten any food.

They probably won't believe me when I tell them Josh is doing okay. That mom will insist on seeing for herself. I can't blame her. It would be my instinct as well. Yes, that was it. I had to put myself into their situation to answer their needs. I should give her a chance to be the caregiver. I can be the teacher, but she won't feel good unless she knows she is helping her boy.

Neither parent was in the waiting room. I checked the cafeteria, and then learned that the head nurse had allowed them to see Josh in the ICU.

When I approached, Dr. Schmidt was at the bedside, giving the parents a run-down on what they'd found. Both parents looked terrified. Words like "perforation" and "peritonitis" would be foreign to them. Later, I would try to describe what organs had been pierced, and explain to them that we had to treat Joshua for an infection in the lining of his abdominal cavity. I could tell them that Josh would recover. Maybe then they would relax and see that we could be trusted.

The next day I waited in the Paediatric Unit. The double doors from the main corridor banged open and the gurney, with side rails raised, was wheeled in. An IV was connected to the mound under the blankets. The mound moved. Josh was awake and back from intensive care.

I turned and saw that Mr. and Mrs. Shumaker had caught up with the gurney.

The mother bowed her head. "Oh, Lord, what have we done? Lord, forgive us." And turning to the father she said, "Aaron, we've got to take him home now. I'll get him dressed. Oh Lord. Please forgive us."

I blocked the door to the private room. "Mr. and Mrs. Shumaker, could you please wait until he's moved and settled? We'll call you," I said, speaking gently but with conviction. "We can't leave the lad in the hall." I had decided that there were occasions when it was best not to have relatives on the scene.

Looking defeated, the parents stood aside. It surprised me that somehow I had learned to voice a directive with a confidence that got results.

"Thanks. Josh will be much more comfortable on the bed."

"Joshua," Mrs. Shumaker corrected.

"Yes. Joshua," I said, smiling at this sign of spunk from the mother.

The parents looked so pathetic, all dressed in black, lumbering along side by side as though they were exhausted, down the corridor and back to the waiting room.

When Josh was back on the bed, I noticed that the IV fluid had infiltrated again. If I hurried, I could insert a needle into a different vein before the parents came into the room, but as I opened the sterile package with the needle, the door quietly opened.

Mr. and Mrs. Shumaker hastened to the bedside, and the mother grabbed for my arm again.

No way. When will they learn? They're like our enemy.

"Look," I said. My patience was running out, but I could control myself. "Your child's got a fever. He needs water. His stomach has just been sewed up so he can't drink. If you interfere, we will have more edema—more swelling." I held up the needle to give her a minute to compose herself, and stood with one hand on my hip.

Joshua opened his eyes.

"Look, Aaron!" the mother called. "Aaron, our boy is awake." There was joy in her voice. "We're going to take you home, sweetheart."

"Mom," the boy said. He began to smack his lips.

"What, sweetheart? Are you hungry? Aaron, you have that apple we brought?"

"Mrs. Shumaker, he can't have anything to eat or drink. He's just had his tummy sewed up, and he can't have any liquids for a few days either." I felt at my wit's end.

What was it Dean Jacks said at our welcome tea—about empathy? At the time I couldn't imagine the Dean being able to put herself into anyone else's place, or being able to understand the patient's point of view, but I must have been wrong. She had pointed out a skill essential for nurses. I needed to see this situation from the parent's point of view.

I modified my tone. "He's thirsty, you see. This IV is the way he is getting a drink." Then I waited for her to understand.

The little boy rolled onto his elbow and spoke to me. "Did the demon go away?"

"What's that, Joshua?" his mother asked. "Tell him he is all right," she said to her husband.

"Daddy, did they get the demon?" Feebly, the boy touched the arm with the IV.

"What does he mean?" the father asked me.

"I'm not sure."

"Wait a minute, didn't you just say that, if you didn't get the needle in just right, he'd get—what was the word you used?" his father asked. "Sounded like demon."

"Edema," I said, nodding now that I'd caught onto the misunderstanding. "Daddy. Did they get the demon?"

Mr. Shumaker smiled; so did his wife, and so did I.

"Yes, the demons are gone," I said. *Well, you could call germs demons, couldn't you?* "The doctor has fixed your tummy and the edema is disappearing. You're thirsty and I'm giving you a drink through this vein." I pointed to the dextrose and saline bottle that was hanging from the pole. "Now your body will heal itself."

The boy dropped back against the pillow. "Gee, my teacher will be surprised." Joshua was weak and had to take a breath before continuing. "Nobody else in class has had a demon that the doctor fixed."

"Tell your teacher that you fell on a broken bottle, and that the doctors fixed your tummy. The only demons around are the germs we are keeping away." I picked up his hand, and used his index finger to trace a line down his other arm. "Can you help me choose where to start the IV again?" We chose an appropriate vein. "It's going to hurt for a moment," I said while cleaning the area with an alcohol swab.

When Joshua's mother reached out, he said, "Mom, it's okay," and she put her arm down.

I leaned close to Joshua and smiled. "Make a fist for me—like you're a boxer." Then I turned to speak to his mother. "Mrs. Shumaker, could you hold his free hand?"

Joshua squeezed his eyes shut. "Okay. Do it."

Mrs. Shumaker took the boy's hand, but she looked away.

The needle slipped in easily. I attached the tube from the IV bottle and adjusted the drip.

Mr. Shumaker smiled. "We've got a strong boy. Let us ask God to help him." He bowed his head. "Lord, we thank you for bringing us to this place and for the care of doctors and nurses. Amen."

"Amen," Mrs. Shumaker repeated.

"Amen," I said. Now all of us could focus on his recovery. I decided that there were no heroes in the emergency ward, and then, upon further reflection, I realized that there actually were: the patients who trust the doctors and nurses, often without understanding what is happening. Those who endure pain, and struggle for the strength to recover, are the real heroes.

The nurse is the facilitator, and that's fine with me.

Chapter 14
The Swim

Early September, 1962. It was the last day a lifeguard would be on duty for the season, and so we'd gone to the lake for a picnic and swim. It was a free Sunday for both Kenji and me. The sky was blue, with a few clouds that looked like cotton candy. The water had finally warmed after a long summer, and we didn't mind that a cool breeze was ruffling our hair. The sun was beating down on us—Kenji in his black trunks, and me in my aqua and white one-piece swimsuit. Kenji rubbed suntan lotion on my back. I shivered from his touch. The lotion being left behind by his caresses was like a blanket wired to transport me out of this world. I wondered how *he* felt, when I applied the lotion to his back and arms—hairy arms with such capable hands. The afternoon was going to be like heaven, but a torment as well, because we wanted each other so badly but couldn't give in. I thought that, if he asked me to marry him, we could abandon every inhibition.

It was okay to sleep with your lover if you were getting married. That seemed to be the unwritten rule—probably in my mother's day, too. My brother was born seven months after her wedding. Kelly must have known that she wasn't going to follow through with her *two* wedding plans. She was engaged twice during our first year of nursing, but still hadn't gotten married, and Roxanne was engaged for three months before calling it quits with her lover. I didn't blame them. No one labelled an engaged girl as promiscuous, but ... well, I couldn't chance getting pregnant. I wasn't engaged. I'd be labelled "loose." Any illegitimate child I had would be revealed on every application for a job or an apartment. People would ask, "What about your husband?" and, "Where is the child's father?" My parents would disown me. My friends would shy away because I'd been so foolish, and if Kenji did marry me, I'd never feel loved—afraid that he had only married me out of duty or obligation. I'd languish in loneliness.

Even counting the days from my period wasn't safe enough. I'd have to lie, like Kelly did, and tell the doctor I was getting married in order to get a diaphragm fitted, but I could never carry off such a lie. When Elsie *did* get married and got fitted for one, the diaphragm hadn't work. She got pregnant after two months and had to quit nursing at the end of our first year.

If only Kenji would say he *wanted* to marry me, but his parents did not approve. During many long evenings, while parked down by the lake, we talked about the family we might have. He must have told his mother about our discussions, and repeated her response: "As you get older you will appreciate the security of your own native background. Furthermore, the mother passes along the culture, so your children won't feel at home in Japan."

Kenji didn't know what to do. "I will be very unhappy if the two women in my life don't get along," he said. How could I argue? I felt sure that, when we lived in Japan, I could win over his Japanese mom, but who knew for sure? I'd seen, among my patients, mothers or fathers who were determined to split their son or daughter from the soul mate they had chosen. My parents didn't approve either. They thought that I'd be abandoning my religious upbringing if I married a non-Christian. "You won't be accepted by either culture," they told me.

On that day in September, we walked over the hot sand to the west side of a rock formation, stopping occasionally to lean on each other and shake the burning grains of sand out of our sandals and laugh, just because we enjoyed each other. Few people went very far from the parking lot and the lifeguard stand, but one family had already opened their basket and were eating when we spread out our blanket just beyond their spot.

Both Kenji and I were quite taken with their little family scene. I wondered if Kenji was diagnosing the overweight mother or the little girl in yellow who walked with a limp. She must have been about ten. I watched how the dad disciplined his son, who was around two and a half years old and intent on running here and there and touching every rotting fish, fragment of drift wood, skeleton, or piece of seaweed.

Kenji would understand our little fellow's curiosity, and let him touch new things.

As I watched the second girl, who was about eight, I was reminded of how I used to help our mother at family picnics. The girl, who was wearing blue, poured five cups of juice, and passed them around, making sure that her sister, in yellow, had a secure place to rest her cup. Then she picked up two wrapped sandwiches; she seemed to ask her something, although we couldn't hear what she said, and then she opened one, and put it on a paper plate within reach of her big sister. The younger girl must have asked which sandwich her older sister wanted. I became more interested in the girl in yellow. I had noticed that she limped, and now realized that she wasn't able to use her hands very well.

After a while, the heat and the loveliness of the day got the best of us, and Kenji and I chased each other into the water. I hated dunking down all at once, but he had challenged me to race to a rock not far out, and my blood surged just to be beside him. He was a good swimmer—the best. I had to turn onto my back and float for a minute to catch my breath. Leisurely, he stroked back to me and held my hand as though he were going to tow me to the rock. We laughed and I let him pull me along. Suddenly, he told me to hold my breath, and when I was ready, he pulled me under water and straddled his body against mine. His sex was so close that I became limp with desire and felt helpless. Then he pushed me up to the surface. "Are you okay?" he asked. He looked worried that he'd done something wrong.

I laughed, hoping he would see my big smile and know how happy I was. We swam side by side to the rock, climbed its steep side, and perched on the pinnacle, glancing around to see if anyone could see us. There was a rough stone outcropping that shielded us from the beach. Reassured that we were alone, Kenji pushed aside my bathing suit, cupped my breast, and kissed it. I fell into his arms, all resistance spent.

Gentle waves swished against the rock and fell back into the lake. The rhythm seemed to match my breathing, which was in tune with Kenji's. I knew that before the day was over I wouldn't be a virgin. I only waited for him to say *when*. There was a moment of quiet joy between us, and his eyes swept out across the water. I was afraid that the moment would be spoiled if he was reminded of his homeland, or what his mother had told him. I shivered, at least partly from the cool air, and he pulled me closer, with his hand once again stroking my breast. "The water is so blue," I said.

"Reflection of the sky," he answered, and then—unexpectedly—he stood up. "Over there," he said.

I leaned out past the rock toward shore, and saw the family chasing the toddler. They were teasing him, both the parents and his eight-year-old sister. The father caught the giggling little boy and tossed him into the air.

"No!" Kenji exclaimed, sounding stressed. "That way!" Kenji pointed to a spot much closer to our rock. He dove into the water, and I realized that he was swimming toward something yellow that was bobbing up and down in the waves.

I immediately knew what it was, and shouted for help, but we were too far from the lifeguard. Kenji reached the girl and started towing her toward shore. Eventually the father heard me yelling and stopped the chasing game. A moment later he was racing out into the water with a rubber life-saver he'd grabbed from the sand.

I arrived back on the beach just as Kenji and the father were positioning the older girl for artificial respiration. Kenji took over. Soon, the girl sputtered, spit out lake water, and gasped for air.

The mother grabbed the younger sister by the shoulders. "You were supposed to keep an eye on Stella!" She chastised the girl, shaking her violently.

"I'm sorry," the little girl in blue said, with tears running down her face. She ran to where Kenji was treating her sister and crouched down beside her. "She'll be all right, won't she? Please say that she's all right."

"Coming around," Kenji said, observing that the girl he'd rescued was finally breathing on her own.

I hurried to get our blanket and wrapped it around the prostrate girl.

"Do you know what you are doing?" the mother asked Kenji.

I looked her in the eye. "He's a doctor," I said. I understood her anxiety, but couldn't she see that Kenji had saved her daughter?

The mother pulled on the younger sister, standing her up. "Go get the lifeguard," she commanded, and to her husband, she added, "I knew we should have stayed on the other side of the rock, or did you hope that Stella would drown? I suppose you hope I'll drown too."

I was taken aback.

Heavens! Their daughter has just about drowned. What are they arguing about?

"Aggie, please." The father stood and dusted sand off his trunks.

Kenji moved back while I massaged Stella's hands. "You're okay," I said, more to reassure myself than the little girl.

Stella smiled up at me.

"She contracted polio," the father said. "She has trouble with her arms and legs."

Kenji and I each nodded to show that we understood.

"It's very crippling," I said, attempting to show some sympathy.

"Our punishment," the mother said.

I must have looked startled.

"Aggie, don't start up with that," the father said.

"God has marked me, and there is nothing I can do about it," the mother said.

'Now, Aggie, you know that's not true. My wife—" The father was interrupted by the arrival of the lifeguard.

After an examination of Stella's eyes, pulse, respiration, and a testing of her reflexes, the lifeguard advised that she go to emergency to be checked out. He ran back to his stand to phone for an ambulance.

The younger sister was holding her brother, bouncing him up and down, and trying to pacify him while he squirmed, wanting to run about. I approached her and she said, "I didn't mean to leave her. Stella never went into the water before." Her eyes betrayed the worry she felt.

"It's not your fault. No one blames you."

She raised her eyebrows. "Mom is tired," she said. "Stella needs a lot of attention and then there's the baby."

This little girl is wise beyond her years.

"Looks like you're a great help to her."

The girl shrugged.

Ignoring all their children, both of the parents began to gather up their gear. I offered to lend a hand.

"You want kids?" the mother asked me.

I glanced at Kenji, but he was rolling up our blanket and didn't look up. "Yes, I'm looking forward to us being a family some day."

"Family? You better be sure your guy loves you."

"I agree."

"Look at Stella. She's my punishment."

"I don't see how it was your fault. Polio is a terrible virus. Thank goodness kids can be immunized these days."

"Yeah, I'm lucky the next two are healthy, so far."

"They look very active and healthy."

"Alex only married me because I was pregnant with her." She tossed her head, indicating Stella.

"He loves you; that's obvious. He seems very considerate. I can't believe—"

"Oh, he knows his duty. He's loyal, because he was brought up that way."

The lifeguard and a man with a stretcher had arrived.

"Aggie," the father said, coming over and putting his arm around his wife's waist. "Let's go, honey. Stella's going to be okay. We owe this doctor a lot for saving her."

The mother began to cry.

"Aggie, Aggie," he said, wrapping his arms around her. "You're such a good mother. I know it's hard for you, day in and day out. I admire you."

She looked up into his eyes, pleading.

Why doesn't he just say that he loves her? That's what she wants to hear.

The father let go of her and began to pick up toys.

"Why is it so hard for a man to say he loves you?" I asked Kenji, but he was occupied too, picking up their toys, and if he heard, he didn't reply. "She doesn't need to hear how capable she is," I whispered to myself. I looked at both men, one after the other, to see if they had any inkling of what she was asking for, but both were occupied with the task at hand.

Stella coughed and the lifeguard was quick to turn her on her side and pound her back, trying to get her to bring up any remaining water and mucus.

Nodding toward the parking lot, I looked at Kenji, and he understood that I was going to volunteer to accompany them to the hospital.

"I'm a nurse," I said. "She might need to be suctioned on the way. If it would be of help, I could—"

The ambulance driver interrupted with a smile, "Thanks, but my partner is waiting at the ambulance. He'll know what to do and he'll sit with her."

I felt relieved. I didn't want to get mixed up with this family, and I didn't like being reminded that an unmarried pregnant woman would always wonder if she was loved or just pitied. I didn't want to be reminded that I too needed to be told that I was loved. Now that the family had left, I was relieved that Kenji and I could resume our day together, but things had changed.

Kenji began to walk along the beach ahead of me. After a few moments, he stopped, picked up a stone and skipped it across the water.

I began to gather skippers, as we called them, rocks that would skim and hit the water several times before they went under.

For a few minutes we said nothing. Both of us sent rocks off onto the glassy surface of the lake. Mine didn't skip well; they plummeted like lead after one skip. Kenji was doing better. He tossed them hard; determination registered on his face. I wanted to laugh and compliment him, but ...

He has the determination to make things happen. Am I in the picture he is trying to create?

He turned to face me. "I think it is going to rain. Maybe we should pack up and eat back at your dorm. What do you think?"

"Hmm." I hadn't been watching the clouds, but it didn't look like rain to me. "Okay. We can just sit in your car and eat." I visualized having him hold me again, and then ... when it was dark ...

We slipped our clothing on over our semi-dry bathing suits and ambled back to the car. He turned on the radio while I unwrapped the ham and cheese sandwiches. I began to think that our situation would soon be perfect once again, and slid over to sit tightly against him, but he turned sideways and fidgeted with the radio.

When I'd eaten half of my sandwich, I wrapped it up and put it in a bag for trash. Neither of us had anything to say. I hadn't touched the bottle of Coke. Kenji swigged some pop, ate the last bites of his lunch, wadded up the wrappings, and added them to the waste. Then he started the engine without once looking at me.

I put my hand on his thigh.

"That's dangerous," he said, concentrating on the driving.

"I don't care."

He took his eyes off the road and stared into mine. "When I take you, I'll have to be sure."

"You act like you love me. It's okay if you can't say it."

"You are so sweet ... you drive me crazy, but ..."

I bit my lips to keep from crying.

He sped between lights and kept changing the stations on the radio. News about the Cuban missiles sent by Russia came on, but he flicked the dial to find music. I sat with my hands folded in my lap. There were so many questions I wanted to ask.

"I've got to check some of the lab results from one of my patients," Kenji said as we neared the university. "I'll drop you off."

"I could go with you. Maybe I could help you write up the findings. You used to ask me for help with English."

We turned into the driveway at my dorm. He stopped at the entrance but left the engine running. "I'll call you," he said. He must have noticed my wet eyes. "Hey, hey ... We can remember a good swim, can't we?" He was smiling tenderly, and I hoped it wasn't just an act.

I watched his car circle down the drive, stop, and then move out into the traffic.

Chapter 15
Visiting Nurse

Mrs. Donovan, age 75, was my patient soon after I started my visiting nurse rotation. She had a chronic heart condition. Though she never missed a clinic visit, and claimed to be following doctor's orders, the fluid in her chest and edema in her ankles were at critical stages. I was sent to assess her diet and her habits and find out why she wasn't improving.

When I walked through the neighbourhood of 1930s clapboard houses, adjacent to the river, people smiled. Children ran up to me, calling "Nurse, nurse," skipping at my side and asking if I was going to see their mothers that day. I felt like the pied piper as the flock gathered around. Old folks hobbled out to stop me and ask for advice about their rheumatism, lingering cough, or other health matters, or just to show me pictures of their grandkids. No one seemed to realize that I was new, and that their community nurse changed from month to month. We were generic. The blue and white checked uniform identified us, and together with the local priest, each nurse became everyone's friend and caregiver. In my black leather satchel, I carried all of the equipment I would need: soap, paper towels, a thermometer, stethoscope, blood pressure cuff, an antiseptic, gloves, masks, bandages, pamphlets, and a clean newspaper to put under my bag on tables, so I wouldn't transmit diseases or bugs from house to house.

Mrs. Donovan lived in a derelict mansion that had been converted to a rooming house at the corner of O'Reilly and River Street. The oak door from the veranda of the stately house was open, so I walked into the hallway, which was lit via a dangling, forty-watt light bulb hanging from the molded plaster ceiling. Ahead was a scuffed oak newel post and wide staircase, carpeted with rubber mats that, on the damp day, were emitting a pungent smell. That odour mixed with the smell of plaster dust, which was escaping from crumbling holes in the sidewalls, where the painted green surface had eroded away down to the wooden lath. The tobacco fumes were so strong that I would have wagered that nearly everyone in the house smoked. On top of that, someone had been boiling cabbage. I began to breathe though my mouth.

At the end of the hallway, I knocked on the door of unit 3. The sound of a hacking cough came from inside—not surprising considering Mrs. Donovan's diagnosis. The knock was answered by a white woman of average size, who motioned for me to enter. She panted at the effort it took to walk seven steps across the floral linoleum to plunk down onto the worn cut-velvet sofa. Her legs were so swollen that they would have looked at home on an elephant. After reaching over to turn off the TV, she leaned back against a roll of bedclothes, and nodded that I was to sit beside her. We'd been taught not to sit on upholstered furniture, though, so I spread the paper on the table, deposited my satchel there, and then perched on one of the straight chairs that was pulled up to a painted, drop-leaf table.

The room was devoid of pictures, and fitted with drab furnishings, but a bay window with healthy geraniums on the sill gave the space a friendly countenance. The sash windows in the bay were propped open with sticks, allowing a light breeze to ruffle the bedraggled lace curtains. There was a pantry, now converted to a kitchen. I surmised that the room had originally been the dining room when some wealthy family had lived there in bygone days. It smelled strongly of cigarettes, even though at the clinic Mrs. Donovan had claimed she didn't smoke. Not wanting to alienate her until I'd assessed her diet, I let that matter rest and clarified the reason for my visit.

"Course," she said, leaning toward me expectantly. "I'm glad you came. It is frightful getting around these days." She crossed her hands, which were resting in her lap over the print dress.

"You been living here long?" I asked.

"Six years—no, seven," she said. "Had to manage with just the social security coming in after I retired, so I took this single."

"What did you do for a living?"

"Cleaner. I cleaned houses. Did that for over forty years, ever since we came north."

"And your husband?"

"Homer? Gone. Rotting in hell, I imagine. Frigged around with women, to say nothing about booze. It finally took him."

"Do you have children?"

"No." She shook her head and looked up at the ceiling as though she were visualizing how it might have been. "That man had grand ideas. When we was young, we moved up from Carolina. Music just came to him naturally, and he was going to make it as an entertainer. Played the piano like he was born to. Well, right away I started cleaning, did it till my heart started to act up."

I nodded that I was interested, and she continued. "The old man tried this and that. Wound up working in the electric factory, screwing parts together—not all he was screwing, either." She laughed, making sure that I understood her humour, and then wagged her index finger at me. "Don't ever marry a good-looking fellow. I was a sucker and believed all them lies. You married?" she asked, seeming to size me up.

"No, I'm single," I answered.

"Good. Don't suppose you will be for long though. Looks like the boys would be after you pretty thick. You got gold streaks in your hair and a pretty good figure. Those breasts are enough to make some men pant," she shrugged, "but you'll heed nothing I'm saying." She wagged her head from side to side like all was hopeless. "You'd think I would have had dozens of babies but something went wrong, so I just kept cleaning at the girls' school all those years."

A wave of pity made me feel low, but I realized that my mission was to better her life, so I pulled myself together to assess her situation. *If her health continues to deteriorate, who's going to look after her?* "Do you have family? I mean brothers and sisters, nieces or nephews?" I asked.

"Got a twin somewhere. My brother went to California when we came north. Think he married, but I lost track. I wish I knowed if he is still alive." She crossed her fingers. "We was just like that, when we was kids."

"Maybe someone in your hometown has his address. Have you written to ask?"

She shook her head. "Nobody left there anymore."

"Your health was good?"

"Yes'm, 'till my heart gave me trouble. Now it's worse. I hope you find out how to fix my legs so I can walk better." She began to drum her spindly fingers on the sofa cushion, impatient for action.

I explained that I wanted to wash my hands and do an examination. She said that the washroom across the hall was communal, so I opted to wash my hands at her enamel sink, which was fitted between a small refrigerator and a two-burner gas hotplate in the former pantry. While there, I inspected the contents of the wall cupboard along one wall for salt, but there was none.

She complied readily when I put the thermometer in her mouth, took her blood pressure, listened to her chest, and looked for other signs of poor circulation. Her fingers and toes were cold; her temperature was slightly elevated. At the time, the slight temperature hike seemed insignificant and unrelated to my reason for coming.

Noting her swollen legs and feet, I asked, "Are you wearing your elastic stockings?"

"Mostly."

"It's good to take them off every eight hours, but you *should* be wearing them. The swelling in your legs might not be so bad. You should elevate your legs and feet whenever you can as well. I guess you sleep on this sofa. Can you put your feet up when you watch TV?"

"I do."

"I'm told that you have a good understanding of the doctor's orders."

"Yes'm."

She insisted that she had no calf pain, no apparent tenderness or redness that would indicated thrombosis. I was relieved that those masses of blood weren't sitting in a vein ready to dislodge and float to the brain or lungs or heart.

She tried crossing her ankles, and then gave up. "I soak my feet in warm water, and I use those elastics most of the time."

I doubt that, but she does know what is expected. "That's good. You have to help yourself."

"And don't I know it?" she spit the answer back at me, stretching her neck to appear confident. "You going to give me a pill or not? I thought that's what you said you come for."

"I'm here to ascertain why you are retaining fluid."

"You got your answer yet? You're a bit nosey; I saw you looking in my cupboard."

I was taken aback. She'd noticed that I looked in her cupboard and didn't understand why. I realized that I could have asked permission.

I stammered a reply, "Y-you're an orderly person, a-and I'm trying to figure out how you get sodium. I was looking to see if you had salt in your kitchen."

"Course not. I told the doctors that at the clinic."

"I don't see any salt substitute, either. There are salt substitutes you could be using. Don't you miss salt when you eat meat or vegetables?"

"Not a bit."

I was really puzzled.

There's something going on here that I haven't discovered. I can't leave until I find where she's getting the sodium that's causes the water retention.

"Never saw *you* at the clinic. Why'd they send you if you can't find answers," Mrs. Donovan said.

"The fact is you *are* getting salt from *some* source."

"You call me a liar?"

"No, no," I shook my head.

Damn it. I've put my foot in my mouth. Claire, you have a way of doing the wrong thing whenever that's possible. How am I going to re-establish a good rapport with her?

I got down to examine her feet, and decided to talk about another topic entirely. "You like to watch TV?" I asked.

She laughed. "Think watchin' TV is going to cause the swelling?"

I laughed too, even though I didn't feel like it. "Well, I used to watch *General Hospital*, and I've always wondered what's happening these days."

"Can't see you watching soaps," she said, bending over to push something farther under the sofa.

I looked down to see what it was—an overflowing ashtray. I confronted her. "You smoke, and you told the doctors that you quit."

Well, I've caught her, and now I've got the upper hand.

It was a good feeling, but this confrontation would only expand our rift, and I'd never get her to tell me where she was getting sodium.

'Cool down,' as my little grandma would say.

"I do *not* smoke. I said I don't, and I don't."

"Then how do you account for that?" I looked down at the ashtray.

"Lorna's. She's my neighbour. We watch TV together."

Maybe she's right. I don't smell smoke on her breath.

"A-all right," I stammered, "sorry to jump to conclusions. I just want ..." I exhaled loudly, flustered. "Look, let's get back to what you eat. What do you like to cook?"

She gave a cocky lift to her chin, and then said, "Vegetables, potatoes, and such, liver if it's cheap, and hamburger."

"How about ham and bacon?"

"Are you crazy? You don't know a thing about my case. I was told not to eat pork and I don't."

I held up my hand, as if to stop her accusations. "I was instructed to check. It's good that you follow those instructions."

Mrs. Donovan got up and walked toward the door. *Is this an invitation for me to leave?* I stayed seated and proceeded with my questioning, though I couldn't control my voice and thought it sounded weak. "Tell me about a typical meal. What did you have for dinner last evening?"

"I don't eat a lot. Some says I eat like a bird," she said, as she hobbled over to her flowers and snipped off a dead geranium leaf with her fingers.

"And last evening?"

With a hand on her hip, she faced me to explain, "I got some chicken liver at the meat market. He sells it cheap. So I cooked it with onions and potatoes."

"Go on. You cooked it on your stove, over there." I gestured toward her hotplate. "Just tell me everything you did."

"I put the water on for tea. I drink it black, in case you're wondering." She returned to sit on the sofa.

"So you dished your food onto a plate and then what?"

She laughed. "I did the same as you would. I sat at this table and ate."

"Hmm," I said. "Mind if I look in your refrigerator?"

She sneered, but extended her right arm as if to give permission.

The top shelf of the refrigerator held a pint of milk. Below it was a dish of margarine, a loaf of white bread, and a box of donuts. The margarine, bread, and donuts would all contain salt. I would have to try to get her to make some substitutes if that was possible, but I didn't think that those three items were the main sources of the sodium she was apparently getting.

I moved the remains of a head of lettuce and a carton of eggs, and was about to shut the door when I noticed a tin of something. I held up the tin so that she could see it. "What is this?" I asked.

"It's juice I put on my food. Food tastes just as good with sauerkraut juice as it used to with salt. I just sprinkle some on." She looked very proud of her solution.

"Sauerkraut juice? It's made of cabbage and brine!"

"Sure, I know that."

"Brine is salt! You cut up the cabbage with salt and it ferments."

"Girl, I've made more kraut than you can shake a stick at."

"Brine is pure salt water!"

"If you know that, then why are you asking me?"

"What I mean is, when you add the kraut juice, you are *adding* salt."

"Well, you can fault the doctor for not telling me that! He said to me, 'Mrs. Donovan, throw out your box of salt and your salt shaker.' You can see I done that. Cut out the weenies too and the baloney."

"Yes, I see. Well, now we know why your swelling persists. Could you please promise me not to use sauerkraut juice anymore? And if you think of something else to put on your food, could you ask if it's okay first, when you come to clinic?"

"I can do that. Is there anything else you want to scold me for?"

"I'm sorry. I didn't mean to be scolding you. I was just frustrated because … well, it doesn't matter now. I guess we've found the reason for your swelling, and if you quit using the juice, I think your swelling will go down. You should give up the donuts too. Maybe substitute an apple. And try salt-free crackers instead of bread. I'll give you a list of food substitutes." I fished in my satchel for the pamphlet and passed it over.

"If you say so."

It seemed that we had reached a measure of understanding. "That's it for today, unless you have some questions about the substitutions."

"I do have something to ask."

I was at the sink, washing my hands again, and didn't look her way.

"What are these red spots behind my ears? Lorna noticed them. And a couple of days ago, I felt like I was coming down with a cold, and I had white spots in my mouth."

Red spots, white spots.

A queasy feeling hit me. I shook my hands dry and went back to look behind her ears.

How could I have missed that rash? And the temperature elevation! I was so focused on finding what I thought I'd find that I didn't really look for any other trouble.

"Have you ever had measles?" I asked.

"Can't remember."

"Did you ever get the measles vaccine to prevent you from getting measles?"

Mrs. Donovan laughed. "We didn't even have a doctor for miles around, so my answer has got to be 'no.'"

Now I felt anxious. "How many people live in this building?"

"Nine, plus Tilley's kids. She's got three. There's a new man moved into number eight. I never saw him yet though."

"I think you have the measles. The virus is very infectious. You don't have a phone, do you?" I looked around to be sure. "I'll go make a call, but please don't go anywhere until I come back."

"I ain't going to leave. Has that got something to do with my swelling?"

"No, if you stop using the juice, your swelling will go down and you'll walk better. This is about an infectious disease. I've got to report it to the Health Department." I hurriedly washed my hands again with extra soap.

"Then what?" she asked, sitting forward on the sofa.

"I'm afraid they will quarantine this house. Put a red sign on it. You won't be able to leave, but Community Service will bring you some food or whatever you need. Wait right here. I'll make the call and be right back." I grabbed my bag and left.

After phoning from the corner store, I waited on the porch for the public health nurse. We put on masks and gloves and went to see Mrs. Donovan, to confirm my suspicion and give her instructions. I realized with a groan that I'd be visiting Mrs. Donovan frequently. No medication would cure the virus, but with luck the rash would disappear in about a week and she wouldn't get diarrhea or stiff joints or more severe complications like pneumonia and encephalitis. We advised her to drink plenty of liquids, take aspirin if her fever got higher. We gave her masks to wear when he went outside her unit after explaining that the virus was transmitted through the air we breathe and could be left on door knobs by someone who coughed or sneezed or had a runny nose or was even crying. The nurse tacked up the red quarantine notice, and then we went door to door informing the other residents about the restrictions. Two of Tilley Smith's children were in the late stages with full-blown red rashes. Their mother had kept them home from school, but unfortunately, not before the virus could have spread to their schoolmates. The Public Health nurse was going to notify the school and speak with parents of children who might be infected.

"Too many parents aren't giving their children immunizations these days," the public health nurse said. "These kids need not have come down with measles, and Mrs. Donovan probably got it from them.

The residents were pretty angry at me for bringing on the quarantine, but since I dropped by nearly every day to see if anyone else had come down with the measles and to check on their healing processes, they began to warm to my presence and to look forward to any news I brought. I wrote to the library in Mrs. Donovan's South Carolina hometown to ask if anyone there could locate her brother. To celebrate the end of the quarantine period, I made little paper plaques of thanks to hand out to each resident for their cooperation, and gave each one an apple, paid for out of my personal allowance. My last mission in the area before finishing my rotation, was to re-establish the small community's faith in future visiting nurses.

"You won't be coming no more?" Mrs. Donovan asked during my last visit, and to my surprise, she sounded sad.

"Don't you worry. Another girl will take my place. You're walking pretty well these days, aren't you? You're one of our success stories."

"Yes, I'll be your success story. Now you take care. You've got gold in your hair and your figure is pretty special—those big boobs will turn many an eye, but you fight off them boys that only wants you in bed! You hear? Find a good man."

"Good advice." I was smiling.

I think I have.

Chapter 16
A Family Affair

I first met Stephen Swidersky during my first clinical experience, when we were practising basic nursing procedures like turning patients in bed, teaching them how to use crutches, and giving bed baths. He'd had a heart attack and was on strict bed rest, which meant he was completely dependent on me, as his nurse, to help with daily ablutions, meals, and finding ways to alleviate stress. He was tall and so thin that his shoulder blades showed through his hospital gown. His dark hair was slicked back, and every day, he insisted on using a straight-edged razor, even though the activity was against doctor's orders. He wouldn't let the orderlies shave him or use the electric. His eyes were always alert and inquiring, and his manner gracious. Though he was only in his late forties, I thought of him as an elder statesman. He liked to speak to me in French, and I was flattered that he assumed I was cultured enough to understand. That boosted my self-confidence immensely and helped me overcome the feeling that I was only good at tasks that one could do mindlessly. He called me Mademoiselle Nurse, and after he learned my name, he called me Mademoiselle Claire, which made me feel different and appreciated.

He was Polish, and had escaped from his homeland during the Second World War, when he was a very young man, eventually working for the Underground in France—carrying out random interference with the German occupiers, and was later given the job of interrogating German prisoners. I couldn't begin to picture what dangers he'd encountered, just getting from Poland to France.

He had met Julia, a French girl twelve years his junior, and married her. In their wedding picture, the sixteen-year-old bride stood a foot shorter than the groom. She beamed at the camera while leaning against his arm. Her black hair was curly, and she wore a gathered white dress with a wide ribbon at the waist. In France, when they couldn't see each other for days, they'd exchanged love letters. He'd kept them all.

Was he Jewish? We never talked religion, but that could explain why his sister, mother, and father had been killed, and why he wasn't in the military. His father had been a banker and he had just joined his dad's firm when the war intervened. From pictures he showed me, of his family estate in Krakow, I gathered that he'd grown up with privileges. He thought the family's house still existed, and described the furnishings and gardens in detail. I loved hearing about what their Biedermeier furniture looked like, and imagined listening to him play Chopin on their ebony, grand piano. It was fascinating to imagine being led though the salons, and testing the Louis XVI *fauteuil* with its padded seat, gilded arms and legs. I pictured a château with servants and groundskeepers.

I was in awe of his ability to speak English, Russian, French, German, and Polish. He taught me to say good morning in Polish. It sounds something like *gin dombri.* I became accustomed to his accent, and learned much about philosophy as well as Polish history. I was already learning about Japanese customs from Kenji, and to speak a little Japanese, but this man had a more extensive English vocabulary than Kenji, and spoke poetically. I looked forward to my work day, in large part, because of our conversations.

Unable to get into banking in the U.S., he had accepted a job selling shoes. I thought it was admirable that he had been willing to take a rather unremarkable job when he had so much education and talent. As he said, immigrants had to start wherever they could. During the long days in bed, if he wasn't reading, he'd be writing letters to Julia, which he passed to her when she visited.

Julia came regularly. She was about thirty-five, but her petite stature, black ringlets, clear complexion, and gentle manners made her seem younger. Her big, dark brown eyes reminded me of those of a bewildered animal that had wandered into a strange city. Mr. Swidersky liked to tell me how he chose her clothes, and scarves, and bought her perfume, chocolates, and dainty gold jewellery. When I dressed up to go out, I remembered his descriptions, and sometimes tried to imitate the way he'd taught her to use scarves to make herself look alluring.

She brought him oranges, and sat close to his bedside, speaking in French while she peeled the fruit and handed him segment after segment. She questioned him about everything: how to pay the phone bill; where to buy her favourite smoked turkey; and how much to spend for their daughter Tanya's new coat. They looked at each other longingly, and their goodbyes brought tears to Julia's eyes. *If a man loved me that much, I'd be the happiest girl on the planet.* But few men allowed themselves to be that romantic, or to care enough to reach up and correct the tilt of one's tam—as I'd seen him do. A photo of Julia and Tanya, their five-year-old daughter, was displayed on his bedside table.

During my second year, Mr. Swidersky was back in the hospital. He was recovering from heart surgery and was assigned to my care on the surgical ward. Julia greeted me warmly, "Oh, Claire, Stephen is pleased to have you back in his life." She was still a pretty woman, but looked harried. Once I saw him scold her because a button was missing from her coat. She laughed and said that she hadn't had time to sew it on. "You've got nothing to do but talk to nurses, Stephen. I'll bring *you* a needle and thread."

When he offered to write post-dated checks to pay their rent, she smiled and said that she could take care of it. The visits this time were short—sometimes to drop off a magazine or report on Tanya's accomplishments—and then she'd give him a quick kiss on the cheek and leave. I didn't notice the exchange of notes.

As I was going off shift one day, Mr. Swidersky asked me to drop back later with a *Time* magazine. I was going out that night, but I had time to run to the drugstore to buy a copy. He sat up straight in bed and reached out with both arms as I approached, carrying the magazine. When I held back, he puckered his lips and blew me a kiss. Then he asked me to twirl around so that my black, taffeta dress rippled. I did, hesitantly. "Beautiful," he said. The fellow in the next bed whistled, and I felt myself blush.

In one way, I felt like a little girl, all shy and coy, and in another way, I felt anxious and uncomfortable to be getting this attention.

He said that I needed a sequined clip to pull up my hair. "If we were in Paris," he said, "I would take you to Maxim's."

Norma had witnessed this, and warned me that Mr. Swidersky might be falling for me, but I brushed her suggestion aside. I was in love with Kenji and Mr. Swidersky was in love with Julia. We just admired each other, and besides, I really thought of him as an old man.

One day they were arguing in French when I came on the scene. Quickly, they put on smiles. "Stephen asked me to give you this." Julia handed me a small box.

I hesitated, but Mr. Swidersky said, "Yes, please. Something from my country. Julia doesn't mind, do you, Julia?" He looked at her quizzically when he spoke.

I opened the box. Inside there was an unusual piece of amber on a silver chain. I drew in a large breath. "I can't take this. You have so few keepsakes." I offered it back.

"It is for you. Stephen gave it to me years ago, but I have no use for it these days. You keep, please," Julia said. She straightened her shoulders, like she was pleased to have carried out a mission.

I hesitated again.

"No, no," she said. "From Stephen."

"Well, then I have to thank both of you. This is certainly very special." I was still uncomfortable taking the amber. It seemed unlikely that Stephen would ask Julia to part with his present, so why was she insisting that the gift was from him? Of course, there must be a logical explanation. Maybe he'd asked her to bring *something*, and he was surprised and not very pleased that she'd brought the amber.

When Julia was leaving, we passed in the hallway. "How is Tanya?" I asked.

"Fine. We manage. I won't come often, only on Sunday." Her manner was brisk. "Stephen says you take good care of him, and I'm working at two jobs, so ..."

I nodded. "He is doing well. You'll soon have him back." When she had gone, I checked on Mr. Swidersky, intending to return the amber; he wouldn't hear of it.

"I don't suppose you can wear the necklace at work," he said. "I shall just picture you wearing it tonight. Are you going out?"

I don't think it's a good idea to be discussing my private life—makes me feel uneasy.

"I'll wear it on special occasions," I said. "It is really a special gift."

"As you say in English, my pleasure," he said, with a laugh.

I really don't want to keep this amber. Why did I take it in the first place? Oh, God, Claire, you do some of the dumbest things.

I didn't ask if Julia had brought new letters. It seemed obvious that she hadn't or he'd be reading them. No fruit either. I took an orange for them to share during her next visit, but when I reported to duty on Monday, the orange was still on his bedside table. She'd been in, he told me, and asked him to thank me for the fruit.

"How is she doing?" I was beginning to be anxious about their relationship.

"She doesn't seem to need me." He wrinkled his brow and sighed. "She insists that she's got the bills organized, and she manages two jobs as well as attending to Tanya."

"That must be a relief."

"I suppose," he said, and then he reached for my hand, but I pulled back. *Darn. Maybe Norma is right. I'm so naive.*

I wasn't on duty when Stephen was discharged the following week, but he left a thank you note written in his curly-cue scroll. He signed it with his full name and added his phone number and address. When the head nurse gave it to me, she said, "Nice note. It's great to be appreciated. You don't need boxes of candy, just a show of appreciation."

I agreed, but I decided not to tell her about the amber and my worry that Mr. Swidersky was taking too much interest in my personal life. I was sure that she would think I had a good imagination.

During the last year of training, we nurses got to be charge nurses, managers of all that goes on on the ward. I was assigned the night shift on a man's medical ward, where the patients were being treated with medications and non-surgical procedures. My responsibilities were to insure that requisitions were ready for the next day's procedures, sterilize equipment, dispense medications, and look after the seriously ill. An orderly was on duty to help men use the washroom, and turn those in bed who were helpless.

"None of our patients are seriously ill," the evening nurse said during report. "Should be an easy night. Well, Mr. Swidersky might be trouble."

I glanced down the list of patients and saw Stephen Swidersky's name. He'd had a Cerebral Vascular Accident.

"Mr. Swidersky had a stroke? I know him from before. How is he?" I asked.

"He's in bad shape. Left side partly paralysed. Speaking is difficult."

"He's got a thick Polish accent."

"Oh, I wasn't aware. I suppose that contributes to our problem. The orderlies can't understand a word he says. He's always flailing his arms about, striking anything in his way, and making horrific, agonizing sounds that scare the other patients."

"I can see why."

"He cries easily. Probably a symptom of the stroke," the evening nurse said.

"He was always very sensitive. His wife comes often?"

"No. She was in today to show him the teddy bear she'd bought for their daughter's birthday. He insisted on keeping it. Maybe she'll have to buy another or maybe she's coming back. I've no idea how old their child is."

"Haven't you seen Tanya's picture?"

"No. Well, if he talks about family, we simply don't understand him. Watch it when you take him his medicine. He kicked an orderly who was trying to help him with the urinal, and he upset his bath water yesterday. If that behaviour keeps up, he's going to be moved to a psychiatric ward."

"That would be terrible! He's extremely bright. There must be some way to communicate. He's just frustrated. Wouldn't you be?"

The evening nurse only smiled. *She doesn't think I understand the situation, but I know what's happening better than she does, and I can make a difference.*

"His wife could interpret for him. Has anyone talked to her about his needs? Certainly she can work out some gestures to convey what he wants."

"That woman? This is the first day she's seen him since he was admitted last week. Days ago she came for an appointment with the doctors, but didn't even stop to see him. She told me she's worried about the care he's going to need if he goes home."

"What's the prognosis?"

"Not good. He doesn't seem to try. The physiotherapist says he refuses to cooperate. The speech-therapist reports the same."

"I know him. Maybe I can make a connection."

As soon as the report was finished, I went into the ward to greet him. Mr. Swidersky recognized me, called me Claire, and reached for my hand. He held it tightly. I had to disguise my shock when I saw him. The skin on the left side of his face hung loosely so that the eye was almost closed. His beard had several days of growth, and saliva dripped from his mouth. I straightened his limp arm and arranged a pillow so that it wouldn't get wedged under his body. "How's Julia?" I asked. "How's Tanya?"

I understood him to say that Julia didn't come often. As he moved his right index finger like a clock hand, I understood that he was saying she worked long hours. Then he pointed to the teddy bear. "Tanya's birthday," he said manipulating his mouth with great difficulty.

"She'll be seven or eight?"

"Seven." He turned on his side and reached into his drawer to get her picture.

She hasn't changed much. Looks like a healthy child.

"She plays baseball," Mr. Swidersky said, and I understood his words.

The man in the next bed chimed in. "What's he saying? Can't any of us understand that guy."

I turned to answer. "His daughter plays baseball."

"Really?"

"He's Polish. With the accent and the stroke, it's hard for him to say the words."

"He ought to be sent back to Poland. He's a danger."

"I've known him for years. He's very gentle."

"My foot. I thought he was going to break his wife's arm when she was in. He twisted it till it was bruised for sure. I don't know the words, but he's a vengeful guy. Better watch it, nurse."

I can't believe what he's saying. Mr. Swidersky's demeanour can't have changed that much!

At that moment, Swidersky lay back against the pillow and pulled the bear to his chest.

"They was fighting over that bear," the neighbour said. "A grown man wanting a teddy bear. Now tell me, is that normal?"

"It's a present for their daughter, and he wants to keep it around for a bit." I was getting angry with the neighbour.

I understand his sentiments, but can't others see how he feels?

As I was about to pull the curtain between the beds, Mr. Swidersky grabbed my hand and it took some time for me to get it released.

When I got back to the nurses' station, I considered what I could do for Mr. Swidersky and decided to phone Julia. For him to cooperate and try to get better, he needed the support of the woman he loved.

She answered the phone, and I identified myself. "Claire Winchester, your husband's nurse," I said.

"I don't want to talk about Stephen." For a second, I thought she had hung up on me, but then she said, "What's happened?"

"He's doing okay. He misses you though, and I just thought I could tell him when to expect you again," I said.

"He's so ugly. I can't stand to look at him."

Her pronouncement shocked me.

How can you stop loving someone you know so well just because he's had a stroke?

"He's still the same Stephen. With time the paralysis can improve. Remember the happy times."

If I had a man who wrote love letters and made love the way I picture them loving each other ... well I could hold those memories in my mind forever.

"I want him to die," she replied.

I gasped but quickly regained composure. "You've had a rough time."

"He wants me to stay a little girl. Well, I grew up!" There was anger in her voice, and then she began to cry. "I work and I manage and I don't need to please anyone."

"He's told me how capable you are."

"I'm sick of being chained to a-a—"

I interrupted to ask, "Could you write to him?"

"*You* write," Julia said. "Stephen thinks you're *so* sparkly, *so* genuine."

"But, Julia, I'm only his nurse. He loves you and I just want him to get better and go home to you."

The phone went dead.

I checked my watch. It's so late!

I'll tell the head nurse what's going on in the morning. Better call social service too. What else should I be doing?

Just as the night supervisor came onto the floor, I heard sounds of a great commotion coming from the ward. The voice of Mr. Swidersky's neighbour sounded above all the others. I called out for the orderly, and the three of us rushed into the ward. There was a puddle of water and shards of glass at the foot of Mr. Swidersky's bed.

"That guy's a nut case," the neighbour said. "He's crazy. Crazy!" When he saw the supervisor, whom he recognized, he said, "Can't you do something? That guy is dangerous."

It appeared that Mr. Swidersky had thrown his glass pitcher of water at his neighbour, and luckily, it had been deflected by the curtain and hadn't reached its mark. Mr. Swidersky was cuddling the bear and crying.

"Yes, it's time," the supervisor said. She motioned for the orderly to clean up the spill and began to walk away.

What's she thinking?

"What did you say to him?" I asked the neighbour.

"Not much."

"What did you say?"

"Only goodnight," he replied.

"Only goodnight?" I repeated, skeptically.

"I went to the washroom and stuck my head behind the curtain to tell him to have a good night. There he was hugging that bear. I couldn't stop myself. I guess I said something about him being a fucked-up guy who had to sleep with a bear because no woman would have him."

I didn't reply to the neighbour, but hurried after the supervisor. She was already on the phone arranging to transfer Mr. Swidersky to the locked Psychiatric ward. She wouldn't listen when I tried to tell her about all the hardships that had plagued his life, and about his wife and her troubles.

Two orderlies came and wheeled him off. They were going to leave the bear, but I pleaded with them to take it. Before Mr. Swidersky's cart entered the elevator, I gripped his fingers, told him I'd visit in the morning, and that I would see what I could do about a transfer back.

He squeezed my hand, closed his eyes, and didn't speak.

The next day, when I saw him in the Psych ward, he lay rigid on his cot with his eyes closed. His hand was cold and clammy. His eyes opened wide when he heard my voice, but he said nothing. The nursing staff said that he didn't speak. He died that night.

It's terrible. He must have felt that I'd let him down. His family let him down. Surely some human contact could have saved him. Julia? She's too tired. Her assertion that he had romantic thoughts about me ... well that seems absurd, but maybe ... no, I don't want to go there.

When the psychiatrist talked with me about the case, he said that a patient couldn't *just* depend on others. "We each need our own strength of character to bring us through adversity."

I tried to tell him that Stephen had *had* strength of character, but that life had dished out trial after trial until there was nothing left. Everything seemed hopeless.

"But weren't you telling me that he depended on his wife's attention?"

"Of course. He loved her so much."

"Did he love her or love the control he had to make her into the person he wanted? You seem to be saying that he kept her dependent--didn't want her to grow up."

Why is he clouding Stephen's image like that?

I was furious. When I didn't answer, the psychiatrist said, "Think about it. Love has to be reciprocal, given freely and received without strings. Strength of character requires having faith in yourself *and* in others."

Later, when I was alone in my room and getting ready for bed, my blood began to boil just thinking of the psychiatrist's remarks, but then I remembered that Julia had used the words "chained to," and suddenly things started to make sense. Maybe, thrown into a situation where she'd had to manage her own resources, she had grown to like thinking for herself. Maybe it wasn't the physical care or his appearance that she disliked. Maybe it was being asked to revert to being a dependent person under his control. I wouldn't want that kind of relationship. I'd want a relationship where sharing with my husband meant that I made some decisions by myself, some would be made by him alone, and some would be shared decisions. There would be times when I could feel dependent upon my husband, and I hoped that he would, at times, feel dependent upon me. My tactics with Stephen Swidersky had been wrong. I should have encouraged him to let Julia bloom, encouraged him to pursue new interests. With so many physical breakdowns, he might not have lived long, but he might have died a happier person if he'd become proud of the person Julia had become.

Chapter 17
The Letter

I wanted the sky to be black. I wanted a blinding snow storm to tie up traffic, smash cars, and make people fall on slippery sidewalks. On this particular day in February, 1963, I wanted everyone on earth to suffer the way I was suffering. I knew that the Negroes suffered—but their pain was different. Jan had taken Jeff to march with the Freedom Walkers in Detroit. Her pain, as a coloured girl, was nothing like what I was going through. In January, Charles de Gaulle and Konrad Adenauer had signed a treaty of cooperation between France and West Germany, for which we were supposed to rejoice. Did that treaty have any significance in my life? I felt like a tree uprooted—all sustenance deprived, and life ebbing away. My nursing pals had been right. Norma said that I had to pull myself together and concentrate on my assignments, but I moved through each day like a robot. Our psychology professor said that if there was another war, nurses might be drafted and sent to the front. Well, I'd be one of the first to enlist, not because I liked the fighting, but because, in the midst of war, I'd be too busy to think.

I decided to write Kenji a letter, and remind him about our good times—about learning to dance the Twist the first evening we met. Even choked with tears, I wanted to smile when I remembered his fascination with the word "wow." That had become a standard expression for every fun thing we did. At Niagara Falls, I'd discovered that we had a lot in common, even though we were from different cultures. I liked to learn what he thought about things, and what Japanese students did for fun, which was not so different from what we were doing. He'd met my crazy family and accepted them. Everything seemed to say that we'd be a couple forever.

I faced a sheet of blank notebook paper.

How should I address him? My Dearest? No, I should be more formal.

Dear Kenji.

I put down the pen. My heart wouldn't let me continue.

Stupid. Stupid. Why didn't I see it coming?

Last Friday, I'd prepared for going out to dinner. Kenji said that we'd go to an Italian restaurant, not the usual White Castle or Colonel Sander's Kentucky Fried Chicken.

This is going to be an occasion.

There had been other fun times: picnics, parties, hikes, concerts. When the music was joyful, I knew we both felt it. At the concerts, we had breathed together when the sad passages moved us to identical feelings. The swim.

How can I forget the swim?

I tore up that sheet and rummaged through my desk for better paper. Norma stuck her head in my door. "What are you doing? Oh, writing. Good idea."

"I'm writing to Kenji, but I need better paper. Do you have any to loan me?"

She returned with pink stationery.

"I can't use pink," I said. Pink seemed to imply mushy words.

The letter has to be business-like, but stir his feelings.

"Brown. I've got some brown stationery," Norma said.

Not brown either.

"It's okay," I said, intending to write a rough draft and copy it later onto some blue-linen writing paper.

Last Friday, I'd known that it was the day my life would change. And it did, but not the way I had envisioned. I'd thought that, after knowing me for two and a half years, Kenji was ready to make a personal commitment, and I wanted to follow him wherever life took us. I lamented that he hadn't taken me to a motel after the swim. I'd been ready to toss all my rigid upbringing aside. "We can't," he'd said. "Pregnancy, too dangerous. I won't take you until I know I will spend my life with you." It was as though we wore iron chastity belts. We were so bound by our cultural mores.

He hadn't told me, but I'd heard through the grapevine that he'd just turned down an offer to join a clinical partnership here. That revelation didn't come as a surprise. It seemed to me that, no matter what, our lives were moving closer. I really expected that this would be the evening that he'd propose and ask me to move to Japan with him.

Norma came with a Coke. "Thought you needed some liquid," she said, obviously worried about me.

"I've got to finish this." I picked up my pen.

I really want to die. Others might get over this sort of thing. I won't. Has she guessed that I've tucked away a big stash of sleeping pills?

I decided to write a simple note, to say that I hoped we could stay friends. Maybe if I put it off a day I could think of a poetic way to say it.

There's always the pills. Not yet, though. I have to write a letter that will make him change his mind. Oh, dear. I'm too upset to do it now.

Half-heartedly, I put on my coat and joined the girls as they were leaving for the student union.

Over the next few days, I couldn't concentrate on book assignments, but did manage to drag myself to the ward for work on scheduled days. I was assigned to a women's surgical ward, nursing women with hernia repairs, gallstones, appendicitis, and even a tonsillectomy—nothing serious. Those women whined, moaned, and fussed about whether the drinking water was cold, why their roommate took so long in the bathroom, and why their hubbies were late.

Gee whiz. Such small stuff. Okay, I know ... they're frightened and worried about home.

I shut out their complaining voices and mechanically gave them the physical care they needed. Life was tolerable. Friends helped, but in bed sleep wouldn't come. Then I would check that the bottle was still hidden under sweaters. I'd thought Kenji would drop me after meeting my family—Uncle Harry in particular, but Mom and Dad hadn't made him feel welcome either. But he didn't, and he didn't seem to mind that my brother was gay either, although he may have been covering up his true feelings. *No, he'd always been honest with me.* Damn, I hated my family for their righteous, prejudiced, ritualistic ways. They were content, but they lived like robots—following strict rules. They were machines that plugged into the energy socket every night and operated on automatic pilot every day. Tick, tock, tick, tock. Drive, work, eat, sleep, drive, work ... I was convinced that both my parents had buried their true passions.

Passion. They must have had passion once—three children to prove it, and one of them born too soon. That darn sex drive. Was it only sex that brought a couple together? How many times had Kenji and I smooched in his car while I sat on his lap, aware that only a couple of layers of clothing were between us? I thought he felt the same. No, sex wasn't the only feeling between us. Kenji and I, side by side, have a mission in life. I'm sure. We understand each other. We can encourage and console each other perfectly. We share a passion to improve the health of others. He must have made his mind focus on Japan. Obligations to his country came first. Damn, damn, damn.

Norma and Jan were in my room when I got home earlier than usual. "Oh, oh," Norma said, when I surprised them. "Hope you don't mind. We wanted to borrow a red pen."

"Of course not." I handed Norma one from the jar on my desk.

They didn't need to go rummaging through my drawers. They're looking for pills. I should have handed the bottle to them right then, to put their minds at rest; they are true friends. But I still might need those pills.

After they'd gone, I moved the bottle to my cupboard, inside a pair of shoes.

I remembered the conversation that I'd had with Jan when she split with Bud. She'd taken that breakup better than I ever could have. She'd come to realize that her conception of Bud had come partly from her imagination. In her mind, she had made him into the person she *hoped* he was. His acceptance of her race, for example. She'd said that she first woke up to the reality of it when she introduced him to her parents. Her mom is light, but her dad is quite dark black, and Bud had gasped when they met. In retrospect, she'd realized that he'd never introduced her to his old friends. Though she is light brown, and used to straighten her hair, she has full lips and a nose that is fairly typical of her race. "He wanted me to pass for a white girl," she'd said. "I can't be happy pretending or hiding away."

I read somewhere that you have to rewrite your story to get over a disappointment. Jan rewrote her story so that it was *her* decision to part with Bud. She incorporated his weaknesses in her telling of it, even though I knew she really liked him.

How can I rewrite my story? I love Kenji. I really do. I'm not Jan. My situation is different.

I started another letter.

Hmm ... Hi Kenji? Wrong. That's not the way I ever addressed him.

I wrote: "Dear Kenji. We have so much in common. I'm a supporter of your devotion to work, and I know you have feelings for me. I know that the passion between us is so great that it's hard for us to be together. But it's more than sex. Friends ... we were friends. We can still be friends. Maybe I can help you write out reports. Take in a movie. Remember how we used to discuss the movies we saw. Remember ..."

Did I dare to mention "Love Is a Many-Splendored Thing"? When we saw that movie, I cried and cried and he comforted me. "Don't cry," he had said. "I won't die in a plane crash."

"I know, I know," I'd said, and he held me tight. We felt secure with each other. I'd thought our whole lives were in front of us. I was soooo happy.

I resumed writing the letter, not mentioning the film. "I never asked you who your favourite movie star is. Marilyn Monroe, I'll bet. You're a sexy guy. Wow, wow. I could learn to pose like she does. They say she uses her tongue in a flirty way. I'll show you. There are other parts of me that match her physique. Talk about breasts. I know you."

I stopped writing.

Phony. That's not me talking. I don't know what to write. Okay, how about phoning? Yes, I'll phone. I've got to dream up some excuse to call. The Yamadas. I can ask him if Fred and Yoshiko are taking that trip to Japan they talked about. I could ask him if he thinks Yoshiko would teach me more Japanese, like she did when we visited them.

I tore up the letter and got ready for bed.

Norma didn't know the whole story. Some girls told all. I couldn't. I only remembered. After the swim, and all during that fall, I had accepted Kenji's claims that he was very busy, or that his car was unreliable so he couldn't drive. Our dates had just been to movies or concerts or getting snacks. At Christmas time, he'd gone on a tour of Harvard and New York with his former Japanese professor from the University of Tokyo's medical school. They must have talked about life in Japan. Somewhere in my desk I still had his postcard from New York City, dated December 24, 1962. I missed our long walks, and cuddling until daylight, but I knew that he needed time and that, on that February evening, I would reap the reward for waiting. I had been so certain.

Dumb me. Dumb me. How could I have been so wrong?

I got out of bed and dug through my drawers. I found my black under-wear—the set I'd worn to dinner that evening: Lacy bra, lacy black panties, and a girdle to make my waist look skinny. Thinking it was sexy, I'd polished my toenails, dabbed perfume on my cleavage, and put on pale rose lipstick.

This isn't a good idea. I'm going to cry again.

The clock said midnight. I thought of the pills, but didn't check. I threw myself back onto the bed, holding back the tears.

The next day, I bought blue stationery, and white too in case I changed my mind. That evening, I arranged the sheet over lined paper, so that my writing would be neat.

Kenji is always neat. I want to be just like him. Okay, my classmates have gone to bed. They won't interrupt me.

It was useless. I could only relive that disastrous evening. Well maybe that's a good thing. I let myself recall everything. At Mario's, he had been very attentive. "What would you like to order? Let's have wine instead of beer." He had scotch—one glass, two ... three glasses and a sip of wine. That was unusual, but it was an unusual night. I didn't need anything to feel high. I was ready to change my life forever. He talked about the job in Japan. I could tell from his tone that it was likely he had already accepted an offer from his former professor and was anticipating the weight of new responsibilities. "To a man, career is the most important," he said. He'd sat up straighter and adjusted the knot of his tie. He wasn't used to wearing a tie. I remembered thinking how thoughtful he was to dress up for the occasion. "A woman thinks about relationships, but to a man, career comes first."

I'd nodded. I understood and I agreed. I was like many women, wanting to focus on making a happy home. Marriage was a partnership. A wife could help her husband succeed and give him a wonderful family life.

He'd put down his fork and looked straight at me. "If I found that having a foreign wife hindered my promotion, I could grow to dislike you."

I'd cringed.

Foreign? Was I foreign? I didn't think of him as foreign.

His eyes terrified me.

Could he imagine hating me?

Something like a tight band seemed to squeeze my head. I was woozy.

Kenji continued. "I considered staying in your country."

Yes, yes. We could be happy here. The doctors respect you. The nurses like you. Your patients will trust you.

"But," he was saying, "I would not advance. I must return. I have duty to my country and my parents." His speech reverted to the grammar of our early days together, when his English was unsure.

It should have been obvious what he was trying to say, but I wouldn't face the obvious. I'd found it hard to breathe.

"My mother cannot accept foreign wife. You would not take care of her as Japanese wife can."

But I'm a nurse. Of course I can learn the Japanese ways of taking care of your parents. I know you will be devoted to your work, and ...

I couldn't speak. I only swallowed and looked down. My shoulders sagged. A sense of weakness filled my being. No longer could I deny what was coming—the end of my world.

"We will not have dessert," he said, in a commanding tone I'd never heard.

Like a sleep walker, I'd followed him to the car. He forgot the western etiquette of opening the door for me, got in himself and slammed his door. He turned the ignition as soon as I was seated. We'd hit every red light with a jolt, and then raced to the next intersection. At the dorm he stopped, and reached across me to open the door. "What I want to say is that I cannot marry you. It is very painful for both, but you are sweet, sweet girl and you will be happy. You will have clever husband and babies and you will have much happiness. I cannot forget ..." He took a deep breath. "I will not see you again. It is best way."

Those memories made me cry. There would be no letter written that night.

The next day I started a new letter, and another the following day. I waited for his phone call. It never came. I looked for him at the student union. If his name came up, it was about how busy he was finishing a research paper. He used to ask me to read his English—no more.

As the months rolled by, I wondered if he'd come to my June graduation. I could invite him. When I was shopping, I intended to look for some sort of card, but I never found one that was appropriate. Then someone told me that he was leaving early, going to New York City to a convention, and from there to Japan.

I set out paper to start a new letter. Why? If he had no faith in us as a couple, what was the use? I was doing all the wishing, all the loving. It was tiring. My patient Stephen Swidersky was the only one loving in his relationship with his wife. I don't think it was that way when their relationship began, but things changed. Maybe things had changed between Kenji and me. Certainly one-sided love relationships didn't work.

I'd learned a lot from my patients. Faith. Caring for little Joshua, with his faith in our medical team, had shown me that one needs to have faith in others and faith that, no matter how serious things may seem, we can heal ourselves. *Persistence ... yes persistence to follow through on what needs to be done.* We aren't all born equal, but we each have a gift for doing *something.* Mrs. Rossi didn't realize it, but she had a talent for looking after those old folks she had been stuck with when her husband had died. When we use the gifts we have, we can be happy. I drew a happy face on the sheet of paper in front of me, and smiled at my crude drawing.

More memories of Stephen Swidersky came back. From him I learned that we have to develop our own strength of character. We can't depend on others to make us feel good. Love has to be reciprocal—given freely and received freely. I drew a stick body under the happy face I had drawn, and found myself laughing at another memory, this time of one of my very first patients, Mr. Bronsky. *Darn, that guy, climbing ladders with only one leg, setting his chair on fire, and getting drunk on the ward. He put us through a lot, but we loved him. What a sense of humour! That's what he taught me. The importance of laughing.*

I looked for the pages from my last attempt at writing Kenji's letter, and tore them up. I went to my closet, took out the pills, and flushed them down the john.

There were more tearful nights. In the daytime, I'd look in the mirror and remind myself that I had years to live. If I could love once, why couldn't I love again? I'd will it to be so. I'd build tough scar tissue around the wound in my heart, and bite my lip, in preparation for facing the day. Then I'd toss my head in a come-hither way, adjust my shoulders, and head out to face the world and whatever adventure was in store. Strength of character is built by facing adversity. Wasn't that what our staff psychiatrist had been trying to tell me?

There is always room for hope.

Chapter 18
Blind Date

Kelly barged into my dorm room one evening when I was trying to memorize which antibiotics treat which infectious conditions. "Busy?" she asked, putting her hands on my shoulders and massaging my tired deltoids.

I was surprised that she'd dropped by, since she'd only joined our group a couple of times since that episode after the Dean's tea party when she had a seizure. I spun around on the chair to face her, and gasped. "What have you done to your hair?" Her frizzy dark hair was now flaming red.

"Just thought I'd be different. But I came with a proposition. Serge has a friend who's looking to meet a nice girl. You two could hit it off. How about it?"

I leaned back, stretched out my arms and legs.

Me on a blind double-date with Kelly? Maybe. She's moving in a new circle these days. Could be interesting.

She readjusted the ties on her polka-dot pyjamas. "We're going to the Saturday races."

"*This* Saturday? Tomorrow?"

"Yes," Kelly said. "Got something better to do?"

No time to mull it over. I've watched the Kentucky Derby on TV, but I've never thought of going to a horse race myself. I need a new adventure though.

"Come on." She played with her hair.

She was rather cute. With a halo of frizzy hair, her face looked small. Her eyes were close together and tiny, and her lips like a bow. She was the playful type, and immature in some ways.

Her crowd could be fun.

"What have you got to lose?" she asked.

In my hometown when someone fixed you up, you already knew the guy.

So what if I don't know him? Kelly does. What else is there to do on Saturday? Laundry, or passing some time at the student union?

"Okay, I'll go," I said.

Kelly and I picked out what I'd wear. My seersucker sundress. Heels for sure. "You've got good legs. Show them off," Kelly said. "I'm wearing my flared skirt, the red one, with a white top." With her index finger, she drew a scooped version of the neckline on her chest. "Let's see your sunglasses."

I fished in my purse and pulled out a horn-rimmed pair.

"That'll do. What about a hat?"

I reached to the top shelf of my cupboard, got a broad-brimmed hat, put it on at a sassy angle, and strutted back and forth.

"Groovy," Kelly said. "Mine's got a sort of bill in the front. You'd better borrow my lipstick unless you've got some that's really red. I mean scarlet."

"Well, I have, but I never wear it. I bought it once when Charlotte and I were out shopping."

I remember how Kenji liked me to look natural. I wear bright rose, but that's the limit, and my cheeks are rosy enough without any blush.

"Let me see." After checking my cosmetics, Kelly agreed that my unused tube of lipstick would do. "If you had a brush, you could paint your lips a little bigger. Oh well, Claire you'll do fine."

The next day I was ready when Kelly knocked on my door. "The guys expect us to be at the bottom of our driveway." Her eyes surveyed my room. "Got everything?"

I'd been up early and was more than ready: my make-up was on, and I was carrying my glasses, hat, a rain hood, umbrella, and cash for the bets—two twenties. Even that was more than I wanted to lose, but I could always babysit if my allowance ran out. I'd never ask Daddy for pleasure money.

Serge's friend, Rudy!

Heavens, he could be a movie star! Long legs, curly black hair—a bit on the long side, and side burns. Sexy sideburns.

I wondered how Kelly had described me.

I suppose, in her eyes, I'm the book-worm type, even though I'm not, but she must have told them something spicy—maybe that I'm adventuresome and a lot of fun. I've got to stop being so self-conscious and live up to that image.

When introduced, I grinned.

His eyes took in every inch of me, and seemed to focus on my ample breasts. Many of the guys back home, hanging out in front of the drug store, whistled when I walked by. I knew that they were just giving my ego a boost though. Those hometown guys thought of me as John or Tommy's little sister. Rudy said nothing. He just gestured toward the back seat. We climbed in.

What do you say to a guy you just met? Heavens, I can't possibly lead a conversation.

As we motored along, Rudy unfolded a racing form, which he proceeded to explain. He was so excited, like he'd just discovered a gold mine or something, and his talk hurried from one sentence to the next. Tattered papers, well marked, spread over his lap and onto mine. He explained the odds, track winning records, and stopped to recite pedigrees of his favourite horses. Of course he had to explain some of the racing terms, like "place" and "show."

Fascinating. Another world.

As my understanding grew, I came up with questions. Soon we were sparring for time to speak. He was so excited that he'd interrupt and hold up a finger to stop me from talking.

At the entrance, the guys got out of the car to pool money for parking. While they were negotiating, Kelly turned toward me from the front seat. "Hey, I forgot to tell you that it's dutch. We should pay our own admission." As the four of us walked to the gate, Rudy remembered something and both fellows hurried back to our car. It was just an excuse, I thought, to avoid offering to treat us.

I wish they'd said at the very beginning that everyone pays, but I suppose they feel embarrassed.

Kelly and I paid to get in and waited just inside the gate. When the fellows returned, Rudy took me by the arm and led me to our bleacher seats. He was high on the excitement, naming the horses we saw warming up on the track, and telling me to bid this much or that much on the ones he liked.

As soon as we were seated, he reached out his hand, saying, "Give me three bucks and I'll place your bet."

"Hey, let me decide what I want to do first," I said. "I think I should skip the first race." I looked up at him and smiled. "Haven't you been telling me to work out a strategy?" I was being more assertive than usual, but that seemed like the way to impress Rudy.

"Okay, okay," he said. "If that's the way you want it."

The sun was in my eyes. I put on my hat, got out a pencil, and began to study the racing form.

He's peeved. Should I cave in? If I'm going to enjoy the race, I need to get involved, don't I? We're talking about my money after all.

I stood up so that he could get by me on his way to the window. He stomped off, taking two steps at a time. I reconsidered my decision.

Should a girl let her guy pick the races? He is the expert, and it's supposed to be a fun date. I don't want to upset him. It's too late for that race though.

Rudy didn't come back until the first race was over. "Look." He fanned a roll of bills at me. "Don't try being so smart. Take a little advice."

He's won that much already? Maybe I am being foolish. I've got no experience. Why do I think I can pick the winners?

When the horses were off for the next race, Rudy shouted and gestured with his fists. Then his horse lost and he slapped his hip and pounded his head. He slid over to talk to Kelly and Serge, leaving me out of the picture.

If he'd asked, I was ready to hand him a five, but he ignored me completely.

Okay. If he's playing it cool, maybe I should place my own bets.

I said, "Excise me. I'll be back," but Rudy was still chatting. He looked over his shoulder as I headed up the steps to the window.

I'll try betting on the jockeys that have won in the past.

"Hey, hey," Rudy ran after me. "Let me. I've got to buy mine anyway."

"Bet on Moonlight," I said. "I like his rider."

"Jockey," Rudy corrected with a wink. He held out his hand for my money.

Friends again. Whew. I guess it was an insult that I didn't let him advise me in the first place.

I returned to my seat, and when the race started, I joined the exuberance of the crowd. "Come on Moonlight. Good boy, Moonlight. You can do it. Pass that black horse. Come on." I jumped up and down when Moonlight came in first. No wonder racing was addictive. I was panting almost as much as the jockey.

"Hurrah. Hurrah, I won." I hugged Kelly and turned to Rudy. "How much? How much, Rudy? My first bet and I won!"

"You bet on *Money Market*," he said.

"No, I didn't. I bet on Moonlight." I drew away from him, puzzled.

"Well, maybe I misunderstood. Money Market would have paid much better."

I clenched my teeth, sighed, and shook my head.

How could he have misunderstood? No matter, I couldn't stay angry. I took a deep breath.

Rudy laughed and threw out his hands. "Okay, honey. Okay. Maybe you're psychic. We'll do it your way from now on." He made a gesture as if he were bowing to royalty. "Come on, love. I'm your servant. What do you want to bet on in the next race?"

He laughed when I picked White Fang, and raised his eyebrows when it lost. "Well, only three bucks down," he said, using a deep voice. "Excise me. I'll collect my winnings."

"Winnings? What did you bet on?"

"Wild Wonder. He came in second."

"Congratulations."

"I owe you one, remember?" he said, and I thought he was going to pay for my next bet, but when he returned, he was carrying a hot dog and a Coke for us to share.

I don't know how much Rudy had won, but his mood had certainly changed. He'd slip up happily to place our bets. I let him do the choosing. He would hug me or console me after each race, depending on the outcome. We locked arm in arm to cheer.

I've got to let him hug me, but it feels so strange. Not like ... No, no ... don't let yourself compare him to Kenji.

He lit a cigarette and put it in my mouth.

I suppose that's the sexy thing to do. I won't tell him that I've never smoked. Just don't inhale. Just pretend. If my new boyfriend wants me to smoke, I could take it up.

At the end of the day, I'd won $15 and he must have won a couple of hundred. He teased me. Told me not to be a sore loser. "The day isn't done. The best part is yet to come, right?"

What does that mean? The best part is yet to come.

We did a military strut together back to the car. I let my head bob from side to side, trying to feel happy and free. He pinched my fanny, but it didn't seem offensive. Most girls must consider that a compliment.

We stopped for dinner at a restaurant with dim lights, water trickling from a fake waterfall, and waiters in tuxedos.

"It's on me," Rudy said, flashing a stack of bills.

"Fifty, fifty," Serge said. "I insist."

I hadn't paid any attention to Serge's betting. Every time I glanced their way, he and Kelly were smooching. I felt uncomfortable seeing them display so much affection in public. Kelly had only met Serge a month or so earlier. How could she love him that soon?

"I'll contribute something," I said.

"No, no. Our treat. Yours is coming."

Did he mean that I'd like the food?

I was confused.

Wine bottles popped open, and steaks arrived. The guys were light-hearted, full of jokes and teasing. If I'd known an off-colour joke, I might have told it. Ten o'clock was our curfew, but it was only nine when we were leaving the restaurant, plenty of time to get back. Rudy pulled me close as we walked, and I cuddled up to him.

He's still a stranger, but I've got to go along or he'll dump me before we even get fully acquainted.

It was dark as we drove along the highway, with no moon, and only the headlights of approaching cars, and the pale glow from the passing street lights. I had a sense that we were going east, instead of west into the city. *The wine ... it must be the wine.* Kelly and Serge were kissing as he drove.

He isn't watching the oncoming cars. I really don't like this. Oh my god, Rudy is kissing my ears!

Our car slowed and Serge pulled our car onto the shoulder.

Are we out of gas? Why are we stopping? I don't like this. We'll miss the curfew.

"What the matter, honey?" Rudy said, and I tensed.

The car rolled off the highway onto uneven ground. Our headlights illuminated grave markers and tall tombstones. Rudy parked the car. The engine was turned off. Kelly and Serge disappeared from view in the front seat. When I finally caught on to what was happening on the bench seat in front, I wanted to protest—for Kelly's sake—but Rudy put his hand over my mouth. He uncovered my breast and licked my nipple. I was wedged against the seat back, so I couldn't move. With one hand, he reached under my skirt. "Relax, honey," he whispered.

I froze.

This isn't happening. Oh my God!

"No!" I tried to protest, but he was squeezing my lips closed with the fingers of one hand. He moved on top of me. I thrashed from side to side, but he managed to get his hand inside my panties. My squirming only made it possible for him to begin edging them down.

"You want it, honey. I know you do."

His hot, stinky breath was in my face.

I hate you. I hate. hate you!

His eyes were wild with determination. He clutched my panties, ripping them off.

I was breathing hard.

Oh God, what's left to protect me? Think. Think. His thing is against my leg! My first sex isn't supposed to be like this! It should be tender, sweet, and mutual!

Those thoughts gave me strength. I wiggled my lips, and shook my head until one of his fingers slipped between my teeth and then I bit. I bit hard.

He pulled out his hand and shook it. Then he slapped my face.

It stung, but I'd had enough time to free one knee, and I jammed it toward his crotch. Summoning all my strength, I heaved my hips and threw him off balance. Then I kicked and kicked. Maybe I hit his groin, maybe his legs. I don't know. I just kicked.

Suddenly both of his hands were around my neck. I couldn't get air. My brain wanted to shout, but instead, I had to concentrate on trying to suck air in though my nose.

"You slut," he said. "You beg for it and then you ..."

I was getting weaker.

I've got to explain that I was only trying to be friendly. I'm not the kind of girl you take me for. How? How did I lead you on?

The will to fight was waning.

Is this how it feels to be raped? Do some girls find a way to fight off the molester?

He relaxed his hold. Maybe he realized that I was going under.

I managed a hoarse sound. "Kelly ... Help ... Kelly ... Please."

"Hey, what's with you two?" Serge called from the front seat. He must have reached over the back to pull on Rudy, because Rudy's body seemed lighter. "Buddy, hey, Buddy. You don't want trouble."

Rudy sat up.

I freed myself, sat up, grabbed my purse, opened the back door, and pulled my dress into place.

Serge was getting out of the front seat when I stepped onto the ground. We had driven several feet into the cemetery, but I could hear the traffic nearby. I ran in that direction.

Kelly was out of the car. "Claire! Come back Claire," she called. "Claire, wait!" She was panting as she followed me.

When I got to the highway, I paused to get my bearings.

Which way is home?

Kelly ran up beside me. "It's okay. Serge is talking to him. We'll wait here until they come with the car."

"Are you crazy?" I asked. "I would *never* get back in the car with that lunatic!" I started walking as fast as my heels would allow.

"Gosh! You must be a virgin," Kelly said, trying to keep up.

"Of course! And that brute was going to rape me!"

"I guess he had too much to drink."

I turned to scowl. "Damn you, Kelly. Are you going to make *excuses* for him?"

She reached to take my hand, but I shook her off.

"No, I guess you're right. He was out of line."

"Out of line!"

Are you so naive? What kind of girl are you? Did you know that your date with Serge would end up in sex?

I wanted to look her in the eye to get an answer, but I couldn't stop walking.

A car was creeping up behind us on the gravel. I didn't look back.

Will they try to run us down? There's a rest stop ahead. With luck there'll be a phone.

I began to run faster, but twisted my ankle on the rough ground. Now every step was painful. I cried from pain and fear.

Kelly had stopped running. "It's Serge. Come on, Claire," Kelly called to me. "He'll protect you! How else are we going to get back to the dorm?"

"Claire!" Serge called, as he got back out of the car and ran toward me.

"Go away," I shouted. "Go away!"

Soon he was beside me, jogging along at my pace. "I'm sorry, Claire. Let me take you home. You and Kelly can sit in the back seat. Rudy won't be any more trouble, I promise. We let him drink too much."

Every step hurt. I could no longer run. I shivered from the cool air and from the terror, but I could see a phone booth, and I made myself move toward it.

Serge got to the booth first. I panicked again.

Will he keep me from phoning? Do I have any coins in my purse? Thank God I had the presence of mind to grab my purse back there.

Serge was putting the receiver on the hook. "I've called a cab for you. Fifteen minutes, they said." He pressed some money toward me, which I refused, but he kept his distance. I leaned against a lamp post a few feet away.

"We'll wait in my car until the cab comes. I don't want to leave you out here alone. Do you feel safe taking a cab back?" Serge asked.

Did I feel safe? What was that supposed to mean? Did he really call a taxi?

"I'll be okay. I don't want you to wait," I said.

I'll call a cab myself as soon as they leave.

Serge walked slowly back to his car and turned off the headlights.

I leaned against the glass door of the booth. Just as the cab arrived, Kelly came running toward me. "I'll ride back with you. Can I?"

How can I refuse? Maybe she's a victim too.

We both got into the taxi.

"We're in trouble, aren't we?" Kelly asked.

"What do you mean?" I asked. "Do you think you might be pregnant? The monster didn't get that far with me."

"I mean it's after curfew. How are we going to get in?"

"I'll signal at Norma's window. She'll let us in the fire door and bring some money to pay for the cab."

"Good. You solve all our problems."

Dumb girl. Didn't Kelly know that the brute was trying to rape me? All those years ago she took that beer and gave herself a seizure. I was pleased to notice that she only drank Coke tonight, but right now she must see that my dress is torn, and my hair's a mess. She hasn't even asked how I feel.

Kelly began to sniffle.

"You okay?" I asked.

Those tears make me angry. What right has she to cry?

"Are you going to report him? My parents will find out and make me quit nursing."

Damn her. The world revolves around her. I want nothing more to do with Kelly or her crowd—Rudy in particular. He drank too much! Some excuse. The goon. The pervert. The drunk.

Then I began to wonder.

Had I precipitated the rape? This is a secret I'll have to live with. No one must ever know how I cuddled up to that guy ... let him kiss me, tried to kiss him back. Norma would probably agree that I brought it on myself. I'll tell no one. Well, maybe Norma. She'll help me sort out what happened. Oh, I'm such a people pleaser. In the beginning, I'd been myself with Kenji and he'd liked me. Then at the end I was only trying to please him, and it didn't work. I've got to learn to be myself. I'm an okay person. Please God, help me be a fun person without being a people pleaser. I'm myself with Norma, Jan and Jeff–my friends from the student centre.

Chapter 19
Marilyn

"No symptoms," I wrote in Penny Star's chart. Then I signed my name, and put on my jacket to leave for the day. For two days I'd seen no cause for her hospitalization in the psychiatric ward. She was like a friend, instead of my patient.

The head nurse stopped me to verify that I'd given Penny her four o'clock meds. None of my classmates liked that particular head nurse. In fact, we referred to her as "The Pillar" because she not only looked rigid in her white uniforms—looking like we pictured Lot's wife, from the Bible, who had turned into a pillar of salt—but also issued orders like a commander, and never consulted any of us students.

Okay, I'll grant that psychiatry is complex, and that we're neophytes, but we've been studying nursing for nearly three years and our experiences have given us some *insight.*

"Yes, certainly I have," I replied, not without trepidation, since I was always afraid in her presence.

She put her hand on her hip. "You're sure that she swallowed the capsules?"

Swallowed them? Why wouldn't she swallow them?

I was taken aback by that line of questioning, and in my mind, I replayed the scene to reassure myself. When I had taken the medication to Penny, she was brushing her hair. We'd talked about Hemingway, and I put the paper cup with the capsules on her table. I could see them in my mind's eye on her bedside table, next to a glass of water. Of course she'd take them eventually. She wanted to get out of here. She'd do the expected to prove she was sane.

When I didn't reply promptly, the head nurse answered for me. "No, you *did not.*" Her bony finger waved in my face. "Didn't your instructors tell you that some patients save them up, even hide capsules under their tongues so that they can try to commit suicide later by taking an overdose? That happened on the men's ward a few weeks ago and it *must* never happen again."

I forcefully controlled my shaking. I pictured us nurses using a flashlight to peer into mouth cavities, wiggling a tongue blade around to see if a capsule was stuck under there. It seemed so absurd.

So Mrs. Pillar, what do you expect me to do?

"And another thing," the head nurse continued, "did you give Miss Star a book? There's one with your name on it in her nightstand."

"I loaned one to Penny." It was Salinger's *Franny and Zooey*.

How is she going to hurt herself with a book, I ask you?

"Don't you know that everything that comes for patients on the psychiatric ward must be cleared by me or Dr. Giacomini?"

"I thought that only applied to things from outside."

"Well, you are 'outside,' as you put it. I don't suppose you put razor blades or running-away money between the pages, but we also have to clear what the patients read."

"I understood about food and trinkets and ... I just didn't think."

The head nurse turned to walk away but stopped short. "Wait a moment; did I hear you refer to Miss Star by her first name? Always address her as Miss Star. You must be professional. Keep a patient/nurse relationship or you will harm the patient. Too much fraternizing is bad."

I said that I'd try harder, and she dismissed me by turning sharply and walking away.

In the hall, I pounded the elevator button.

Come on. Come on. What does The Pillar mean by "too much fraternizing"?

I walked back and forth as I waited.

Fraternizing! Really! Does she think that there's a potential for something sexual? I'm not gay. Neither is Penny—I mean Miss Star. Really! Absurd! I'm not like Maxine.

Maxine, my dorm neighbour, got expelled for dating one of her patients—well, more than dating. It started when she went in after hours to look after him. First, she let him walk in the hall, not realizing that the doctor had changed his order because the graft on his burns was bleeding. That infringement was excused with a warning, but when they caught her in his bed ... ? They'd become engaged, but that didn't matter. They kicked her out. I could see the school's point. But my case was nothing like that. Penny—Miss Star—and I just liked to talk about the same subjects.

She's my age and she needs a friend. Isn't it good for patients to have normal conversations like they'll have once they are released from the hospital?

I headed for the cafeteria to get a coffee and hopefully let off some steam. I paid for the coffee and joined my friends, eager to relate the reprimands The Pillar had just given me. "Miss Star *does not* belong in a psych ward. She needs a normal friend like me," I said, and then let out an exasperated sigh.

Jan agreed. "I don't see anything wrong with her."

"She's as sane as I am," I said. Then I had to laugh, because I knew they were ready to remind me that I had sleepwalked a few days earlier. "Okay, sleepwalking is not a psychosis, no matter what you say. I *am* sane."

Everyone chuckled.

"And I *wasn't* chasing after a man," I added.

When I'd sleepwalked, my classmates had teased me and asked if I was after a man. They reminded me that Miss Penny Star told the hospital staff that she had seen her boyfriend standing outside the fourth floor window. How could that be? There was no way he could climb the outside hospital walls and how could he stand on a narrow window ledge? My friends said, in jest, that I might be running after Penny's beau too. I'd laughed with them, but I didn't like being teased about the sleepwalking incident, or being labelled, even in jest, as a possible psycho, just because I had walked in my sleep one time.

Norma tapped my hand. "That joke was pretty sick. We won't tease you again."

"Thanks, Norma. It won't happen again, because I put a chair against my door. So there!"

"Don't take it so personally. We aren't comparing you with Miss Star."

"Penny Star is sane too," I said.

"Sometimes I wonder," Norma said. She leaned back and tapped her fingers together. "Yesterday she was still claiming that her boyfriend comes to the window and talks to her."

"She never told me that," I said.

"Nor me," Jan added.

"With me she talks about Margaret Laurence and other authors I've read," I said. "Do you know that she speaks several languages? Japanese and French, of course."

"Even I can say a few words of French and German and Italian," one of the girls said. "That doesn't make her brilliant, or sane for that matter."

"She knows a lot of Japanese," I said. "Kenji taught me some, and when I speak to her, she knows what I'm saying."

"Maybe. Maybe," she scoffed. "She could just be guessing from your gestures."

"I don't think memory or languages have anything to do with schizophrenia, anyway," Norma said. "It's about believing fantasies are real, losing touch with reality. That sort of thing."

Jan spoke up. "We really should have been taught the symptoms before we were put on the psych floor."

"She fantasizes that she's a movie star. Haven't you noticed?" Norma asked.

"No," I said, "but don't most of us dream of being movie stars? I don't know why you have it in for her."

"Maybe you just talk too much and don't let her expose her fantasies," one of the girls said with a chuckle.

I was still smarting from The Pillar's scolding. I pounded the table, and my coffee spilled over into the saucer. "Why are you siding with Norma?" I asked.

"We aren't taking sides, for goodness sake. Norma has just read up on schizophrenia," one of the girls said, while patting my arm to calm me. "She's a good observer too."

I looked from one classmate to the other. "And I'm not? Don't you think I listen?"

"We're just teasing," one girl said.

Oh, no. You aren't just teasing. You think Jan and I don't understand Penny's situation. Now I'm really angry.

Sometimes I'm quiet when I have something on my mind, but this time I felt like making a grandstand speech in defence of Penny. I didn't though. I kept the peace.

The following day, Penny—Miss Star—was my patient again. She wore a white halter top and a black and white polka-dot skirt, which showed off her curvaceous figure. She wore a hospital gown open over it, fanning out in front. Her feet looked dainty in four-inch red pumps. She sighed like she was bored. "Hi Miss Winchester. What's the weather like out there?" Her voice was breathy, almost a whisper. "I wish you could take me for a walk one day. I see all those trees—Red Pine, White Pine, Spruce; I think there's a Cedar." She walked to the window. "There's a real forest behind this place."

I won't let that melancholy tone get to me.

"How can you tell what kind of trees are there? They're so far away." I said. *I'll test her knowledge about trees and prove that she isn't just fantasizing.*

"The shape. I can tell from the shape." She gave me a warm, understanding smile.

Hmm ... that smile could mean that she knows I'm testing her.

But I was amazed. I could identify some trees from their needles, but not from the shape of the whole tree.

Should I go down into the woods to see if she's right? If she's identified the trees correctly ... well it means she isn't fantasizing about that anyway. How nice it would be if I could get permission to take her out of this prison. She must feel like she's bound and gagged. This ward is like a cell, even if there are *other patients around her.*

I looked down the rows of white cots, covered with white spreads and separated by white curtains. And I looked at Penny's fellow roommates on this ward.

Trying to be friends with any of them would make anyone insane. Mrs. Mosby with her paranoia about poison in her food; Violet Ramsey, who thinks her side rails are bars of a jail. Penny, you don't belong here.

"Maybe we *could* go walking one day," I said. An idea was churning in my head.

"John might come tonight," she said. "Did I show you his picture?" She ambled to her cubicle, looked in her drawer, and in the cupboard below. Her brow furrowed. Rather frantically, she pushed things around in her closet. A jacket toppled off the hanger, but she left it where it fell and slammed the door shut. "Oh, my God, that battleaxe head nurse has taken his picture! I knew it! She says I made him up. She doesn't want you to see his picture. That woman wants to get me in trouble. She'll see how real he is. He's coming to see me."

Well if there's a picture ... I really want to judge for myself.

"Let's retrace your steps," I said calmly. "When were you looking at the picture last?"

"Hmm," she hesitated a moment, and then ripped back the covers on her bed. She tossed her pillow out into the centre of the room, looked under the bed, and finally put both hands on her temple like she was trying to remember. Tears came. She threw herself onto her bed and cried.

I can't interfere. What will she do next? She's acting rather hysterically, but under the circumstances I might do the same thing. This isn't a sign of psychosis.

"Maybe you left it out and the nurses didn't know whose it was. I'll go and ask all the nurses if they have it."

I'll leave her alone a while and see if she persists in hunting for it or calms herself down.

I walked away, got myself a glass of water from the refrigerator in the locked nurses' lounge, brought it to our nurses station, and sat down to put in some time.

When I got back, Penny Star was sitting on a chair, and filing her nails while a nurse's aide remade her bed. "I need a manicure," she said, splaying long fingers.

"I could polish your nails," I said.

She didn't look up. She'd made a quick recovery.

Is that normal or a characteristic of schizophrenia? I'm really confused.

"I think that woman in the housedress took it," she said. "Wait until she goes to the washroom, and I'll look through her stuff."

She's talking about Mrs. Mosby! I guess she's still preoccupied with that missing picture.

"Why would she take it?"

"Jealousy," Penny answered. "That woman wants to believe John is her boyfriend."

"Has she seen him too?"

"Heavens, no. She's just seen his picture."

Poor Penny. The only thing wrong with her was a nervous breakdown. The pressures of university could do that to anyone. She's just burned out. What kind of parents does she have to bring her to this loony hospital over a simple breakdown?

Penny waited until the accused woman left the ward, and then made a bee line to the woman's bedside.

I shouldn't have allowed her to pursue that invasion, but before I could stop her, she had yanked the woman's nightstand drawer open, stirred things about, found nothing, and banged it shut. Next, she stormed off into the women's washroom.

Thank goodness no nurse was around. Any of them might report me to the head nurse.

I won't let Penny do that again. Heavens, why didn't I intervene?

Moments later, Penny calmly came out of the washroom. "Someone broke a tumbler," she said, nonchalantly pointing back over her shoulder, toward the washroom. "In there. I nearly stepped on a piece."

The head nurse appeared out of nowhere and went to check the lavatory. "Miss Winchester," she called to me. "Come and stay here until I get housekeeping to clean up this glass. Did you give Miss Star a tumbler?"

"No. No I didn't."

She pulled me out of hearing distance of Penny. "*Someone* gave it to her or left it where our patients had access. I wonder if Miss Star broke it herself. We'll have to watch her. She may have intended to use the shards to cut her wrist."

"She wouldn't do that. She's—"

"Make no assumptions. I'll have to get to the bottom of this and find out who left something glass where our patients could get at it."

My throat constricted. I swallowed. "It could have been me. I got a glass of water from the nurses' lounge. Maybe I left it at the nurses' station when I finished drinking. But patients aren't allowed there."

"You? I must say that you have a lot to learn." She stood with hands on her hips. "Do you get the message?"

"Yes. I'm sorry."

"Patients aren't supposed to be in the nurses' station, but you can see that they sometimes get around the restrictions. Wait here. I still need to find out which patient took the glass." She stomped away.

I didn't wait for housekeeping, and when the head nurse returned with a housekeeper, I had just finished the clean-up and was about to take the broken pieces of glass down the hall to a chute.

"That's good," the head nurse said to me. She turned on her heels and walked away.

Has she written me off as hopeless? Do other students make as many mistakes as I make? No wonder she gets so upset.

When I returned to the ward, Miss Star came hurrying up to me with a photo in her hands. "Look," she said. "Someone threw it in the trash. Why would anyone do that? Poor John. Oh, sweetheart, I don't want to lose you."

I watched while she kissed the picture repeatedly while walking to her cubicle. "Jack, Jack, Jack," she said. "He wants me to call him Jack." She began to hum. After standing the photo on her nightstand, she sat down, swung her shapely legs over the side of the bed, and crossed her ankles. Looking at me, she said, "Could you really take me for a walk?" She hugged herself. "You're the only friend I've got."

"I know," I said.

I'm the only one that understands you, and I want to do something better than pushing pills and treatments. You aren't mental. I will find a way to take you out into the fresh air. Can I get permission? Perhaps not, but I'll find a way.

I picked up the photo. It wasn't the standard photo on glossy paper, and the picture was so scratched that you couldn't see any details, only that it was a photo of a very young man with dark hair. He looked vaguely familiar. "Tell me about Jack," I said.

"He's very important," she said. "You'll meet him. He's a loooong way off now, but he's coming." There was a wide grin on her face.

"Do you hear his voice?"

This can be another test. Norma said that Penny told her she heard voices.

"Silly," she said. "I'm not allowed to get phone calls."

Okay, she isn't hearing voices.

"You get letters?" I asked.

She giggled, and from her bosom, produced a bundle of envelopes bound with a rubber band.

Are they real letters? If I can read one, I'll know whether she is making things up. I wonder if she'll show one to me. Girls like to share secrets, especially love secrets, with their best pals. That's what she's always carrying when she takes that bundle of towels into the shower with her—the letters are wrapped in them.

"Very mushy are they?" I asked, hunching my shoulders like I could imagine something romantic.

She slipped one out of the pile and kissed it.

Is she going to hand one over? No, she's putting it back and tucking the whole bunch inside her bra again. If I bump her, will she drop the bundle? One might fall onto the floor and I can grab it and tease her till she lets me read it. I have to see if the letters are fantasy or real.

She slid back away from me to lean on her pillow, and the chance was gone.

"I don't have to see the words," she said. "I know them by heart. My dearest Lala." She cocked her head. "He always begins that way. Calls me Lala because he says my tongue is always going, you know ... la, la, la. I talk so much, don't I?" She giggled. "And I sing. Someday I'll sing for you. When's your birthday?"

"It's a long way off. You'll be home by then."

"So sad." She spoofed a pout as she leaned toward me. "I'll tell you a secret. Jack might come tonight."

"How? When?"

She looked away.

Where's she looking? At the window?

"I can't have visitors yet, but Jack knows how to get in."

"He does?"

She laughed again.

"He won't do anything illegal. Were you thinking he'd come in the window? You've got some imagination. That would be impossible." Her index finger waved at me playfully. "We're wayyyyy up on the fourth floor, aren't we?"

That's a very sane answer.

"Please, please, pretty please," she said. "Take me for a walk. Five minutes. If I could breathe some fresh air, out in the woods. I want to touch leaves, touch those beautiful, sharp, pine-tree needles."

Sharp needles! Crazy thought. You can't commit suicide by sticking yourself with pine-tree needles.

She inhaled deeply. "Oh, I want to smell the trees."

"Leave it to me," I said. The tests I'd tried proved to me that she did not hallucinate. She needed me, and if I didn't look after her, who would? I was her only friend.

The head nurse summoned me. "Miss Winchester, sit with Miss Dougherty. She's just back from electric shock therapy. You're needed there."

I sat beside Miss Dougherty's bed, but there wasn't much I could do for her. She would sleep for hours. I *could* help Penny, and I made plans. I'd be taking her to the appointment with the psychiatrist on Thursday.

We won't walk through the tunnel this time. We'll go across the quadrangle ... not just across, but under the arch and out into the woods behind the hospital. I'll take her in a wheelchair. If anyone sees us, they'll think she's a long-term patient who gets a daily visit to fresh air. It's so unlikely we'll get caught. Yes, the plan'll work.

On Thursday things started off as planned. Penny didn't want to sit in a wheelchair, but I convinced her to trust me. It was then that I revealed my plan, and her eyes lit up.

The head nurse questioned why I wanted a wheelchair. "Isn't it better for her to walk and get some exercise?"

"I can get her there quicker," I said, "Otherwise, she'll try to wander off."

The nurse seemed to weigh the possibilities, and then nodded. "Miss Star does saunter along." She turned to Penny, "I know you like to go to the gift shop. Don't ask today. Miss Winchester isn't allowed to take you on any detours. You and I will go there one day next week, okay? As long as you keep taking your medication and your symptoms are under control, I can take you." She smiled. Penny smiled back and the head nurse nodded approval of the plan.

We had to take the elevator to the ground floor and wheel down a long corridor to the outside door. I saw no one I knew. In the quadrangle, I practically ran as I pushed her along the walkway between the flower beds that were sprouting daffodils and tulips, and only slowed down when I rolled the wheelchair under the arch and bumped along on the cinder path that led into the woods. It was a warm spring day; like us, no one wore jackets, so we didn't look out of place. There was time to give Penny five minutes in the fresh air and still arrive at Dr. Giacomini's office on time.

One of the gardeners was coming toward us. The path was narrow so I stopped to let him pass. Penny sprang from the chair and started to run to him. "Don't you recognize me, Jack?" she said, stumbling in her red pumps as she traversed the uneven ground.

Can he be someone she knows from home? Oh, my!

I was getting suspicious.

"Jack. Oh Jack, I knew you'd come," she said, having caught up with the man, who had stopped to see what the shouting was about. "You'll remember this." Penny posed, with one knee bent against the other. She leaned her head toward her left shoulder, licked her red lips, and began to sing, "'*Hap-py birth-day to you.*'" Her hand delivered a kiss into the air. "'*Hap-py birth-day to you! Hap-py birth-day Mr. Pre-si-dent ... Hap-py birth-day to you.*'"

I gasped.

Oh, God. What have I done? She is *psycho. What if she takes off? Does she have running-away money?*

"Help us," I said to the gardener. "Ask her to sit back down. Please, could you just lend a hand? Please?"

"Is she some weirdo?" he asked.

"Please, please, just ask her to sit back down."

He tossed his head like it was a crazy thing for me to ask, but took her hand, led her back to the chair, and bowed like he wished her to sit.

While complying, she kept singing, and reaching out her hand toward him as he backed away.

The man looked at each of us and then shook his head. "Is this a gag or is she a bit ..." He tapped his head, indicating some mental instability. "You want me to call someone?"

"Thanks," I said. "I'm taking her to her appointment. We'll be okay."

"An appointment? What are you doing out here?" He eyed my checked uniform and white apron. "You're just a student nurse, aren't you?"

"It was an experiment, but we're okay. And thanks for your help." I pushed the chair around him and ran with it toward the hospital door before he could decide that I should be reported. Nor did I look back. The alarm—the one that was used when there was a fire or when someone took off—did not sound, so I slowed my pace, entered the building, and pushed the chair down the corridor toward Dr. Giacomini's office.

The Pillar was standing outside the doctor's door.

Had she followed us? I'm in for it.

I eyed her pleasantly, but said nothing.

Did she guess my plan and let me break the rules so I could be kicked out of nursing?

Penny was admitted into Dr. Giacomini's private office, and I turned to leave.

The head nurse took my arm. "Come with me, Miss Winchester," she said.

I felt horrible.

I'm going to be expelled. Three years down the drain, and I really love this job. I'm a good nurse, too, only ...

I went willingly. I pictured the march to the Dean's office, and the Dean lecturing me and finally telling me that I was out. I bit my lip to keep from crying. My palms were wet. I carried my hands in front of myself like they were handcuffed.

Two months before graduation. What a fool I've been. Kenji's gone and now...

The head nurse took me to the coffee shop, ordered, and served me black coffee. *So I'm to get a lecture before she turns me in. Prolong the torture. I suppose I deserve it.*

"Look," she said. "You let your heart rule your head. It happens to many of us. We choose nursing because we care about people. We identify with their feelings and our satisfaction comes from doing something to make them better, emotionally as well as physically."

I put a Kleenex to my eyes and looked down at the black coffee.

"In our eagerness, we sometimes overstep the bounds. We do things that harm the patient."

I was tempted to say that I hadn't meant any harm, but I bit my lip and kept quiet.

"I know you care for Penny Star. I know why you feel that your relationship is the only way for her to recover." The head nurse sipped from her cup.

A tear ran down my cheek.

I just wanted to do more than push pills or oversee shock therapy. No one else seemed to care. No one was being her friend. Obviously I made an error of judgement. Penny is sick.

"I'm going to tell you my story," the head nurse said. "When I was a student, we had a patient—a physics professor and a brilliant man. I guess I had a crush on him or maybe he reminded me of my dad. Maybe I thought I could save *him*, when I hadn't been able to save my dad from cancer." The nurse tapped an index finger against her lip. "At any rate, electric shock didn't help. The drugs available in those days didn't help. I thought that if someone really cared, he'd recover. I read to him, played pool in the recreation room, joked, and found a radio station with classical music that he liked." She leaned her elbow on the table and looked at me. "I was sure that someone could bring him out of the depression. His face lit up when I came on duty. He trusted me. I decided that he needed to be reminded of what the outside world was like. One evening, when I wasn't on duty, I borrowed my mom's car. We sneaked out. He was very nervous, but I thought that he'd be happy when we got away from the hospital." She hesitated and then tapped the table with one finger, as though wondering whether to continue the story. "Some drunk ran the light and smashed into our car. We were shaken, but not hurt physically. He was taken back in an ambulance. The wife came into the picture again. She wanted me arrested. Fortunately that didn't happen, but she took me to court. I got off on some technicality, but I should have lost. I quit school before they kicked me out. It took me three years to understand what had happened. Caring does make a difference, but we can't let our hearts overrule our heads. Finally, I did go back and finish the nursing program."

I looked up at her and nodded. "Thanks." My tears dripped onto the table. I was crying for her, and for getting myself kicked out of a job that I knew was right for me.

She handed me another tissue. "I'm not going to write this incident on your record. No one was hurt. You are a sensitive girl, a fine nurse. Nursing needs you."

"I've done something very bad."

"You've learned how vulnerable you are." The head nurse stood up and put her hand on my shoulder. "I'd like to have you on my team one day." She smiled, and left without looking back.

As I trudged slowly to my dorm room, mulling things over, it came to me why she was so rigid.

Protection from her own vulnerability. I'm vulnerable too, but I'll find a way to be compassionate. I'll use better judgement. Psychiatric nursing might be my choice when I apply for a permanent job. Yes, I'll think about it. Nursing is rewarding. I can make a difference in the lives of my patients.

As I passed the dorm kitchen I remembered that my class was having a meeting. I was the last to arrive and quickly slid into a chair next to Jan. We'd decided to have some sort of celebration of our graduation. Of the forty-eight girls who started in 1960, only twenty-one of us remained to graduate. The Dean's prediction was coming to fruition, but not necessarily because my classmates hadn't tried. Some had married and moved away, one girl left to care for her mother, one got pregnant and her parents sent her to California to live with a cousin, and some did find that nursing was not for them.

At first we had grandiose ideas of renting a hotel ballroom for a dance, but none of us had money. That problem was remedied when we all signed up to work for pay during our days off. We pooled our earnings but it wasn't enough for a ballroom. The next idea was to hold a dinner party—perhaps at a nearby restaurant, but that idea had to be scratched. Norma, Jan and I went to make inquiries at two of the nearby Italian places, and we'd been told that the restaurants were reserved—reserved for seven nights in a row! Though none of us said a word, we all knew what that meant. It could be difficult to find a place that would allow Jan and the two coloured guys who were our Intern and Resident friends to attend. I grabbed my classmates by their hands and pulled them out of The Spaghetti Palace, remarking that I had a new idea. Why didn't we reserve the dorm's recreation room, have food catered, get Jason, one of the new med students, to be our disc-jockey and invite our friends? That idea was affordable. The one drawback was that the room had to be vacated by twelve-thirty, but we reconciled ourselves to that alternative. This meeting was to make the final plans. We formed committees to order the food, choose the music, decorate the room and then Nancy, our class president, said, "Anyone want to take dance lessons? I've found a studio nearby where we can learn the basic steps or those of us who are good can get advance instruction. If ten of us sign up, it will be really cheap."

Jan, Norma and I waved our hands and we were joined by ten other classmates. Some intended to bring their boyfriends, so the cost was going to be even better.

At our first dance session I was paired with Paul, a young assistant curator at the museum. He was taking a job in Boston in September and had been warned to buy a tux, that there would be many formal money-making events, including fancy balls, so he needed to learn to dance well. He was very shy. I had a job on my hands to get him to laugh at our mistakes, stop worrying about being perfect, and just let go and dance to the rhythm. We all looked forward to our lessons.

Chapter 20
Child's Play

Sunlight shone through windows into the hospital's fifth-floor playroom. The space was furnished with shelves of toys, low tables, and chairs. Tempera paintings the children had made decorated the pale yellow walls. Many children wore street clothes, even those in wheelchairs or on carts who worked on puzzles or played with dolls. At the centre, children grouped around work tables, making roads in sawdust, constructing clay animals, or tapping castanets to the tune of the Mickey Mouse theme song, which was coming from a 45 on a record player in the corner.

This was my final rotation, two weeks spent playing with the patients, to learn how children expressed their thoughts and fears through play, and how the child life specialist helped them through hard times. A cluster of older kids were playing dress up. "You're the prince and I'm the princess," one girl said to her companion, handing the little boy a satin jacket from the box of dress-up clothing.

Every little girl's dream. I can identify with the story she's inventing.

The friendships with hospital playmates must have tempered the strangeness of the hospital experience.

I concentrated on what Kathy, the child life specialist, was saying. "The child doesn't have the vocabulary to talk about his or her loneliness and fears. The little girl washes the doll's hair like Mother does for her, and thus she relives the comforting memory of Mother, whereas adults will be comforted *talking* about getting a hairdo and the things they did with their moms. The boy paints a car and puts his dad in the driver's seat. He's comforted by playing that he's with his loving dad. You and I might tell a friend about a drive we enjoyed *with* our fathers, or someone else close."

I pictured my mom, dad, brothers, and Kenji, my lost boyfriend.

I'm constantly talking about them. Yes, even about Kenji. Makes me smile and feels like they are near.

Kathy nodded across the room toward Trevor. The six-year-old boy was at the easel, painting in red. His subject had the contours of a boy, with a round head, eyes, and no mouth. The red paint ran down the paper. "Trevor is going to have his umbilical hernia repaired tomorrow," she said. "I'm going to ask him what he thinks will happen to the boy in the picture. We'll learn what he fears about his own surgery."

Hmm, the red paint is probably blood.

"We'll play at giving anaesthesia to a doll," she continued. "He may believe that he won't wake up, but when we play, the doll *will* wake up. I'll try to straighten out his misconceptions."

I listened when she spoke with Trevor. "So, what's happening in your picture?"

Trevor had finished and was putting the paintbrush back in the pot of red tempera paint. "He'll have his *nabel* fixed."

"Just like you're having yours repaired, right? Have you noticed that your navel sticks out? It's not like other little boys' navels."

"Yeah."

"How do you think the doctor can fix it?"

"He'll cut it off."

"Well no. He'll make a small cut." She indicated the space of a couple inches with her fingers. "Then he'll sew it so that it looks like everyone's navel. We call the problem with your navel a hernia, but your hernia will be gone—no more problems for you."

Trevor seemed to be quietly taking in what he'd been told.

"You look worried." Kathy said to Trevor.

"It's going to bleed."

"Not as much as your picture shows, in fact very little, and you have pints and pints of blood." Kathy pointed the the pint jars that held the tempera paint. "Your body is constantly making more. When you skin your knee, it might be frightening to see some blood, but your body heals very quickly and makes more blood. Then what will happen?"

Trevor looked distraught. He whispered, "The doctor's going to cut the other thing off." He made a subtle gesture with his hands, pointing toward the front of his pants.

Oh my gosh. He thinks he's being castrated.

"Your penis is just fine. Nothing wrong with your peepee. The doctor won't touch it. He is only going to fix your navel."

A hesitant smile brightened Trevor's face. "I won't die?"

"You won't die. Your mom and dad can come to see you wake up and you'll be right back here in the playroom before long."

Trevor was smiling brightly now.

Kathy said, "You choose one of our dolls and we'll play what's going to happen in the operating room." She had the mask, the blood-pressure cuff, and all the equipment needed to play at going to sleep with anaesthesia, and I could guess how their game would progress.

She'd told me to look around and pick a child to observe. I gravitated to two girls playing with tiny, flexible dolls in the dollhouse. Connie was about four, with golden ringlet hair and a tiny bow mouth. Lucy, who was eleven or twelve, was tall for her age, with brown hair reaching her shoulders, and wore gold-framed glasses. The older girl bossed the little girl around and the dynamics interested me. I wondered if Lucy had a younger sister at home, or if there *she* was the young one getting bossed around.

"The mother must cook dinner," Lucy said, putting her own hand on her forehead and signing like she was contemplating what to fix.

I bet that's just the way Mom gestures when she's thinking.

"You set the table," Lucy said to Connie.

Carefully, Connie straightened the chairs around the dining table. She pretended to distribute plates. "Daddy is here. Mommy is here, and Granddad is here," she said aloud as she worked.

Lucy hummed, *One little, two little, three little Indians.* "Okay, now you eat," she said, "and don't spit anything out."

How long is Connie going to put up with all that bossing?

However, it was still a cozy scene that brought a smile.

Lucy turned to me. "You want to play? You can be the dad."

"Sure." I picked up the daddy doll and bounced him toward the chair at the table.

"This is lunch," said Lucy, in a commanding tone. "You're at work."

"Oh, I forgot," I said.

"You have to wait till very late to come home."

I suppressed a chuckle. This little girl was willing to include me in their play, but only with a minor part. Playing with Lucy meant playing by her rules. In her experience, daddies worked late. I was learning a lot about her family dynamics, and I sensed that she was imitating the way she was treated. I sat on a chair beside them, juggling the man doll against my knee—ready for action.

"Who am I?" Connie asked, sounding afraid that she wasn't included. "You're the little girl. You sit next to me. I'm the mom."

Connie put the replica of her character on the appropriate chair.

Apparently the meal was consumed quickly. "Now we're done. You got to take a nap." Lucy said to Connie.

"No. I'm not sleepy." Connie shook her head forcefully.

"Yes, you are." Lucy forgot the dolls and shook her fist in Connie's face.

"I'm not." Connie looked ready to cry.

Should I intervene? No, better give them time to work things out.

Lucy arranged the furniture in the master bedroom. "I sleep here and my husband sleeps here." She pointed to the double bed. "Kiss, kiss, kiss." She giggled.

Oh my. This little girl has seen a lot. What's next?

"You have to sleep in the room with Granddad," she said, arranging twin beds in the second upstairs room.

"No. I don't want to," Connie sniffled.

I thought I should remind both girls that this was only a game, but I'd begun to sense a terror in Connie and wanted to find the root.

"Why don't you want to sleep with Granddad?" Lucy asked, putting her hands on her hips. "Does he tickle you?" She laughed.

My body tensed.

This sounds serious.

Connie began to cry. I put my arms around her, and she cuddled in. I had to find out what was behind her terror. As for Lucy, my blood boiled because of her aggression.

Oh, wait ... she's telling us something about her own past, too.

Lucy eyed us angrily. "She's just a bad girl. She's bad."

Connie caught her breath and sobbed louder.

"She's not a bad girl. You're not a bad girl," I said, as soothingly as I could, because I knew that something frightening had happened to both of them.

"Shut up. You can't play anymore," Lucy said to me, and to Connie she said, "Did he give you money? I know what you did. You are a bad girl." She stomped her foot and walked away. There were tears in her eyes, too.

I reached out to stop her. "What do you mean?" But she shook off my hand.

An old horror came back. I could barely breathe. My eyes, my face, even my skin tensed. A terrified feeling filled my being. I'd almost managed to block out the time when I'd gone on that blind date, which had turned into an attempted rape. I'd talked it out with Norma, my pal, and with one of the guidance instructors, until I'd begun to let my brain take over and rewrite the story, giving me a sense of control, because I saw clearly how it had come about and wouldn't let it happen again.

If only I can get both girls to talk. I'm sure Lucy is hiding her guilt and fear. But I'm moving on shortly. There might not be time for me to draw them out. I'll tell Kathy.

Lucy had snatched a colouring book from the table and gone back to her bed.

"Let's take a walk," I said to Connie, and she grabbed my hand. We started walking up and down the corridor outside the playroom and she leaned into me. Her little hand was damp and cold.

"Does Granddad want you to do things you don't want to do?" I asked. She nodded.

"Did you tell your mom?"

Her head shook back and forth.

"I think your mom would want to know."

"Can I stay here with you?" She hugged my arm.

"Your mommy and daddy will miss you."

"I don't want to go home," she said, hiding her face behind her hands.

"We'll see about changing things before you go home. Kathy and I are going to talk with your mom. It's okay if we can fix things, isn't it?"

She gripped my hand like I was her only defence.

When Kathy, the specialist, and I talked to Connie's mother, she objected to the suggestion that the grandfather was molesting her daughter. "He's a good man. He loves her. He would never hurt her. He pays half our rent and he likes to give Connie quarters for her favourite candy. You should see how pleased she is when he reads her stories. I can't believe it." The mother clamped her lips, raised her chin, got up, and walked out of the meeting.

The next day things changed. Connie's mother must have decided to check out our accusations. She'd brought the granddad to visit. Connie screamed and hid in the washroom. That incident convinced the mother that something untoward was going on. She addressed Connie in a way that encouraged the child to talk, and Connie confided how Granddad lay on the bed to fondle her, and asked her to touch him.

The child psychiatrist was brought into the case. When Connie was discharged, she was scheduled for clinic visits so that the psychiatrist could work with Connie and her parents, and she urged them to press charges.

Though I finished my rotation, and was working on a private ward until our graduation, the head nurse kept me informed. Connie's mother and father were refusing to do more than chastise the grandfather, fearing it would bring shame to their family. I remembered how I didn't want to expose *my* molester. I'd felt shame, as though I'd brought the attack on myself. Though the incident had been dealt with logically, and I couldn't even remember his name, the feelings came back. Because of the help from the psychologist, I could talk about it. I repeated part of my story to the parents during their clinic sessions, urging them to act. But it wasn't until rumours of the grandfather's act began to circulate in the community, and a neighbour's daughter told that she had been lured into the family car by the grandfather, and paid a dollar to let him touch her privates, that the parents moved the grandfather out and took him to court.

"I guess we have to realize that my father needs help or he'll continue to molest little girls," the mother said to me, in tears.

I made a point of going to the clinic when Lucy had *her* follow-up appointments.

But, the aggressive little girl refused to look at me, and her mother always dragged her into the washroom each time they saw me approaching. It didn't matter to me that they blamed me for suggesting Lucy might have been molested too. Luckily, Lucy's mother had agreed to let Lucy meet with a psychologist, not because she believed Lucy had been molested, but because Lucy was becoming more and more aggressive toward her younger sister.

Is the little sister being molested too?

I wanted to do more, but there seemed to be nothing I could do for any of these girls. Compared to their suffering, my hurt seemed minimal.

Many children must be homesick and terrified about what will happen to them in the hospital. I could make a difference there. I saw how Kathy used play to help the children express themselves, and how she taught them about procedures. I saw how the nurses helped the child go through treatments with the least possible trauma, and taught the parents about the child's care. As I thought about the future, I reviewed all the medical specialty services we had studied and practised. I could identify with these frightened children. The hurts I had survived—losing Kenji, the near rape, as well as many other disappointments, had taught me that we can survive. We are better able to emphasize with those in pain because of our experiences. This was my calling. Every day, I would see the frightened faces of children and bring them hope and confidence that they could meet any adversity. I didn't wait until graduation to apply for a job on the pediatric ward.

Our graduation dance had to be held in late May. Classmates were scattering. Two girls were joining the army. Four of the girls were getting married and bringing their husbands before they left the area. Norma was going to miss the graduation ceremony; she had taken a job back in Toronto. Jan was moving to Vanderbilt to teach in the nursing program, the first coloured instructor on their faculty. Jeff was taking a senior residency in orthopedic surgery and would join her in July. They'd become fast friends, but it wouldn't be easy for a red-headed guy and a coloured girl to maintain their relationship in Tennessee. Bud was in private practice, but still single, and said he'd love to come. Only Kenji was missing from our original crowd. Bud had heard from him, pulled a post-card from his pocket and passed it over. I read Kenji's neatly scribed note about his teaching duties and getting resettled with his parents in their new home, and then passed it back. At the party, we all tried to laugh and tease, but there was a sense that it was the end of an era. Would we ever meet again? Jeff took us to a happy ending. He lifted his glass of wine in a toast, and began to sing, "We'll meet again, don't know where, don't know when, but I know we'll meet again some sunny day." And every guy and gal made the rounds to be sure they danced with everyone.

Chapter 21
After 40 Years

Air Canada flight 01, from Toronto to Japan, landed in Narita at three in the afternoon. We took the train into the city, and then a taxi to our Shinjuku hotel. Spring in Tokyo begins in February, and I'd been told that it would be jacket weather. Plum trees, resplendent with white and pink blossoms, would be drawing people to the parks, and students would be flocking to the temples to attach their prayers to the branches—prayers for passing marks on their entrance examinations.

Peter and I had never travelled. It would have been so romantic to see the pyramids of Egypt or even the Grand Canyon, but my husband's idea of fun was just sitting in a motorboat with a fishing line in the lake. I have to chuckle when I remember the time we won a romantic night at the Royal York Hotel in Toronto. We were given dinner and ballroom tickets, but Peter had brought a copy of the biography of Theodore Roosevelt, which he thought we would read to each other. Roosevelt led a fascinating life. We both liked history and that biography led to plans for visiting Roosevelt's birthplace at 28 East 20th Street; but we never got to New York City.

I couldn't complain. Peter was thoughtful, and a good provider. Even our Muskoka cottage had the latest conveniences. He was almost six feet tall, and handsome, with brown hair, blue eyes, and a quiet, thoughtful demeanour. He used to tell me that he wasn't popular in university, but I think he just preferred books and nature to hanging out with the gang. Between the two of us, I was the social one, but that's not saying much, because I liked to focus on my home and career.

On the Tokyo express train, I had a comfortable recliner in a temperature controlled car, with plenty of leg room and picture windows. Somehow I expected to find terraced rice paddies, gnarled pines, and trickling streams running along a valley floor, like in those pictured in early guide books of Japan. Instead there were walled, jammed-together houses, and bumper-to-bumper cars on the throughways. No one was carrying paper parasols or wearing colourful kimonos. No rickshaws, no three-wheel contrivances carrying everything from a pig to an office desk. It wasn't like the land I'd imagined when I thought I might be living there all those years ago. As I looked out the window at the scenery, my thoughts were somewhere else, in a different time—a time when life was full of possibilities.

Three of us had been invited from Canada: Dr. Sommers, who had coordinated management of the 2002 SARS crisis in Toronto; Mr. Roberts, who was chief information officer; and me, the "authority" on the part nurses played in treating and inhibiting the spread of Severe Acute Respiratory Syndrome—a coronavirus respiratory disease. I had been called back to work when the epidemic progressed, because I was experienced in caring for those with communicable diseases. I'd worked with Dr. Williams in the U.S. during the polio epidemic years ago, spent years with children who were ill with tuberculosis and other infectious diseases, and had earned my doctorate studying AIDS and other communicable conditions. During the last years of my full-time employment, I taught at the University of Toronto. Japan was well prepared, should a similar epidemic occur, but the Japanese health officials felt that they could learn from others. We'd been invited to describe the successes and shortcomings of our program. *En route*, the three of us had relived the sleepless days and nights we'd spent in consultation, and now, too jet-lagged to talk, we watched the suburban landscape go by.

I wondered if I could remember any of the Japanese phrases I'd learned from my Japanese boyfriend years ago. Recalling brought back scenes from the past. Some left me smiling and some I tried to put aside.

Would I recognize Kenji if I saw him on the street? What part would be the same? His voice? His eyes? The bouncy way he walked?

The Japanese delegation was waiting in the hotel lobby. Two men and a woman. I caught my breath. He was taller than I remembered, was bearded, and nearly bald—all that bouncy hair was missing—but I recognized his laugh as they approached. He grabbed my hand to shake even before the introductions. "Cl—Miss Winchester, I would have known you anywhere." The others looked on in surprise, and Kenji Akiyama explained that we'd once studied together in the States. He continued to pump my hand up and down. "Amazing. Both of us are still working," he said. "You did not change."

"Dr. Akiyama," I said, and introduced him to my friends. We said our names and exchanged calling cards.

The Japanese man involved with public relations introduced us formally. "Akiyama *Sensei* is Director of the Institute of Infectious Disease Research at the University of Tokyo. I believe he worked with the famous Dr. Williams in the U.S., when polio was prevalent," he said, and then turned toward the woman in the group. "Yamaguchi *Sensei* is head of the University of Tokyo's School of Nursing. She took graduate studies in California."

The nurse smiled and said, in well-rehearsed English, "I am glad to meet you."

"And I am Sato." The public relations man bowed. "I spent two years in the U.S. at Harvard." It was all very staid.

The three waited downstairs until we settled our baggage in our hotel rooms and then took us to a western-style buffet dinner. We weren't being kept out late since it was assumed we needed a good rest to recover from jet lag.

I wasn't sure how I felt about running into Kenji again.

Did I hope to meet him when I agreed to come? Possibly, and yet I don't want to relive those painful days after we parted.

He'd put on a few pounds, but still had the same erect carriage, with his straight back and head held high. His eyebrows were bushy, and his hair formed a rim of closely cropped white hair across the back of his head, from ear to ear. He'd grown a beard, adding to his already distinguished look. Through small steel-framed glasses, his dark, sparkling eyes still latched onto whomever he addressed. The others did most of the talking during dinner, entertaining us with tales of their mishaps and adventures in the States.

The next day, many professionals from the medical field gathered at the United Nations University building in Shibuya to hear us speak. We were introduced by Kenji—Dr. Akiyama. With able translators, the event progressed formally and without a hitch. Dr. Akiyama was so formal that it appeared he had forgotten our past.

That's good. He won't do anything to make me remember.

After lunch the meeting resumed— more presentations and time to answer questions.

I glanced at Kenji several times as I spoke about the complete barrier precautions nurses had taken in order to avoid catching the virus during the SARS epidemic, about fever-reducing methods we'd used, the oxygen and ventilation nurses had provided to patients, and about house quarantine for patients who weren't hospitalized. He seemed to be interested in every word. He wasn't using the simultaneous translation, but listening to my voice instead.

Come now, Claire. After all these years, and a happy marriage, you aren't still under his spell.

My delivery was more subdued than usual. I felt flat. My colleagues, who knew me, must have thought that I was tired. Somehow though, I was able to force a cheerful closure to my presentation.

A banquet followed, and when it was finished, Kenji approached as I waited for the elevator. My body tightened.

What can I say to him? It's so uncomfortable, just the two of us.

I hesitated before pushing the button.

I'm past sixty—an old woman, and a professional nurse, here on a mission to exchange information. Nothing about this trip is personal.

"Good, I caught you," he said, smiling. "I won't be able to join you tomorrow for sightseeing. I am very sorry."

I shrugged.

Had I expected him to join us? Maybe? Unconsciously? Why is my heart pounding?

I swallowed. No words came. I looked down, wanted to exit his presence as quickly as possible. Where was this passion coming from?

Peter was a wonderful husband—a steady, caring person who had made me feel comfortable with life. Hadn't I moved on?

These thoughts made me angry enough that I was able to push aside the passion, adopt a blandly pleasant expression and say, "You're a very busy man. I'm sure you've arranged a grand tour for us."

He stood blocking my way. "Tomorrow night I will clear my schedule to have dinner, if you could join me. The others go to see Kabuki, but maybe you don't mind to miss it?" he asked.

I felt flushed.

It would be rude to refuse, but what would it be like if we met alone? Well, the day tour is going to take my mind off the past, and I'll have so many exciting things to tell him about our visit. I'll ask about his family, and about his career.

I bowed in Japanese manner. "That would be nice."

The tour took us to many sites, and had many highlights: Meiji Shrine; Ueno Park; the Canadian Embassy Prince Takamado Gallery; and the observatory atop the Tokyo Metropolitan Government building in Shinjuku, where we saw Mt. Fuji in the distance. The Japan Open-Air Folk House Museum was a glimpse of the Japan I'd pictured years ago. As we awaited our tour bus in the hotel lobby, a nearby television was broadcasting the local news about a sporting event. Yamaguchi *Sensei* nodded toward a woman on the screen. "That lady used to be Dr. Akiyama's wife," she said. "She promotes the Olympic teams."

Used to be. Was she saying that Kenji wasn't married?

The woman appearing on TV was close to my age, and attractive with cropped black hair and a trim build. She radiated self-assurance. I couldn't understand her words, but she was obviously a woman of strong opinions. I didn't want to think what kind of marriage they'd had, but having seen so much of Japan that day, I could understand why his culture would mean a lot to him.

He belonged here. His career has been successful. His dreams have come true. I'm just a friend from the past—an outsider, and a foreigner. He rejected me because I was a foreigner, and I still am.

I'd never felt so tired. Finally, the tour ended and we were dropped back at our hotel. The others left for dinner, which had been scheduled for an early hour because they were going to the theatre. I asked myself why I hadn't declined Kenji's invitation.

Can I make the evening enjoyable?

I took a shower and dressed in my black suit, brushed my hair, which was now restored to its original colour—shorter than before but clipped back almost like I used to wear it. My complexion was still rosy, so I needed only a bit of lipstick. I chose to wear the pearl earrings Kenji had given me one Christmas years ago.

In spite of what I told myself, was this really a ploy to jog his memory?

Kenji greeted me in the hotel lobby. "I am taking you someplace special," he said. "I have proposal to suggest." He looked quite formal in a navy blue, silk suit, his blue and burgundy patterned tie knotted perfectly and standing out against a white shirt, with gold cufflinks.

Proposal! He always was full of surprises. Darn, he's teasing just like in the olden days.

We boarded a taxi. When our hands brushed, that familiar flutter filled my being. The eyes of the taxi driver stared back in the rear-view mirror. The driver was like the Japanese culture, inhibiting our thoughts and any acts that might betray the mores of Japan. Kenji was staring at the traffic and keeping his distance.

At the the rooftop, Italian-style restaurant, Kenji had Scotch and I ordered white wine. The waiters wore tuxedos. Tables were set with linen, white porcelain, and heavy silver cutlery. An orchid floated in a crystal bowl as a centrepiece on our table.

Does this splendour mean that he is glad to see me or that he feels obligated to entertain me in style?

We looked at each other and laughed, neither knowing how to start our conversation.

Finally, with a lilt in his voice, he said, "You haven't changed. You look very young."

"I have a good hairdresser but so have you. That goatee. And with those glasses, you look very wise."

"If I can't be wise, I should appear to be so." He laughed, and squinted playfully as he appeared to size me up. "Maybe you are a bit wider."

There he goes. Sure I've gained a few pounds, but I'm not fat. You might say, I have good curves. You used to like my breasts. Sometimes your teasing hits a sore point, but I can still deliver a return punch.

"Just soft spots, but you missed your chance."

Making an apologetic face, he said, "Hmm, I am not so wise. Now tell me, did you visit Japan before?"

"No, I never made it," I said.

"You used to be very interested in Japanese ways," he said.

Stupid. Stupid. What a stupid thing for you to say. Of course I was. I had a reason. I'd expected to marry you and live in Japan.

"Well, I see there are no more paper lanterns, or wooden clogs, and few kimonos. I guess a lot has changed from my original impression of Japan."

"Much changed."

"Have you been happy?"

"What is happiness? I've been lucky with my career." After a reflective silence, he said. "You have wedding ring."

"In private life, I'm Mrs. Peter Wilson. Do you remember Norma, the Canadian girl whose father was teaching in the med school? I married her brother. He was a GP in our small town near Toronto. We met when I went to Canada to visit Norma a year after our graduation. He passed away four years ago—cancer. He had a wicked time. That's why I took on some nursing duties again during the SARS epidemic, even though I'm so old."

"I am sorry for your loss. You have children?" Kenji asked, stoking his beard.

"Our son is a high-school science teacher, married to a Chinese-Canadian girl."

"My daughter lives in Philadelphia. She married American physician."

Our eyes locked.

"I believe that when love happens between races, it is nature's way of breaking down barriers."

Of course. I knew that long ago.

After a pause, I said, "I hope you are pleased."

He nodded. "Nice fellow, but they are too far away." A wide smile lit his face and I noticed that, even though the skin on his face sagged a bit, and his perfect white teeth might be false, the dimple was still there. "My grandson likes to fish. *Ojiisan* very busy when they visit." He tapped his chest, which clarified things for me, reminding me that he was using the word for grandfather. "Junko is a nurse like you. She studied here, so cannot practice in Philadelphia."

I ran my finger around the rim of my wine glass. "You always wanted a daughter."

"Life does not progress as we think it will," Kenji said, before taking a long drink from his tumbler and then summoning the waiter for a refill.

He's only being polite. I've been through enough hurtful times. It was miserable watching Peter deteriorate during those final months. And I remember the motorcycle accident that put our son, Kurt, on life support. Kurt, I worried and worried about you. I've survived it all. Some hardships teach us about life. But, I don't want to relive any of them.

I clapped my hands together, to end those thoughts, and leaned toward him. "Now, tell me about your career."

"I studied endocrinology in the U.S., but changed my speciality to infectious diseases."

"It's fascinating isn't it? But tell me, isn't TB a thing of the past? And what about AIDS? Does Japan have an AIDS problem? Do you offer flu vaccine? Do babies get vaccinated against the usual childhood infections here in Japan?"

He laughed, made a puzzled face, and put his hands against his forehead.

"I guess I'm asking too many questions."

He smiled. "My research is about drug resistance. If we don't deal with it, the antibiotics we use won't be curative any longer. Viruses are still problematic. And we have stumbled on an insect toxin that we believe will kill some cancer cells."

"Wow. And as a little boy you used to collect insects! That's a splendid pursuit. I hope you get good funding and a lot of cooperation from drug companies."

"We always wish for more." He opened my copy of the menu in front of me, saying, "Now we should order dinner. And later we can have a big dessert, don't you think?"

Dessert! Does he remember that we didn't have dessert at our last date?

While we ate, he told me about students who'd come from other countries to study in Japan, and about his trips to lecture abroad. He'd been all over Europe, to Africa, Vietnam, China, Taiwan, and Korea. He promised to send me copies of articles that had been written about the research undertaken by his institute.

Once or twice, as he was speaking, I remembered his reference to "a proposal," but I didn't let my mind dwell on what that could mean.

Now I get it. He hopes I can introduce him to researchers in Canada who are working on drug resistance. Business. This date is all about business.

When dinner was nearly finished, he said, "Did you enjoy spaghetti? I chose this restaurant because we used to eat spaghetti so many times."

"I remember," I said.

"Do you cook rice?" he asked.

"Yes. Often. I finally bought a rice cooker."

"I used to tease you. Say I would have to eat spaghetti every day, because I didn't think you could cook rice."

"I remember."

"You made good *miso* soup for me. I knew you were good cook."

"Did I?"

"And *sushi*. You were rare American girl to like *sushi*."

"Where did we eat *sushi*? There were no Japanese restaurants in those days."

"I cooked for you. I am good cook, too." He puffed out his chest. "Those were happy days for me. Maybe happiest in life."

"And for me," I said. I put my hands in my lap and squeezed them together.

"Many picnics. We used to go to swim."

"Yes, I remember when you saved the life of a little girl with polio," I said. Immediately, the family scene came to mind, and I pictured his dive to save the little girl. "I hope she got proper treatment."

Kenji was summoning the waiter for a dessert menu. "Pick your favourite dessert. Big one."

"Thanks," I said, putting aside the painful memory.

We chose an exotic mixture of berries, topped with ice cream on meringue—not a typical Japanese dish.

"And I have a proposal to make you," Kenji said, while toying with his spoon and looking right at me.

Yes, you want me to help you with your mission. We'll see.

"I will go to Africa for six months with the Doctors Without Borders team. AIDS is big problem and so are childhood diseases. I'm old, but I still speak English and they think I can offer some instruction. And they need nurses who can teach procedures. You have good credentials. I said I would ask you."

"Africa. Me? When?"

"I will leave in April. If that is too soon, you can join later," he said.

"Quite a challenge."

He touched my arm, and his look seemed to encourage me to accept.

"Well, I'll have to consider ..."

Kenji gripped my hand and squeezed it. "Please do. The committee wants you, and I would very much like for you to join."

"It would be a great adventure. Hmm ... I will give it serious thought."

"I knew you were one of the delegates," he said. "I was very excited to find out that you were coming. I've read many of your articles, and I believe you specialized in infectious diseases. I didn't know about your husband, but I noticed that you were listed as being single on some of the documents regarding this trip to Japan. I am sorry that your husband has passed on." He nodded a gesture of sympathy.

"Where are you going in Africa?"

"We will be told shortly. We will work with medical colleges and nursing schools, and I hope we will go into the countryside, to small clinics."

I suppose I'd be working with young girls. Perhaps teaching the basics, like sterilization techniques. I wonder what equipment they have.

"When do they need an answer?"

"Soon. I-If you have no other commitment. I hope ..."

"I'm considering," I said. But my mind was way ahead of this conversation. I was thinking about my house. Who would look after it? Who could take the lectures I'd promised? Peter would say that I should go. He'd been content with his practice, and with time to relax at our wilderness cottage, but he'd recognized my drive to tackle new things. My granny, who used to give me advice, would certainly say, "Go for it!" How would I break the news to Kurt? Maybe every son thinks his mom is too old for new projects. "What do I have to do?" I asked.

He pulled a form out of his inner coat pocket. "Please submit this as soon as possible. They are holding a place until they hear from you. See, I've been preparing this proposal for several weeks."

As usual, my next thoughts were about reasons for saying no. *I'll have to review what I learned about AIDS. Six months is a long time. What will it be like to see Kenji every day? It'll be just business; is that okay? We will get to know each other again. I'll have to buy some books. What's the climate like?* I grinned and said, "Interesting. Could be interesting."

"Then it is settled. I am glad," he said, clasping his hands together.

But I haven't ... actually, I guess I have.

Kenji leaned back against the brocade upholstery of the chair. "You used to read to me. Do you remember Wordsworth's poem?"

I was puzzled. Our eyes locked. An orchestra began to play "Love Is a Many-Splendored Thing."

Kenji noticed. "We saw that movie once."

"Yes, and I cried and cried when Mark's plane crashed."

"Good excuse for me to hold you," he said, with merriment in his eye.

"Did you need an excuse?"

"Japanese reticence."

"Hmm."

On the way down in the elevator, he held my hand.

"Sweet memories," he said.

We walked hand and hand to the taxi stand, got into a cab, and said nothing as the cab swept us past the flashing signs of the Ginza, past parks to my hotel. We got out. He stood for a moment facing me, and then, right there in front of all the people coming and going from the prestigious hotel, he kissed me. *So much for Japanese reticence.* "We will meet again very soon," he whispered. "Sweet lady."

I was numb from exhaustion, emotions, and the exhilaration of the unexpected change in my life's direction. In my hotel room, I looked from the window down on the plum trees and across the street where taxis waited for late night travellers. Tomorrow I will be on my way again, and beyond that, the future will be an adventure. Some day someone will tell me about their dilemmas and the decisions they've made. They'll share stories about happy outcomes or heart-breaking tragedies, and I'll share my stories. I've been there, lived through good times and sad times. I'll understand. It's as though my life has been lived in the margins of many lives. Memories linger and beg to be told. In the sharing of life experiences we feel a connection to another person, even a stranger. It is comforting to know that we are not alone, that life is about joy and sorrow—feelings all humans share. I'll tell my friend to watch for open doors, that life has surprises, and that we can benefit from the outcome of any experience. I'd puzzled about why Kenji remembered Wordsworth's poem, and then the poet's words began to come back to me. Wordsworth had written what I was trying to say. From my computer I read: "Ode: Intimations of Immortality and Recollections of Early Childhood."

"There was a time when meadow, grove, and stream,
The earth, and every common sight,
To me did seem
Apparelled in celestial light,
The glory and the freshness of a dream.
...

Though nothing can bring back the hour
Of splendour in the grass,
of glory in the flower;
We will grieve not, rather find
Strength in what remains behind;
In the primal sympathy
Which having been must ever be;
...

In faith that looks through death,
In years that bring the philosophic mind.
..."

Acknowledgments:

Publication of this novel would not have been possible without the superior editorial and management services of FriesenPress, for which I give thanks. The cover design, created by my long-term friend and artist James Rourke, captures the puzzling expression of the young protagonist. My thanks to him for his hours of thought and effort to produce this cover. My sincere gratitude goes to poet and author of books for children, Janet Barkhouse, my friend, who edited an early version of this manuscript, to my friend, Dr. Sey Nishimura, who corrected Japanese terms and to Mary Addison, another friend with useful advice and encouragement. Also I want to thank Ann Ireland together with her class at Ryerson University, Toronto, helpers when I began to write fiction.

I am indebted to the faculty of Frances Payne Bolton School of Nursing at Case Western Reserve University , Cleveland, Ohio, and in particular to Kay Krumhansl and Helen Halfors, for the excellent instruction provided during my nursing education, and to my classmates, colleagues and friends, who were my supporters. And I am thankful to the late Dr. Fred Robbins and the late Emma Nuschi Plank, who created the Child Life and Education Profession and hired me as the first teacher, thus giving me the rewarding experience of attending to the non-medical needs of our young hospital patients. I witnessed many memorable occasions when children conquered great odds.

All of the characters, happenings, and sites in this novel are fictitious. They are products of my imagination, although some scenes were inspired by actual incidents, or are based on recorded, historical events.

CPSIA information can be obtained
at www.ICGtesting.com
Printed in the USA
LVOW11s2253050517
533311LV00001B/4/P